Reader reviews for *Hot Ice, Cold Blood*

"*Hot Ice, Cold Blood* is ind      fully
written, characters so re   ᵻere
in the room with you. Th   ᴐne
that makes perfect sense!   ᴐ a must read."

– Lauren McKinney, reader

"Holly Spofford really knows how to weave a plot. In *Hot Ice, Cold Blood* she starts by introducing the plot line and some of the characters. She tells you just enough to hook you and begin to develop theories about what might happen. I love how she kept me guessing the entire time about the completely unexpected outcome. Her characters are varied, interesting, and relatable. Holly easily keeps you interested the whole way through because of the action and suspense. The ending is highly unlikely to be what you thought. That is the essence of a great writer and great writing, not to mention a great story. Holly is a master of all three. It leaves me wondering when the mainstream publishing industry will recognize her talent."

– Ed Flail, reader

"If you liked *A Letter for Hoot*, you'll love *Hot Ice, Cold Blood*. This is an awesome thriller that will keep you riveted from page one. I loved how Holly developed Daisy and NT into young adults. This book is action-packed and won't disappoint."

– Cheryl Flail, reader

Other books by Holly Spofford

A Letter for Hoot

10/20

HOT ICE,
COLD BLOOD

Dear Debbie,
Happy reading!
Cheers!
Holly Spofford

HOLLY SPOFFORD

Copyright © 2020 by Holly Spofford

All rights reserved. This book or any portion thereof may not be reproduced or used in any manner whatsoever without the express written permission of the publisher except for the use of brief quotations in a book review.

Publisher's note: This is a work of fiction. Names, characters, places, and incidents either are the product of the author's imagination or are used fictitiously. Any resemblance to actual events, locales, or persons, living or dead, is entirely coincidental.

Edited by Kristen Corrects, Inc.
Cover art design by Shezaad Sudar

First edition published 2020
ISBN: 978-0-9994143-1-6

HollySpofford.com

For my husband John
with all my love

CHAPTER 1

Victor Sykes pushed the end call button on his phone. He laid the phone on his desk and sighed deeply. *Good God. Here we go again. Damn you, Hugo.* His eyes fell on the picture of his beautiful wife. *I must tell her.*

He sat for a bit as he wrestled with how his wife Alex was going to take this unsettling news. Not well, he knew. Victor rose from his creaky desk chair and gazed through the immense window onto the bustling city below. The leaden March sky did nothing to elevate his mood. He was the one who organized every part of their lucrative import side business and Alex expected perfection.

Get it over with.

Victor dialed Alex's number. "We have a problem with Hugo." An exhale of annoyance filled Victor's ear. "Don't worry, Alexandra, the African ivory is safe and sound with its buyer. And you and I made a pretty penny."

"Lovely," Alex replied. "But what did Hugo do now?"

"He was in another fight and is locked up at the police station. I'm fed up with him and his crap. I'll be damned if we're going to pay *yet again* to bail him out," Victor answered.

Victor listened carefully to Alex as he walked over to his wall safe. She gave him carte blanche to do what he pleased with pathetic Hugo, even though she knew he would anyway. "Yes, my dear. I'm heading there after we hang up. I'll call you when I'm finished. Have a good meeting."

He opened the safe in his office and removed a syringe and small bottle of clear liquid. He snapped the plastic cap off the needle and pierced the bottle's rubber stopper. The syringe slowly filled with the liquid—potassium chloride. Victor recapped the needle and placed it in a plastic toothbrush container that he dropped into his pants pocket. The last item he took from the safe was a thick brown envelope. *This'll do it.* He slid the envelope into the inside pocket of his overcoat and grabbed his phone.

"Francie, I will be out of the office for a bit."

"Yes, Mr. Sykes," Francie replied.

He walked out of his office located in the Cooper Building, which housed senators, their staffs, IT engineers, and Victor's staff. As Employment and Housing director for the Veterans Administration, Victor oversaw his staff finding employment and housing for vets returning from active duty. When Victor had returned from the Iraq War, he soon learned he and his fellow vets struggled to reacclimate into society. Job and housing searches proved fruitless. Now, his job allowed him access to many veterans' resumes, from which he could hand-pick some of those vets to work for him in his lucrative import side business.

Outside the office, Victor flipped his coat collar around his neck to ward off the day's chilly grayness. He turned to his right and walked the six blocks to the police station for a visit with his old friend, Captain Michael Goodwin. Victor and Michael had known each other for over twenty years. Each had served in the Gulf War and were part of a veteran's group that shared season tickets to the Washington

Nationals, DC's professional baseball team.

Victor entered the DC Metropolitan Police station. Even at midday, the station was quiet, with just two employees busy doing paperwork at their desks. Victor greeted Michael with a handshake.

"Vic, good to see you. Have a seat." The captain signaled for Victor to sit in one of the chairs opposite his desk.

"Good to see you too, although I wish we were headed to a Nats game instead of the real reason why I'm here."

"Let me guess—you're here about Hugo. Again."

"Mike, you know me all too well," Victor replied.

"He's in his usual cell, the one you chose. In a drunken rage, he beat some poor guy senseless. I assume he expects you to bail out his sorry ass."

"Probably. But not in the way I have before," Victor said.

"He's a damn mess. I don't know if he can even talk. He crashed pretty hard in the cruiser." The captain kept his eyes on Victor, who smirked and reached inside his coat pocket to pull out the thick envelope. He slid it across the desk to his friend.

Michael's eyes lit up. They flicked to Victor then back down to the envelope. Its thickness told him it contained thousands of dollars. He glanced back at Victor, who gave an imperceptible nod. Michael looked to make sure no one else was nearby, then opened the envelope. He let out a low whistle. "Vic, that's a lot of money," he whispered.

Victor leaned in. "Yes, it is. I am going to go back now and talk to Hugo if he's coherent. All the better if he isn't. Make sure it's *you* who checks on him after I leave. Kill the video cameras too. Give it thirty minutes. Lucky for you— unfortunate for him—there will be zero witnesses.

Understand?"

Michael held Victor's gaze as he weighed the pros and cons of taking the bribe. It did not take long. Within a matter of seconds, he slid the package into his top desk drawer.

"Wise decision." Victor's smile belied his unctuous demeanor. "Thirty minutes, understand?"

Michael nodded and jerked his head toward a darkened hallway lined with three holding cells. "The door's unlocked."

"Thank you."

Victor walked past two empty cells to the one at the end of the hallway and looked in. He stared down at his former friend and fellow soldier, Hugo Scott, who lay passed out on the cot. His once-handsome face was gray and concave. Grease and mud matted his dark hair. Filth caked his fingernails; scratches and dried blood covered his hands. His sunken eyes were at half-mast and did not register Victor's presence.

Jesus, what the hell happened to you, Hugo? He felt a mix of revulsion and sadness for this once-upstanding, strong soldier who fought in Iraq with Victor. They went through hell together for three years and maintained their friendship even after they were home.

Hugo Scott was a womanizing party boy who came from an affluent family. When his parents passed, they left him a sizeable inheritance that went straight up his nose or down his throat. Broke, he begged Victor for a job—specifically in the import business Victor established and ran with Alex. Hugo promised Victor he would clean up his act and stay sober. For two years, he proved to be a reliable employee until a cocaine- and alcohol-fueled bender destroyed everything.

"Hello, Hugo. You're not looking very well." No response. "Perfect." Victor removed the needle from his pocket and inserted it into Hugo's right arm. Not a single muscle flinched. Victor counted to thirty, patted Hugo on the head, told him to sleep well, and walked out of the cell.

Halfway back to his office, Victor heard the chiming of his phone. He was surprised at the area code and knew it could only be one person—his younger sister, Tammy. *She's probably begging for more money.* Victor exhaled and answered. "Hello Tammy, long time no speak."

"Hi Victor. I know, it's been a long time and I'm sorry." Her soft, syrupy drawl had not changed.

"What do you want? More money I assume?" Victor asked.

Tammy began, "Not money, no." He heard her inhale on a cigarette. "Victor, I need your help with Rubi Lee and Zeke. They're real down on their luck. I was hopin' you could help." Through tears, Tammy told him how her children had done time for petty crimes and currently were in dead-end jobs. "Vic, I can't stomach havin' them turn out like me. I have to live with my failure as a parent every day."

"I'm sorry, Tammy," he answered. "I'm not sure how I can help."

"Vic, I'm asking if you could please help them find a decent job somewhere in that big city. I googled ya and I know you place people in jobs. You're my last resort."

"Did you tell them you were going to call me?"

At first Tammy did not answer. "Um . . ." She inhaled deeply. "Yeah, I did. Please, Vic."

Victor said nothing as his mind traveled back when he

last saw Rubi Lee and Zeke. Two cute innocents playing on the burned-out front lawn of the decrepit double-wide they called home. A fissure deep inside his chest grew wider. He always wanted to be a father, but he was not.

"Please, Vic. At least think about it—for them. They're too young to be broke and hungry. After all, they're your flesh and blood too." Her voice cracked.

Victor sighed and rubbed his face. "Tammy, I will see what I can do."

"Bless you, Victor. Thank you, thank you. I'll—"

"Stop. I did not promise you *anything*. I'll call you back." Victor hung up and took his time to the office. Tammy's call opened a trove of feelings he kept buried for over twenty years. *Rubi Lee and Zeke. It's a wonder they made it past high school. Tammy's right, I can at least think about helping them.*

Back at the office, he called Alex. As expected, his call went straight to voicemail. "Alexandra, my love, I've taken care of the matter we discussed and am headed back to the office. Tonight we will open a nice bottle of wine and decide how to move forward from here."

CHAPTER 2

"Oh, boy. I'm glad today is over," Alex called down the long hallway. She slid off her cashmere coat and hung it in the closet.

"Nice to see you home at a decent hour," Victor said. He gave her a kiss on the cheek and handed her a glass of chardonnay, her favorite.

"Mm, thank you. It's so nice to *be* home at a decent hour," Alex said. She clinked glasses with Victor, then kicked off her shoes and moved into the living room, where she dropped into a chair by the fireplace. Victor joined his wife and they absorbed the welcome solitude of their home. Alex closed her eyes momentarily, trying to decompress from her hectic day. She took a deep slug of wine and said, "Please tell me you have good news."

"Yes, my dear, I do. Hugo is no longer an issue," he said with a smile.

"Well done. What an utter waste of a life. He had looks, charm, and money—things people would kill for. Since he pissed it all away, I feel zero remorse."

"Neither do I." Victor set his glass down, leaned back in his chair, and rested his interlaced fingers against his chest.

Alex glanced at him and snorted. "I know you certainly aren't *praying*. Care to tell me what's on your calculating mind?"

Victor rolled his head to the right and smiled. "Now that Hugo is out of the picture, we need to replace him."

"Ah, you're right. And who's the lucky person?"

"I'm thinking Don Gaylord is our man. We can move him from his current domestic delivery position to the international importing side."

Alex pursed her full lips together. "I like him for this. He's been very dependable transferring packages, especially since he doesn't drive."

Victor frowned. "You are right. He doesn't drive—a major problem."

Alex finished, "Which means he'll need a driver."

"Yes, he will."

Alex finished her wine. "Who do you think we could find? They need to understand how we operate and must be trustworthy."

Victor considered his wife's words and knew she was correct. He noticed she finished her wine and asked if she wanted a refill.

"Of course." She handed it to him.

In the kitchen, he refilled her glass and checked his phone for messages. He scrolled through recent calls and his conversation with Tammy earlier jogged his brain. He looked up and placed his phone on the counter.

He returned to the living room, a triumphant smile on his doughy face. "I feel I have a solution for Gaylord's driver." He handed her the glass.

"Do you now?" Alex sipped her wine and wiped the smudge of mauve lipstick from the rim.

"Yes. Tammy called me today in tears."

"Your sister? What does she have to do with Gaylord's

driver?"

"Apparently, her children—my niece and nephew Rubi Lee and Zeke Dixon—are down on their luck and have dead-end jobs."

Alex frowned. "What else did she say?"

"She asked if I could help them with employment. I promised her nothing, other than I'd think about helping."

Alex stroked her chin in thought. "I know what you're thinking—hire them to drive Gaylord, right?"

"You win!"

Alex was nervous. "Given their parents' proclivity to lie, cheat, and steal, how do we know we can trust them?"

"Because when they realize that I have the means and desire to improve their pathetic lives, they won't say no. You know how persuasive I can be."

Alex nodded as she rose from her seat and settled into her husband's lap. "Oh, *yes* I do. I'm sure Gaylord will sign on too."

Victor wrapped his arms around her. "He won't say no to money. Furthermore, our little import business is thriving, and I will ensure Don continues our success." Alex giggled at Victor's use of air quotes around *import business.*

"And if he doesn't?" Alex asked.

"Then he will be eliminated," Victor answered.

Alex purred, "That's why I love you. You always have a plan."

Victor picked up his glass and said, "Cheers."

"Cheers," Alex replied, and clinked her glass against his.

CHAPTER 3

Twelve hundred miles away, in Louisiana, Rubi Lee Dixon lay on the single bed under a thin yellow blanket and clutched the ratty ballerina doll to her chest—the single treasured item she salvaged from her tumultuous and sad childhood. Early sunlight pushed its way through the metal blinds. She squeezed her eyes shut against the memories of laughing and spinning round and round in her pink tutu as a little girl, the doll held above her head, dreams of being a dancer. *Don't go down that street. Don't do it.*

Her attention was drawn to the birds serenading her through the open window with their cacophonous symphony. Every morning at four thirty they sang, rain or shine. They warbled to each other for twenty minutes until they flew off to find breakfast. Rubi Lee rolled over on her side, closed her eyes, and relished in the warmth of bed for the next hour.

Exactly one hour later, Ozzy Osbourne's voice bellowed from Rubi Lee's phone. For five minutes and nineteen seconds, she escaped into the lyrics of "Crazy Train," her self-proclaimed theme song. As the final note faded, she forced herself out of bed to face another day of chopping up chickens at the poultry factory.

As was his habit, her younger brother Zeke knocked on her door. "Rube, you up? It's gonna be longer than ten minutes to get you to the factory. Traffic is a nightmare."

"*Yes!* I'll be ready in fifteen minutes!" she yelled.

"Back down! I'll be outside, warming up the van," Zeke replied.

Rubi Lee lit a cigarette and took a swig of the diet soda she had on her crowded bedside table. She yanked on black leggings and thick socks. She rummaged in the cardboard boxes on the floor for a long-sleeved T-shirt and sweatshirt. She sniffed them and recoiled. *Am I going to spend the rest of my life smelling like fucking chicken?* In the cramped bathroom she and Zeke shared, she tamped her cigarette out in the sink and looked in the mirror—something she tried to avoid. Overnight, it seemed like the lines around her mouth and eyes snuggled deeper into her pale skin. *God, I look forty instead of twenty-six.* Sickened, she crumpled up the soda can, hurled it off the wall into the trash can. She grabbed her bag and phone and headed outside to the van.

"Son of a bitch! *Come on!*" Zeke yelled as he turned the key over three times. At last, the white van coughed to life. In the driver's seat, he closed his brown eyes, rested his head back and summoned the strength to get through another day. *There has to be something better for me out there.* His intellectual side told him he was lucky to have a job. But the thought of another interminable day standing in the back of putrid trash trucks hosing out clinging remnants was hard to stomach.

Rubi Lee hoisted herself in the passenger seat and glanced at her brother. "What's wrong with you? Are you sick?"

"No, but I'm damn sick and tired of my job and this shitty life. What did we do to deserve this life? I don't know how much longer I can do it. I really don't." He punched the steering wheel.

"Here, have a cigarette. You'll feel better." She handed one to her brother. "Zeke, I know exactly how you feel, but guess what, we got rent to pay and other bills."

Zeke lit up. "I know, I know. But is *this* gonna be our life for the next fifty years?" He sucked in half the cigarette. "Jesus Christ, Rube"—he blew out a long stream of smoke— "I'm hosing shit outta trucks, and you're slicing up chickens! Why did *we* have to have such crappy parents?"

"I don't know, little bro. I simply don't know."

Zeke punched the gas and the van lurched forward into the dark morning.

Zeke and Rubi Lee were what people called Irish twins. There was a noticeable resemblance in their light brown hair and pointed features. At barely twelve months apart, they were placed in the same grade. Their closeness helped them navigate an abysmal childhood. Their formative years were spent in a small, shabby house in west Texas. They witnessed horrible fights between their parents, Tammy and Hank. Tammy bore the effects of those fights in the form of black eyes, bruises, and welts. She toiled at two jobs while Hank worked hard at being a drunk. One night, Hank was passed out on the living room sofa—yet again. "Rubi Lee, Zeke," Tammy said, "pack a few items of clothing in a bag. We're leaving."

Tammy settled in Louisiana, where Rubi Lee and Zeke attended middle and high school. For Rubi Lee, school was a nightmare. During middle school, it seemed all the girls matured except her. She resented both her own flat chest and the tall, pretty girls with perfect everything. She cut her hair into a severe wedge and dyed it jet black, then taught herself how to apply the makeup to complete her look. To her dismay, though, her clothes hung on her small frame and the combination of black hair and goth makeup only intensified the pastiness of her thin face. The only bright spots in school were an elective dance class and painting class. She demonstrated much greater skill at dancing and painting than she did at making friends.

Despite her diminutive size, Rubi Lee was fiercely protective of Zeke—especially since he had a slight lisp. One day in the cafeteria, Rubi Lee overheard kids bullying Zeke. Fed up, she marched over to the group, wielding the dull knife from her lunch tray. The lead bully scoffed at her until she threw him up against the wall, knife at his throat. The entire cafeteria froze until a lunch-lady pulled her away. Rubi Lee was suspended for three days. No one ever bothered Zeke again. By the end of sophomore year, Zeke possessed the build of a running back and could take care of himself. At over six feet tall, he dwarfed Rubi Lee by at least eight inches. He was the clean-up hitter on the baseball team and pinned any opponent who had the misfortune of wrestling against him.

Their names, written in red ink, topped the *These Kids Are Trouble* list that circulated among teachers and administrators. Zeke and Rubi Lee left a paper trail of fights, bullying, and cutting class all the way through high school. The Dixons were distant and mistrustful, thanks to their dysfunctional parents, and they ignored all encouragement and offers of help from teachers and coaches.

Fed up with school, Zeke and Rubi Lee dropped out months shy of graduation. Attending college was never an option. For years, they worked menial jobs and had minor skirmishes with the law. Their lives were at a dead end—until that day in late March when their mother made her desperate call to their uncle, Victor Sykes.

CHAPTER 4

The early April morning air was muggy; the sky hung like a gray blanket. Rubi Lee and Zeke loaded the white van with their few measly belongings. They planned to drive straight through to Washington, DC, from Louisiana. With enough cigarettes, caffeine, and heavy metal, the sixteen-hour drive would be tolerable. Their dreams of a better, different life nearly crashed and burned because of a worn-out carburetor—something they could not afford. Their Uncle Victor wired them enough cash to cover the cost, plus money for a three-month deposit on a new apartment.

As they sped north on Interstate 59, Zeke remarked, "I never plan on going back to Louisiana. Ever."

"Damn straight." Rubi Lee gnawed a stick of beef jerky. She twitched her thin-lipped mouth and asked, "When's the last time we saw Uncle Vic?" Rubi Lee offered Zeke a stick. "Want one?"

Zeke took a stick from the package. "A long time. I think when we were like eleven or so? Maybe younger."

Rubi Lee watched the yellow lines speed by. "I still have all the birthday cards he sent me. He used to write the funniest messages and always stuck a dollar in the card. Remember?"

"Yup. And then the cards stopped coming and Mom told us he was in the war."

Several miles went by.

"I never thought we'd be working for our uncle in an import business. I'm sure it'll be a crapload better than our old jobs, right?" Rubi Lee asked and lit a cigarette. "And as much as we don't like our *mother*, I'm glad she called him."

"Did you talk to her before we left?" Zeke asked.

"Briefly. She tried to apologize again for being a crappy mom. I was like, *whatever*. I just let her babble."

"Was she high?" Zeke asked.

"Who knows and who cares. We're out of her life for good now, right?"

"Yup." Zeke yawned. "Any more beef jerky?"

"Here." She handed him a stick and consulted her phone. "GPS says we have six more hours. Are you okay driving?"

"I'm good for another two hours. We'll switch then."

"Sure. I'll text Uncle Vic and tell him we won't be there till late."

Rubi Lee's phone chimed within a minute. "He said to text when we get there, and he'll give us a little time to settle in. I don't know about you, little bro, but I sure am looking forward to making some *real* money. And I don't really give a shit what we have to do."

"Amen."

Sixteen hours after leaving Louisiana, they stood in the kitchen of their new two-bedroom apartment. Zeke and Rubi Lee threw their sleeping bags in their respective rooms and unpacked their backpacks. As agreed, Rubi Lee sent a text to Victor telling him they had arrived. He responded immediately. Rubi Lee read aloud, "Welcome to DC. I took the liberty of buying you some basic provisions you'll find in the refrigerator. Please be ready at eleven on

Wednesday morning. I will pick you up for an important meeting."

"Thanks, Uncle Vic. See you tomorrow," Rubi Lee spoke into her phone and hit send.

Zeke opened the fridge. Milk, cheese, eggs, bread, and coffee sat on the top shelf of the otherwise barren fridge. A jar of peanut butter, alongside two boxes of cereal, was on the counter. "Decent selection," Zeke said and shut the door.

"We can leave the other stuff in the van until tomorrow. I'm beat," Rubi Lee said.

"Same here. All that driving is tiring. I'll set the alarm for tomorrow. Night, Rube." Zeke went into his room.

"Night, Zeke."

* * *

At exactly eleven the next morning, an SUV parked outside honked.

"He's *here*?! Crap, I still have to get dressed!" Rubi Lee said, looking out the window.

"What do you expect? He's a former *Marine*. Hurry the hell up!" Zeke said.

Victor sat in the driver's seat and thrummed his fingers on the steering wheel. A door slammed from behind and Rubi Lee and Zeke joined him in the SUV. He turned in his seat and whispered, "Eleven means eleven. You're"—he consulted his Movado wristwatch—"five minutes late. First thing you need to learn is to *be on time*. Better yet, be early. Here is a little saying for you to memorize: Early is on time, on time is late, late is left. Understand?"

Zeke and Rubi Lee nodded like admonished school

children.

"Good. Don't forget it." He turned in his seat and hit the gas.

After ten minutes, Victor broke the silence. "Lesson two: You will not be high or drunk when transporting my clients. You do what you want on your own time, not on my time. And three, you will not speed. Officers are constantly patrolling the roads to and from the airports. You will maintain the proper speed and drive safely. Any questions?"

"No sir," Zeke and Rubi Lee said simultaneously.

Victor continued, "In this job, I may ask you to do things you may not like nor want to do. But aren't all jobs that way?" He flicked his eyes into the rear view mirror and saw them nod. "This morning you are going to meet two of my employees. One of whom you will be ferrying to and from both airports. The other one is my inside source."

"Yes sir," Rubi Lee answered for both.

Victor pulled the car to the curb in front of a small coffee shop. "I'll be right back," he said and shut the door.

Moments later he reappeared and motioned to Zeke and Rubi Lee to come into the shop.

"Here we go, sis," Zeke said.

The smell of freshly brewed coffee snaked up their noses and Zeke's stomach began to rumble. Victor sat in the back at a table with a man and a woman. He waved to them to come over. Victor stood up and introduced Rubi Lee and Zeke.

"Don Gaylord, Paula Brown, these are our new employees I told you about. Meet Zeke and Rubi Lee Dixon, my niece and nephew."

Pleasantries were exchanged. But no one bothered to

hide the blatant scrutinizing of one another.

"Please sit, everyone," Victor said.

Don spoke up. "Why do we need two drivers?"

"In case one of them falls ill or is working on something else for me."

Don picked up his cup of coffee. "Can we trust them?" Don asked.

Victor's stare bore holes into Don. "Are you *doubting* me?"

"No! Not at all." Don's cup shook slightly.

"I didn't think so."

"Do they understand the seriousness of what we do?" Paula asked.

"Yes, Paula, they do."

Don eyeballed Rubi Lee and gestured at her with his pointy chin. "She looks like she could barely hold a week-old kitten."

SLAM! Rubi Lee leaped up and thrust her knife into the table inches from Don's hand. She leaned close to his face and stared into his eyes. "Don't you *ever* call me weak, got it *Donny*?"

Don's Adam's apple bobbed as he leaned his head back and slowly moved his hand away from the knife.

"Don't let her petite size fool you. She's tougher than a honey badger. And like I said, they are very trustworthy. I think you will be wise to trust them." Victor grinned confidently.

"What kind of car do you drive?" Don asked.

"We have an older white van," Zeke answered.

"Any other questions?" Victor said.

Victor again ran down the plans for the next few weeks.

Don would be traveling abroad to secure the goods. Paula would monitor the drop spots.

Paula and Don got up from the table. "See you two around," she said. Don said nothing.

Victor walked them to the door. "I'll send you their contact information. Thank you for meeting."

Victor bought himself another cup of tea and coffee for Rubi Lee and Zeke. They sat for two hours and caught up on their lives.

"So, Uncle Vic, how did you start your import business?" Zeke asked.

Victor swallowed his tea and let it sit before answering. "I inherited it from a friend," he responded. He sat back and folded his arms across his chest.

"Tell us more. You have a great job at the Veterans Administration. How did you get involved with your side business?" Zeke pushed.

"Why do you want to know?"

"Because you're really successful and we want to understand why you can pay us all this money."

Rubi Lee quickly added, "Plus, we look up to you and you could give us some pointers about business. It's not like we have a father to ask."

This last comment tugged at Victor's thin heartstrings. Victor sipped his coffee and looked at the young but worn faces of his niece and nephew, debating whether to tell the whole story.

"Fine, you're my only family. What I am going to tell you stays here."

Rubi Lee and Zeke leaned forward and listened intently.

"When I returned from active duty, I found a job, but

made no money. A colleague of mine, Arnie, asked if I was interested in a side job working for him selling goods out of the trunk of his car. Arnie made all kinds of connections around the world."

"What do you mean selling goods out of a car?" Rubi Lee asked.

"Stereos, artwork, ivory, sneakers, and even drugs."

"Holy crap, how could he afford to buy all that stuff?" Zeke asked.

"Let's just say he didn't pay for any of it. He just sold the stuff—hence the import business." He sat back and smiled at them.

Rubi Lee and Zeke mulled the information over. "Oh, all of it was *stolen*," she said.

"Now you understand. I suggested we expand the business by enlisting some down-on-their luck war vets to run the goods into the country for a small fee. Arnie agreed and it worked well. We flew the vets all around the world to"—he looked up—"shall we say, bring back goods. Arnie had connections with high-profile people and they were more than happy to acquire high quality items for lots of money. The very wealthy have exotic tastes, but it was worth the risk."

"So, when you met Alex, what did she think of it?"

"At the time, she obviously was not in her current position. She was a fresh-faced legislative aide. I met her one day in the lobby and was taken by her intelligence and beauty. We struck up a conversation which led to a date and several more followed. On one of those dates, she poured her heart out about her penniless background and she swore she'd never return to poverty."

"And what—did you, like, hire her?" Rubi Lee asked.

"Not exactly. When I told her about the business, she wanted in. After all, she worked among the top echelon of people in the entire city—senators and congressmen." Victor sipped his tea and signaled for the server to bring more water. "And they have money—something we all love."

"How did you know you could trust her?" Rubi Lee was skeptical.

"Because she wanted to *make money* and at her low-level job, she could not afford the lifestyle she craved."

"Kind of like me and Zeke," Rubi Lee said.

"Exactly. Anyway, the money flowed in. I had high aspirations of selling high-end jewelry—diamonds to be exact. Arnie resisted and even threatened to expose me at work. He was content making small money."

"What happened to Arnie?" Zeke asked.

Victor sighed. "Oh, such a pity. His brakes on his car failed. He hit a tree and was killed." Victor took another sip and smiled.

Rubi Lee and Zeke exchanged a surprised glance.

"Now you two know the story of how the business started. Even though we are family, if either of you get greedy or threaten to expose us . . . well, it would be a shame if your van's brakes failed. Wouldn't it?" He placed his cup down on the table.

CHAPTER 5

At the Black LaSalle, one of DC's most popular bars, daffodils pushed to the surface of the large clay pots outside the main entrance. For an early spring evening, the temperature was warmer than usual and happy hour was in full swing. The seats were full; laughter and conversation filled the air.

Erin Driscoll, the manager, watched her two top bartenders, Ira and Daisy, duck, dodge, and reach around each other with the grace of a well-choreographed dance team. There was a tinge of comedy in the movements as Daisy towered over Ira, yet it worked. Patrons returned night after night, and money poured in.

Erin took pride in her knack for hiring excellent bartenders. She never compromised her three hiring criteria: intelligence, drive, and a passion for serving. Good looks helped too. Those qualities helped her make a killing when she tended bar during college. After graduation, Erin planned to travel abroad for the summer before starting her dream job as a Spanish teacher. She saved all her money for the trip as well as for a down payment on a house. Her childhood home was small—four bedrooms and one full bathroom. And with seven siblings, it felt like a shoebox. She grew up sharing everything and could not wait to purchase her first home. Her dreams went up in flames the night her mother left a cigarette burning in an ashtray. Thankfully, her parents were unhurt. Yet they lived on a meager budget and could not afford to buy a new house. Erin gave them all of her savings to relocate. Bartending was familiar and comfortable, and she soon found herself behind the bar again. Eventually, she worked her way up to manager and replenished her savings. She smiled when she heard Daisy gently admonishing a group of men.

"Hey! Stop with the cursing, or I'll toss y'all out!" Daisy yelled to a group of rowdy young men at the end of the bar. She was lenient with her patrons, except for those with foul mouths.

"Aw, come on Daisy! You love us, especially me!" slurred one of the party boys.

"Seriously? My cat wouldn't even date you," Daisy shot back, but tempered her words with a smile.

Daisy Kathryn Taylor loved tending bar at the Black LaSalle. The plush leather stools that lined a hand-carved oak bar coupled with low lighting created a comfortable, warm environment. Behind the bar, floor-to-ceiling mahogany arches supported glass shelves lined with bottle after bottle of every type of liquor imaginable. A striking oil painting of a black LaSalle, one of General Motors' finest cars, hung on the center wall behind the bar. The painting was huge, measuring six by eight feet. The original owner of the bar salvaged the painting from an estate sale, and it was now a popular talking point as the bar's namesake.

When Daisy was accepted into grad school, she knew she'd have to get a job. DC was an expensive city, and even though she secured a student loan and a relatively cheap apartment, a part-time job would help pay the bills. She had experience tending bar her senior year in college and liked the idea of flashing her bright smile to earn a few generous tips. She researched bars close to her apartment and interviewed at three she liked, though the Black LaSalle was her favorite. When Erin offered her a job, she jumped on it.

"You know," joked Erin, "people might mix us up."

"What do you mean?" Daisy asked. "Why would they confuse you with me?"

"Seriously?" Erin put her arm around Daisy and turned her around to face a mirror-lined wall. "Look at us."

Daisy's eyes flicked back and forth. She had not noticed their similar looks before, yet she immediately saw the likeness. She knew then and there she and Erin would get along. "I've always wanted a sister! But your hair is more auburn."

"Don't tell me you don't like your *gorgeous* ginger curls. You're crazy if you don't!"

"I do, I suppose. Your auburn look is *hot* though."

Erin stood and tilted her head to one side as she further scrutinized Daisy's features. "And look. Your eyes are like emeralds. Mine are a more amber color."

Erin was right. In time, people confused the two tall, fit women, each with masses of curls that bounced as they moved around the bar. Daisy's kind, yet direct demeanor was the perfect complement to her wit and humor. Her mind was a sponge and, by the end of her first week, she had memorized twenty cocktail recipes. No one mixed a tequila sunrise or a Manhattan quite like Daisy.

Daisy checked on a trio of middle-aged regulars she and her colleagues had nicknamed Stick, Mumbles, and Moneybags. "You guys ready for another round?" Stick, whose real name was Teresa, drank like a fish, but never ate.

Mumbles, also known as Al, managed to speak without moving his lips. And Moneybags, a.k.a. Donny, paid for his friends' drinks from the stack of hundred-dollar bills he liked to show off.

"Sure, why not?" Moneybags replied. "I'll be out of town for a week, so, bottoms up!"

"You headed somewhere exciting?" Stick asked.

Moneybags snorted. "No. Unless you consider Moscow exciting."

"Moscow!" Stick exclaimed.

"As in Russia?"

Several heads turned to see the source of the noise. Stick jerked her thumb at Moneybags and told the gawkers, "This one's off to Moscow!" The onlookers returned to their own conversations, clearly finding Stick's exclamation neither interesting nor exciting.

Mumbles looked at Moneybags and asked, "Why?"

"It's part of my job."

"In *Russia*?" Stick retorted.

"Yeah, unfortunately," Moneybags answered.

Stick turned serious. "Al, I guess you and I are gonna be paying for our own drinks while Donny's gone."

"Tell ya what," Donny said. "Whatever time I get back, I'll text you, and we'll start the party right away, instead of waiting for an official five o'clock happy hour start time. Sound good?"

"Deal," Mumbles replied. "Assuming you get back any time before five!"

Stick was pleased at the chance to start happy hour early. "Hey, Donny," she asked, "will you bring me back one of those nesting dolls?"

"Nesting what?" Moneybags asked.

"You know. Those nesting dolls where the large one holds a bunch of smaller dolls inside. I always thought they were cute."

Moneybags looked at Mumbles. The two men shrugged at the same time.

She shook her head. "I'll text you a picture later."

"Sure," Don replied.

CHAPTER 6

After two weeks of ferrying Don Gaylord to and from the airport, Victor called Zeke and Rubi Lee and asked to meet him by the Korean War Memorial. "Things have changed," he told them. "Please be there at two o'clock."

"Okay," Zeke said. "See you then." He hung up and relayed what Victor said. "I wonder what's changed."

Entrenched in a game on her phone, Rubi Lee shrugged.

Rubi Lee and Zeke arrived early and took in the sight of the memorial. They were riveted by the nineteen beautiful, ghostly soldiers situated in the middle of the space. The soldiers represented each branch of the military: fourteen Army, three Marines, one Navy, and one Air Force.

Goosebumps crept up Zeke's arm. He stared at each figure. "I feel like they're about to talk or move any second," he whispered.

"Pretty spectacular, isn't it?" Victor approached them from behind.

Zeke could not take his eyes off the soldiers. "Yeah. I've never seen anything like it. I didn't even know there *was* a Korean War," Zeke said.

"These statues are really cool—eerie, too," Rubi Lee added. The painstaking effort of creating the statues awakened her artistic side, a side she buried.

"Yes, they are. This is my favorite memorial because it's

so lifelike," Victor said. He gestured toward some benches. "Please sit."

"What's up?" Rubi Lee asked.

"According to my intel, Don has been talking to people about our operation. He has the tendency to drink too much and talk. As the old saying goes, 'loose lips sink ships.'"

Zeke and Rubi Lee stared at him, blank looks on their faces.

Victor nodded. "Ah, young people. You all don't understand old adages—what a pity. In other words, it means when people talk when they shouldn't, things go *very* wrong. What this means for you is Don Gaylord will meet an accidental death. I want you to do it tonight when you pick him up."

"*Tonight?* That's kind of soon, Uncle Vic," Zeke said.

"Yes, tonight." He reached into his briefcase and pulled out a paper bag. "Bring this with you." Victor handed it to Rubi Lee. In it was a pistol.

She pulled it halfway out of the bag. "You want us to *shoot* him?"

"No—too traceable. You will simply threaten him with the gun."

"How should we do it?" Zeke asked.

"Drive him to the junkyard under Warren Bridge. Order him out of the van with the gun, and then make it look like a hit and run." Victor stood. "Call me when it's done." He walked toward the soldiers in front of him, saluted, and walked away down the sidewalk.

* * *

That night, Zeke and Rubi Lee sat in their white van on an airport side road like they'd done each time Don returned from a job. Rain poured from the slate sky. An orange glow from their cigarettes punctuated the darkness inside the van. Their assignment was to pick up Don Gaylord, whose flight from Moscow was due to land at seven p.m. Given the weather, chances for an on-time arrival were slim.

Rubi Lee looked out the window. She asked her brother, "Do you think we'll hear from him soon?"

"I don't know," Zeke said. "It's raining like hell. If his flight lands on time, I'll be surprised." He lowered the window and tossed out his cigarette butt.

Rubi Lee checked the airline app on her phone. "His flight's thirty minutes late." She let out a sigh, then put out her cigarette and picked up the loaded gun from the floor by her feet. "I'm just anxious to get this over with, you know?"

"Same here," Zeke said.

* * *

Don was awakened by the voice of the pilot informing the passengers that, due to heavy rain, the plane would be arriving thirty minutes late. Everyone around him groaned. *Figures*, Don thought as he looked out the window at the cloud cover below. He hated flying. In one final slug, he tossed back the last of his peptomopolitan—vodka, cranberry juice, and Pepto-Bismol.

Exactly thirty minutes later, the plane's landing gear disengaged and the 747 floated down onto the slick runway. No one paid any heed to the direction of keeping seatbelts fastened. The second the plane taxied to the gate, the passengers around him sprang into action and snapped open the overhead compartments to pull out their bags. *Do they really think they'll deplane first—with some fifty passengers ahead of them?* Don knew the process of getting off the plane and through customs would be slow. He texted Rubi Lee to tell her he was still on the plane and would text her again when he was ready to be picked up.

Okay, we're waiting on a side road, she texted back.

Sweat trickled down Don's back as an ominous reminder of what could go wrong when passing through customs, even though he had made similar trips a dozen times before. Thanks to his drink on board, at least his stomach had settled. And thanks to the lines of people waiting to get outside to their families and cars, the customs agents worked quickly to pass everyone through. Don watched as the agent stamped his passport and waved him on.

From there, he nudged his way through crowds of other travelers and saw his duffle bag winding its way to him on the creaky baggage carousel. He texted Rubi Lee he would see them outside in five minutes.

Through the rain, he saw a white van and waved it forward. Zeke pulled up, and Don yanked on the side door and got in. The odor of crusted food wrappers and cigarette smoke assaulted his senses.

Don greeted Rubi Lee and Zeke with sarcasm. "I see millennials were taught how to clean." He kicked an empty Styrofoam cup out of his way.

"Gee Don, it's good to see you, too," Rubi Lee responded. "You sound grumpy."

"Because I am. I feel like I was born on that plane."

"Any issue with the diamonds?" Zeke asked.

"None. I sewed them into a thick sweatshirt. More importantly, do you have my five grand?"

"Right here." Rubi Lee pulled an envelope from the glove compartment.

Don smiled. "Perfect. Now, just get me home." He turned his attention to his phone and was about to text his bar buddies when the van jolted. Don looked up sharply. "What the hell?" He looked out the window. "Where are we going? My place is in the other direction."

Rubi Lee answered, "We're taking a different route."

"Why are we changing course?" There was no response from either Zeke or Rubi Lee. "Well?"

Rubi Lee glanced quickly at Zeke, who kept his eyes forward. Zeke had turned off the main road onto an access road where he drove slowly under a graffiti-covered bridge. Tires, broken televisions, and other debris littered the godforsaken area.

"What's going on here?" Don demanded.

Rubi Lee turned and looked at Don. She hissed, "Maybe you can tell *us*, Donny. Seems you've been telling people about our operation."

"What are you talking about?" Don yelled.

"Talkin' too much is what Victor called it," Rubi Lee spat back.

Don snorted. "What? Why would I tell anyone about this?"

"Because you're a drunk. Just like our daddy. Alcohol makes people talk. Seems you get drunk and shoot your mouth off."

"For God's sake, I have no idea what you're talking

about. And, yes, I drink. Who cares?"

"*We* care and so does Uncle Vic." Rubi Lee narrowed her eyes. "Someone heard you yapping."

"Again, what are you talking about?" Don's mind reeled.

"*Again*, Don, you were talking to people. Uncle Vic doesn't like you talking about Russia."

Don tried in vain to remember who he talked to about his travels.

"You know what happens to people who talk, right, Don?" Rubi Lee asked.

Beads of sweat broke out across Don's forehead and his heart wanted to explode. *Think. Think hard. These crazies are not messing around.* With Zeke and Rubi Lee facing front, Don reached for his phone and sent a text. *trble here. need help. in white van. near the—*

Rubi Lee turned around when she heard Don typing. "What in the hell do you think you're doing?" She snatched his phone.

"Gimme that, you bitch!" Don lunged at her.

Zeke slammed on the brakes. "Who are you calling a bitch?"

"Yeah. Who're you calling a bitch?" Rubi Lee picked up the gun and cocked it.

Don's eyes opened wide.

"Now, get out, but leave your bags." She fired a warning shot.

Don's bowels loosened as the bullet whizzed by his head and lodged into the side of the van. "Jesus, are you *crazy*? You could have killed me!"

"I know. You're not worth the bullet, though, you lying piece of shit," Rubi Lee said. "Now, who have you told about

Victor's work?"

"I swear to God I haven't told anyone!"

Zeke parked the van under the bridge. He turned in his seat and glared at Don. "Best to listen to my big sis. Get out. *Now.*"

Don looked out at the barren dumping ground under the bridge. "I'm not going anywhere except home. Turn this van around and get us out of this hellhole."

Rubi Lee spoke in a low tone. "Get out now or I'll blow your ugly-ass head off." She leaned out of her seat and pushed the cold metal of the barrel against Don's moist forehead.

Don stared at Rubi Lee and she stared right back with murderous eyes.

"I don't understand . . ." he started. But he knew his efforts would be futile.

Rubi Lee cocked the gun. "Get out. Last warning."

Don stared at the brother and sister team. "You fools won't get away with this. Victor will figure out you took my bag and he'll be after you next."

Rubi Lee glared at Don and continued. "You dumbass. Who do you think told us to do this?" She threw her head back and laughed.

"You're lying. He needs me, and so do you for that matter."

"No, we don't. And Uncle Vic? He *especially* doesn't need a snitch like you. Now, out," Zeke ordered.

The wiper blades swished on the windshield. Don looked out the window, then pulled the door open and stepped slowly into the pounding rain.

Zeke and Rubi Lee watched him walk toward the main

road.

"Ready?" Zeke asked.

"Yep," Rubi Lee responded. "It's time."

Zeke ignored the stabs of nerves inside his chest. *Just get it over with.* Zeke punched the gas pedal and the van lurched forward.

Deafened by the rain, Don did not hear the van. He did, however, see lights reflecting on the asphalt road ahead of him. He spun around and saw the van was headed in his direction. He tried to outrun it, but he tripped and slipped in a futile attempt to get off the road. Zeke and Rubi Lee laughed as the van hurtled toward their panicked prey. Don looked back and put his hands up in a last act of self-defense. He was terrified.

When the brother and sister saw the look on Don's face, they knew he understood these were his final moments on Earth. He screamed as the van sped straight into him. *Thump!* The strike of the van hurled Don into the air. One of his shoes flew back and hit the van.

"Bull's eye, little brother!" Rubi Lee shouted. "We got him! Uncle Vic will be so proud."

Zeke scanned the desolate area. Not a soul in sight. He turned the van around and aimed the headlights at the heap on the ground. There was no movement. Don looked like a twisted marionette. Zeke inched the van closer to the body and got out. He put on a pair of latex gloves and rooted through the dead man's pants pockets. Amid used tissues, eye drops, and keys, he found Don's wallet.

Meanwhile, Rubi Lee scrolled through the text messages on Don's phone and saw his last text was successfully sent, but she did not know to whom. *Shit! That could be incriminating.* She also saw a message from someone named Teresa who asked Don to get her a nesting doll. She yelled out the window at Zeke to hurry up.

In the van, Rubi Lee showed Zeke the text. "Look."

Zeke's eyes widened as he read. "This is bad. These people—whoever they are—know something's wrong."

"You're right. Plus," Rubi Lee added, "whoever Teresa is, she asked Don to bring her a nesting doll from Russia—"

"Which means she's expecting Don to give it to her," Zeke finished. He rested his head against the driver's side window.

"Where do you think it is?"

Zeke shrugged. "It's probably in his bag." He reached behind him for Don's bag and rooted through it. "Is this it?" He held up a wooden nesting doll.

Rubi Lee checked the photo in Teresa's text message and acknowledged it was the doll.

"What's so special about this?" Zeke asked.

"I don't know. It's just a doll with, like, six smaller dolls inside it."

"Okay, whatever. What do we do now?"

"We need—" Before Rubi Lee could finish her sentence, Don's phone chimed and lit up.

"What's it say?"

"It's a text from Teresa asking Don if he's okay and when they're gonna meet at the Black LaSalle."

"Black LaSalle? What's that?"

"No clue. We'll ask Uncle Vic."

"Are you gonna write back?"

"Let me think on it," Rubi Lee said. "But first, you need to wipe the front fender. Use the rag from in back. We'll burn it later."

"Check." Zeke turned off the headlights and got out of the van. The fender showed no sign of damage. Zeke used the rag to rid the van of Don Gaylord's DNA, then stuffed the rag in his pocket before returning to the van.

"We need to call Uncle Vic to tell him Don's dead. He needs to know about this text thread and this stupid doll, too."

Rubi Lee put Victor on speakerphone and told him, "Yes, he's dead, but . . ."

"But what, Rubi Lee?" Victor asked. "I can tell by your voice there's more."

"He, um, sent an SOS text to two people."

Silence, and then, "Explain please."

"Because I have his phone and read the messages. He said he was in a white van and in trouble. And some lady named Teresa asked Don to bring her back a *nesting* doll. There was also something in the text about meeting at a place called the Black LaSalle."

Victor thrummed his fingers on his desk. The sound was loud enough for Rubi Lee and Zeke to hear through the phone. They swallowed hard. Rubi Lee hastily added, "Don't worry, I know what Teresa looks like. There's a picture of her on Don's phone."

After an excruciatingly long silence, Victor exhaled loudly. "That certainly is helpful. The Black LaSalle is a bar three blocks from the Washington Mall. You need to find out who she is and her connection to Don. We can't have this. You will text her from Don's phone and set up a time to meet."

"I'll say to meet at four thirty. We'll get there earlier to check things out and get seats."

"Wise plan. That place draws a large crowd. When you spot them, wait ten minutes until you send a text from Don's phone saying he's not able to make it. Since you know what Teresa looks like, you'll wait to see what they do."

"And then what?" Zeke asked.

"You'll wait all night if you have to until they decide to leave."

"And when they do?" Rubi Lee asked.

"You will follow them and find out if they know why Don went to Russia."

Zeke asked, "And if they do?"

"You will make it abundantly clear to them they know nothing about Don and his trip. Understand?"

"Yes, sir," they replied. Then Rubi Lee asked, "You want us to bring you the money, right?"

"Yes," Victor said. "You also need to find a red Washington Wizards sweatshirt in Gaylord's bag. Sewn inside is two million dollars' worth of raw diamonds. Take it home with you. You will eventually drop it at one of the spots when I tell you."

"Two *million* dollars?" Rubi Lee breathed. *Holy shit.*

"Yes, so don't lose it, understand?"

"Yes sir."

"Oh, and before you bring me that cash, keep two grand for yourselves." He ended the call.

Zeke and Rubi Lee looked at each other and mouthed the words *Two grand!*

"That's a ton of money," Rubi Lee said. "I know he's pissed—the text wasn't our fault, right?"

"Not at all. How were we supposed to know? And since

he gave us a mountain of money, I'd say he's pretty much over it."

Rubi Lee concurred, "Two grand'll definitely be enough for another new tat."

"Maybe more than one!" Zeke started the engine. "Let's get the hell out of here."

They drove off into the inky, wet night.

CHAPTER 7

During her two days off each week, Daisy took care of necessary errands. With her to-do list complete for the day, she headed home. Gussie, her calico cat, greeted her and sniffed at the grocery bags. Daisy flipped on a reggae music playlist. The soft notes floated through her apartment as she unpacked groceries and did some light cleaning. At age eleven, she fell in love with reggae when she and her family vacationed in Jamaica. She had never heard music so intoxicatingly beautiful in her life. Her mother could barely get her to leave the pool where the music floated out of speakers.

I loved that trip, she thought as she sank back on her sofa and admired her first apartment. The walls were a soft gray, which complemented the maple floor. White cupboards and an island were the focus of the small kitchen. The place was small, clean, and all hers. After sharing a tiny house and a bathroom with three older brothers, her apartment was paradise.

* * *

That evening, Daisy handled the crowd with her gracious smile and the tip jar was filling up. Happy hour was just about over when two police officers entered the bar. They stood and looked around at the patrons for a minute, then approached Daisy, who had seen them but continued to work. She assumed the police officers were just doing their usual foot patrol.

"Excuse me, miss. I'm Officer Dunn and this is Officer Norman. Are you the manager?"

Daisy looked at the two officers. Dunn, the male officer stood half a foot taller than his female partner. Both looked to be in their mid-thirties.

"No, I'm not," Daisy answered.

"Is the manager available?" Officer Dunn asked.

"I think she's here. Let me check," Daisy replied. She went to the back of the bar and opened the door to the office. It was empty. Back at the bar area, she said, "Actually, the manager—Erin Driscoll—must've run out for a few minutes. She said she had to go to the bank, if you want to wait. I can text her and tell her to come back now?"

"Yes, please. We'll wait for her. Thanks." The officers sat at the bar.

After Daisy texted Erin, she offered the officers drinks.

"Sure. I'll have a Coke," Officer Norman said.

"Water for me, please," Officer Dunn answered.

"Here you go." Daisy placed the drinks in front of them. "My name is Daisy in case there's anything else you need. Erin said she'll be back in a few minutes."

"Thank you," Officer Norman said.

"You're welcome." As Daisy unloaded the glasses from the heat washer, her curiosity got the best of her. "I don't mean to be nosy, but maybe I can help you with what you need?"

The officers looked at each other and shrugged.

"Possibly," Officer Norman replied. "Are you willing to answer a few questions?"

"Sure, but if it will take more than a minute or two, I need to get someone to cover the bar."

"It might," Officer Norman responded.

Daisy asked Ira to cover while she spoke with the officers. She led them to a quieter area where they sat in a booth.

"We're here to ask about a body that was found yesterday."

Daisy blinked at them. "What? A body?" She was both surprised and intrigued.

"Yes ma'am. The body of a man was found under the Warren Bridge, but there was no identification on him. We did, however, find *this* in one of his jacket pockets." The officer removed a crumpled piece of paper from a small plastic bag and handed it to Daisy.

Daisy looked the paper over and saw it was a credit card receipt from the Black LaSalle. "It's a receipt. From here."

"Do you recognize the signature?"

Daisy squinted as she read out, "Don Gaylord. At least that's what I think it says." She handed the paper back to the officer.

The officer next placed a photo on the table and asked, "Do you know this man?"

Daisy looked down at the picture and gasped. She took in the man's half-closed eyes, partially open mouth, and dried blood caked on his left cheek. "Oh my God. Yes, I know him. It's ... um ... It's Moneybags," she stammered, then realized he must be the man whose signature appeared on the receipt. "Oh, no. He's the man who signed the receipt, right?"

"Yes."

"I can't look at this," Daisy said. She cast her eyes away from the photo of the dead man.

"If you don't mind, take another look—to be sure," Officer Dunn asked.

"Please, no. Once was enough. It's definitely him."

"All right. Thank you for looking."

Daisy sighed. "We called him Moneybags. I feel badly I never knew his real name."

"Moneybags? Quite an interesting nickname," Officer Dunn remarked.

"Yes. My coworkers and I nicknamed him because he always paid in cash." She caught herself. "Well, *most* of the time." She indicated the receipt in Officer Dunn's hand. "He was a very generous tipper."

"Do you remember the last time he was in here?" Officer Dunn asked.

Daisy frowned and tried to recall when she last saw Don Gaylord. "Hmm, maybe a week ago, or longer? I'm not one hundred percent sure. Sorry," Daisy replied.

Just then, Erin entered the bar. She looked around and saw Daisy seated in a booth with two police officers. She approached the booth and said, "Hi. What's going on?"

The officers introduced themselves and explained the reason for their visit. They showed Erin the photo.

Erin immediately recognized the man and inhaled sharply. "Oh, no. Moneybags! This is horrible!" She looked away from the picture.

Officer Norman cleared her throat. "I'm sorry about all this. He was found dead yesterday." She then showed Erin the receipt from Don's pocket.

"I can't believe this. Near here?" Erin asked, horrified.

"No. He was found under Warren Bridge, not far from the airport," Officer Norman answered.

"I'm shocked. He's one of our best customers."

"Do you remember if Mr. Gaylord came in with anyone or interacted with anyone while he was here?"

"Of course," Erin said. "He usually came in by himself, and he seemed to be friendly with two regulars."

"Do you see them here now?" Officer Dunn asked.

Erin scanned the bar, looking for Stick and Mumbles. She looked back at the officer and shook her head. "No. They're not here."

"Can you describe them?" Officer Norman asked.

"One is a woman who looks about sixty and the other is a man about the same age."

"Do you know their names?" the officer asked.

"I do. The woman's name is Teresa and the man is Al." Erin then shook her head and added, "I'm a little embarrassed to admit we have nicknames for them."

"Nicknames?" Officer Dunn asked.

"Yes, my coworkers and I refer to Teresa as Stick and Al as Mumbles—not to their faces, though. She's rail thin and he's hard to understand when he talks. Hence, their nicknames."

"I see." Officer Dunn smiled at Erin and scribbled on a pad. "Any other physical description of them? African American, Latino, Caucasian?"

"They're white," Erin replied. "Teresa is short and has long white hair she usually wears pulled back in a tight bun. I've seen her wear glasses, you know, to read the menu. And her voice is sort of raspy."

"How about the man?"

"He wears glasses too and is taller than Teresa. He has gray hair and seems to always wear a striped, short-sleeved shirt."

"He has a full head of hair?" Dunn asked.

"Yes. Oh, and he has a birthmark on his cheek."

"Left, right? Approximate size?"

Erin scowled in thought. "Right cheek and roughly the size of a dime."

"Do you think they're romantically linked?" Officer Dunn asked.

Erin shook her head. "I don't get that feeling. I've never seen them be affectionate or physical with each other."

"Where do you think Don Gaylord fits in with them?" Officer Norman asked.

"I'm not sure. I think they happened to meet here one time and have hung out together since then. All three of them are friendly and never get out of hand like some of the people who come in here."

"Thank you for your help. When they're in next, please give us a call." Officer Norman handed Erin her card.

"Do you have any leads?" Daisy asked.

"Not at this time. It's early in our investigation and we're canvassing the area to speak with anyone who might have information we can use," Officer Norman replied.

"Well, we hope you find whoever did this," Erin said.

"So do we. Please call if you have more information. Have a good night." The two officers made their way through the crowd to the door.

CHAPTER 8

The air was balmy, even at eleven o'clock when Daisy left. On her walk home, the warmth conjured memories of childhood summers in Cab Station, Virginia. Summers were special for Daisy because of a boy she had befriended— Nicholas Tucker Tyson. NT, as he was called, spent six summers in Cab Station with his grandparents, William and Marian Tyson. The Tysons and Daisy's parents, the Taylors, were good friends. Soon, NT and Daisy became inseparable.

NT. I wonder how he is. Those young summers together were filled with lazy days at Serenity Lake, playing golf, and plenty of ice cream at Sweetwoods. Daisy smiled when she recalled how she adored spending time with him. As naïve seventeen-year-olds, she and NT believed their summers would blissfully roll on this way forever. One winter night, he called to tell her that his visits to Cab Station were over. He explained to her that his grandparents decided to move back to Philadelphia to be nearer to family. Daisy was devastated and NT's hollow tone told her he shared her feelings. They promised to stay in touch and visit each other during Christmas vacations. However, before they knew it, they had graduated from high school and gone off to college. They texted and friended each other on Facebook and Instagram, but these online friendships were not the same. With life and time, they drifted apart.

Daisy's first summer without NT was empty and boring.

She worked one summer serving ice cream at Sweetwoods and one was enough. Daisy grew to hate scooping ice cream and smelling like waffle cones. She complained to her mother, Annie, who suggested to Daisy she caddie, especially since she played golf and understood the game well.

Daisy recalled her mother's encouraging words. "Honey, you love to play golf. Why don't you call or go see Hoot about being a caddie? I'm sure he can help."

Daisy liked the idea and soon found herself as the only female caddie at Cascades Golf Club. Hoot, the caddie master, worked them hard, yet the cash tips were worth it.

Daisy walked up the steps to her apartment building, tapped in the door code, and entered when the door buzzed. She stopped to collect two days' worth of mail, mostly junk. At her apartment door, she slid her key in the lock. As soon as Daisy opened the door, she heard a loud meow as Gussie leaped off a windowsill perch.

"Hi, Gussie. Are you hungry?"

Gussie rubbed up against Daisy's shins, and Daisy bent to give the cat a rub on the head. Gussie meowed again loudly. "I guess you are." Daisy poured kibbles into the cat's bowl and turned on the TV. She flipped to a news channel to catch up on the day's events. Gussie soon joined her on the couch. The cat purred with delight at Daisy's scratching along her back.

The hours she spent working at the Black LaSalle were good preparation for the hours required by her course load in pursuit of a graduate degree in journalism and public affairs. The year-long program would pave the way for her to be a news reporter.

Daisy's career as a reporter was born her freshman year in high school. One night she was flipping through channels and landed on an old episode of the news show, *Entertainment Tonight*. As an impressionable fifteen-year-old, Daisy was enamored with the coverage of gorgeous, rich celebrities, as well as the stunning reporter. Watching *ET* became a ritual. Her brother Brett, whom she adored but also drove her nuts, used to tease her about watching "that crap."

"You should watch the *real* news with *real* stories. Those stories"—he pointed at the television—"are a joke."

"I *like* watching them, so what?"

"You're too smart to watch that crap. And since you *love* to tell stories, maybe you'll be a reporter someday—but not on *ET*!"

In high school, Daisy helped establish CAB TV, the school's cable television network. Three out of five mornings a week, Daisy and a classmate reported stories related to school, sports scores, and upcoming events. She thrived on interviewing people, writing their stories, and reporting it live on the air. The teacher who ran the club told her she was a natural.

Daisy settled in to watch the news. She enjoyed imagining herself in the reporter's seat, her hair and makeup perfect and her eyes lasered on the teleprompters as she delivered the latest news to all her viewers. *I can't wait.*

CHAPTER 9

At twenty-three, Nicholas Tucker Tyson was ready to start his own life, meet new people, and enjoy life in a fascinating city: Washington, DC. He sat up in bed in his mother's house and looked around his boyhood room. Posters of Jerry Rice, Brett Favre, Tiger Woods, and other famous athletes stared back at him. Bags of clothes sat on his floor ready to be thrown into the U-Haul truck.

By seven thirty, he was in the kitchen toasting a bagel and sipping coffee. He saw his mother in the back yard giving her two dogs their first run of the day. The toaster pinged and Nick smothered the bagel with butter and jelly. Georgia Tyson soon entered the kitchen with the dogs trailing closely behind.

"Morning, Mom. Morning, Clarabell. Morning, Geronimo." He reached down and petted each dog on the head.

"Sleep well?" Georgia Tyson asked as she poured creamer into her cup.

"I did. How about you? I heard you get up extra early this morning."

"I tossed and turned and finally just got up, probably because I was thinking about how much I'll miss you."

"I'll miss you too, but we'll Facetime."

"I know. It's not the same, though," Georgia said. "In any

case, I can't tell you how excited I am for you to start this next chapter in life." She squeezed her son's hand.

"Me too." Nick crunched on his bagel and mentally ran through his packing list. Mother and son sat in contented silence and enjoyed their breakfast.

By late morning, the temperature had shot up to eighty degrees, which was steamy for late May. Nick's T-shirt was drenched after he finished loading the truck he rented for his move from Philadelphia. He checked twice to ensure the doors were locked and secure.

Georgia walked out of her house and onto the gravel driveway where Nick was waiting. Close on her heels were the dogs. "It's always good to double-check the locks. The last thing you need is for the back to pop open and all your worldly possessions fly out onto the interstate."

"That would not be good," Nick said. "I think I'm ready to head out."

"I believe you are." Georgia held Nick at arm's length and looked up into her son's handsome face. He had her same large hazel eyes and an angular face softened by arching eyebrows. Years of braces gave him a smile that melted hearts and drew envy. Nick used to complain to his mother he was the runt of all his classmates, and he was destined to be short. Not anymore. Just as his father did, he shot up in high school to just over six feet tall and tipped the scales at two hundred muscular pounds.

"Have you heard from Win yet?" Georgia asked. Win— Winston Wang—was Nick's friend from college. He was three years older than Nick and in the same fraternity.

"He's meeting me later today."

"Do you have everything?" His mother looked at his

packed-to-the-gills rental truck.

"Yeah. I checked my list at least three times." He looked at his mother. "You'll be okay here without me?"

"Yes, I think Clarabell, Geronimo, and I can hold down the fort. Plus, with a new catering staff to train, I'm going to be pretty busy—not too busy to miss you."

"I'll be busy as well. And I'll miss you too."

"You're going to your dad's from here, right?"

"Yup. I just texted him and said I'll be there in a few minutes."

Nick's parents had been divorced since he was in eighth grade. At the time, he had no idea how to handle the resentment and anger that pulsated through him. As he matured, those dark emotions melted away. Eventually, he came to understand his parents and understood it was best they split.

"Call me when you get to DC, okay?"

"I will, I promise." Nick scratched the dogs on their heads and told them to be good. "And guard Mom with your life." He turned to his mother and said, "Love you, Mom." He gave her one last hug.

"I love you too, honey. Drive safely."

Georgia felt sadness mingled with pride as she waved goodbye and watched the white truck rumble down the road and turn the corner. She did not let her son see her tears.

* * *

Nick pulled up to his father's house and honked the horn before getting out of the truck.

Christopher Tyson opened the front door, walked down to the driveway, and stood next to his son. "Hi, NT. It looks like you're ready to roll."

"That's an understatement. Everything I need is stuffed right in here." Nick patted the side of the truck.

"You *do* have truck insurance, right?"

"Yes, I do. I'll be fine."

Christopher walked around the truck and inspected the tires. "The tires are in good shape. I see no sign of balding."

"Dad, trust me, I wouldn't rent some lemon. Plus, the drive is not long. And if, for some reason, a tire blew, I know how to change it, thanks to you."

"I know, I know. I'm being overly protective," Christopher chuckled. "I can't tell you how proud I am of you, son. The senator is lucky."

"Thanks. I'll see a load of grunt work, which is exactly what I expect. I'll be able to move up to legislative aide soon."

"Your work ethic and capacity for patience make you the perfect man for the job."

"Thanks, Dad. I'd better hit the road before it gets too late."

Christopher held his son tightly. "I love you, NT. I can't wait to hear how things are going once you're settled."

Nick hugged his father back. "Thanks. I love you too. I'll call later."

"Drive safely."

"Will do."

Before pulling out of the driveway, Nick texted the rental agent of his new residence. *Hey, Jen, leaving now. Will text again when I get close.*

Jen replied, *See you in a few hours. Safe trip!*

Traffic moved at a decent speed. Nick encountered no accidents. He shook his head at drivers who were entrenched on their phones, driving below the speed limit. He quickly returned his focus to the road and the music he had loaded from his favorite bands. The robotic voice of his GPS interrupted a song to state an hour remained until he reached his destination. At a rest stop, Nick texted Jen again and told her his ETA.

Growing up, everyone called Nicholas by his two-letter nickname, NT. Like many young boys, he dreamt of being a professional football player, and NT Tyson was an ultra-cool name for a pro athlete. However, during one dreadfully lopsided football game in seventh grade, Nick was slammed to the ground by a boy twice his size. A shattered collar bone and minor concussion permanently ended his football career. When he went to college, he insisted on being called by his full name, reasoning that Nick was a more mature name for a college student. Close family and childhood friends still called him NT, which was fine. He knew some things stayed forever.

As a senior in high school, Nick got hooked on the tumultuous, enthralling world of politics. His eighteenth birthday fell prior to a presidential election, and he counted down the days until he could vote in his first one. He researched the candidates thoroughly, watched the debates and formed his own opinions, regardless of what he heard or read.

During Christmas break of his sophomore year in college, Christopher asked his son about his choice of major. "You'll be declaring a major soon, correct?"

"Yes. At the end of this semester."

Nick's father laughed. "Not to tell you what to do, but I'm going to anyway."

"Uh oh, here it comes," Nick teased.

"How about economics? I know you love politics, but that's a tough haul."

Out of respect, Nick let his father do what he did best: be a father. "Dad, I appreciate your input, but—"

"Now it's my turn to say uh oh."

"It's not so bad. I think you'll be pleased."

Christopher raised one eyebrow in expectation.

"I'm going to major in political science and minor in communications. Poli sci is a constant field. I find it mesmerizing. And, as you well know, I'd love to live in DC someday. I know I can make it happen."

Nick's father smiled. "I don't doubt your tenacity and ability to do well in whatever field you enter. I do, however, worry about you making ends meet, especially as a new guy in a new city."

Nick laughed. "Dad, I don't graduate for two years!"

"I know, I know. You're right." Christopher shrugged. "What can I say? I'm your father and I worry—especially about people taking advantage of your altruistic nature."

"Thanks. I'll be fine."

Christopher looked at his son and said, "Yes, you will."

The following year, Nick secured an internship in the office of a state senator in Harrisburg, Pennsylvania. The minute he stepped in the office, Nick felt like he was in locomotive engine barreling full steam ahead. Days were long and often stretched well into the night. Quickly enough, Nick realized his desire to live and work in the capital where the real action happened was stronger than ever. This experience helped to cement his aspiration of becoming a US senator someday.

"In four hundred feet, turn left on Leonard Street," the GPS voice announced. Nick continued until he heard the GPS voice speak again. "Turn left in five hundred feet." Nick turned left down a tree-lined street and drove slowly, scanning each house number as he drove past. At last, "You have arrived at your destination."

Grovedale was a neighborhood in the northeastern section of the city. Its tidy rowhouses and lawns attracted a young, diverse population, most of whom worked in or around DC. Nick parked on the street directly in front of his new home, number 131. He turned off the truck and looked first at his house, then all the houses up and down the street. Each row was comprised of five houses, all constructed with red brick, now worn with age and weather. Homeowners put unique touches on their own home—white shutters, coordinating light fixtures, and front doors painted in a contrasting color. Nick walked up the three steps to his front door and admired the iron placard that displayed the house number.

"You're at the right address," Nick heard from behind him. He turned and saw Jen walking up the steps toward him with her right hand outstretched.

"Jen, good to see you. Thanks again for all your help finding this place."

Jen unlocked the door and ushered Nick in. He was greeted with the deep sheen of dark wood floors. A light, pleasant aroma of something sweet hung in the air all through the house. They walked through the living room, dining room, and into the kitchen where an old fridge sat against the wall opposite the back door.

They finished the tour of the house and agreed everything was exactly as written up in the lease agreement. Nick saw her out to call his soon-to-be housemate, Winston. "Hey, what's your ETA?" he asked.

"I'll be there in about fifteen," Winston responded.

"Excellent. You can help me unpack the truck and move in my bed."

"Perfect," Winston groaned. "I can't wait." His sarcasm was not lost on Nick.

"See you soon."

Nick spent the next few minutes unloading boxes. He was in the kitchen getting a drink of water when he heard an ear-piercing shriek of brakes. *Winston.* He stepped outside and watched a beaten-up truck shudder to a stop behind his own.

"Nice truck," Nick yelled to his friend.

"Hey, it was cheap, and it got me here." Winston hopped out of the vehicle and sized up his new house. "Very cool. This is the nicest place I've lived in since moving down here." Winston's appearance never changed. As a runner, Winston's physique reminded Nick of a Whippet. He wore his black hair spiked—a perfect complement to the horn-rimmed glasses balanced on the tip of his small nose.

Nick greeted his friend with a slap on the shoulder and a one-armed bro hug. "Great to see you, Win!"

"Same to you." Winston returned the hug. "Let me grab my bag and then you can give me a tour of our awesome new house."

"You'll like this place. It's perfect for two studs like us!"

Nick laughed.

Inside the house, Winston looked around and gave a low whistle. The sound echoed in the barren living room. "Man, we've got some work to do."

"For sure."

"Priority number one—hang the TV."

"I was thinking the same thing." Nick pointed at the wall opposite of where they were standing. "That wall is the biggest. How about there?"

Winston stroked his chin. "Good call. Then the couch can go here, opposite the TV."

The two friends went to work rearranging the furniture and hanging their sixty-inch television.

"That was work, but it looks good," Nick commented.

"I agree. Now the fun part of hooking all the wires and boxes," Winston said.

They spent three more hours unloading the truck and arranging their mismatched furniture. Finally, Winston said, "I'm done for now. It's hot."

"Yeah, I've had enough too. We can unpack tomorrow." He went to the kitchen and returned holding two bottles of water.

"You read my mind. Thanks."

"Cheers, man," Nick said, and they clinked each other's bottle before plopping onto the couch. "So, how's work going in the world of information security analysis?"

"It's nuts. I monitor networks for security breaches for hours on end. I sit on my ass in countless meetings about potential cyberattacks from the dark web and how we're going to catch the bad guys—which, of course, requires more security and more money. And then, explaining to our fearless leaders why we need to make protective changes to the network is like talking to kindergarteners."

"Aw, c'mon. It can't be all that bad. Besides, it's better than sitting around doing nothing."

"It's not, except the great wheels of government don't turn as quickly as they should."

"Well, look at it this way. You have a decent enough job to pay the bills."

"Yes, I do. Speaking of work, are you looking forward to starting your job?"

"Yes, I am," Nick replied.

"Tell me again what you'll be doing?"

"I'll be working as a staff assistant to Senator Boyd."

"Staff assistant, huh," Winston said. "You won't be bored, trust me."

"Fine with me."

"I've known many staffers who had a tough time with the frenetic pace of a senator's office."

"I'm sure you have. I remember during my internship some of my colleagues couldn't handle all the multi-tasking. I know I'll be organizing files, researching bills, and reading documents," Nick replied. "And getting all that done simultaneously won't be new to me."

"You don't mind the clerical nature of your job?"

"Not at all. I'll be hustling and the experience will help prepare me for a promotion when the time comes," Nick laughed.

"When do you start? Soon?"

"Not until September."

Winston cocked his eyebrow at Nick. "The whole summer off? Lucky you."

"Actually, no. There'll be no summer off for me. I can't afford not to work. I've got rent to pay."

"You bet you do. I'm not going to carry your sorry ass." Winston laughed.

"Oh, I know, trust me. I remember how cheap you are."

"Can't disagree. What do you have lined up for the summer?"

"Before I left home, I called my friend Hoot. You've heard me talk about him, right?"

"You've known him since you were a kid, right? From a golf club?"

Nick took a sip of water. "Exactly. He hooked me up with a caddie job at Carver Golf Club this summer."

"Right up your alley. Caddying and our daily runs will keep you in shape. You're still running, right?"

"Um, no."

Winston looked down at Nick's sneakers and pointed. "I can tell, they hardly look used. I'll get you back pounding the pavement. I have the perfect place."

"Oh boy. Where? Hopefully nowhere too hilly."

"A place called Margaux Ford Park. We'll go tomorrow since we have all this unpacking to do still." Winston gestured to the dozen unopened boxes on the floor. "It isn't far. And it's got great woods with running trails all over. You'll like the park, especially the scenery." Winston finished his drink and sighed. "Ready to tackle these boxes?"

"Do we have to?" Nick moaned. "I was just getting comfortable!"

"No whining! We might as well unpack now so we don't have to do it later. And, furthermore, the Nats are playing the Orioles tonight and I want to watch it. Got it?" Winston laughed.

"Are you *sure* you don't want to put off unpacking until tomorrow? A cold beer would taste exceptionally good right now."

"Nice try and no way."

Nick was defeated. Winston loved his hometown Baltimore Orioles. "Okay, boss. Here we go."

CHAPTER 10

The next morning, Nick and Winston caught a ten o'clock bus for the fifteen-minute ride to Margaux Ford Park.

The sun was high but the heat of the day before abated and the park was busy on this sunny Sunday morning. People of all ages flocked to the clean, peaceful space. Wide sidewalks and off-trail paths were idyllic for walkers and runners. Strategically located wrought-iron benches allowed people to sit and enjoy Mother Nature. Mature oak trees offered shade in the summer and resplendent foliage in the fall.

"Take it easy on me, Win," Nick warned. "It's been two months since I've tortured myself like this." As the two jogged down the path, Nick drank in the scenery: kids on bikes, seniors playing cards, and young women sunbathing. He almost fell over himself staring at the bikini-clad women. "I think I'm going to like it here."

Winston gave Nick a knowing smile. "I'm sure you will."

"Aside from running, are you getting out much?" Nick asked.

"Not like I used to. Other than dating the hottest, smartest woman in DC," Winston said, referring to his girlfriend of several months. Winston noticed his friend's labored breathing. "Let's slow down a bit."

Relieved, Nick slowed down to a walk. "*You?* After your

last debacle of a relationship, I thought you swore off dating!"

"I know, I know. I thought I did, especially after the drama *that* ex brought. She's different from my other girlfriends."

"How so?"

"She's mature, grounded, and gainfully employed. And besides, who wouldn't want a piece of *this*?" Winston pounded his bony chest.

"Don't hit too hard. You might break a rib!" Nick laughed.

"Very funny."

"Who is—?"

Nick's question went unfinished. A loud, rich voice interrupted him from behind. "Is that the quickest you can run? Better pick up the pace, youngster!"

Winston and Nick turned around and saw a golf cart slowly approaching. In it sat a middle-aged couple. The man drove while the woman stayed put, talking on the phone.

Winston laughed. "Hey, Henderson! I was wondering if you'd be around to bust my chops!"

"Hi, Win. Who's this?"

"This is my friend, Nick. He recently moved here from Philly."

"Hi there. I'm Henderson. Nice to meet you." The man hefted himself out of the cart to shake Nick's hand. The buttons on his shirt strained against a belly that spilled over the top of his gray pants. A gun hung on his right hip.

Nick shook Henderson's hand. "I'm Nick. It's nice to meet you too." He attempted to hide his surprise at seeing a gun.

Henderson noticed Nick's questioning look and patted the weapon. "This was issued to me because I'm a part-time security guard in the park. I'm a retired police officer, and the fine folks who hired me figured I'd know how to use it if I had to. Luckily, I haven't."

Nick nodded. "Got it. Thanks."

The woman in the cart hung up and introduced herself. "Hi everyone. I'm Jackie Bishop. I pal around with this guy"—she pointed at Henderson—"on his rounds!" She laughed and shook hands with Winston and Nick.

Henderson said, "*Detective* Jackie Bishop. She's modest." He winked at Jackie. "She and I used to be partners—years back."

"Detective? Cool," Nick said.

Henderson flicked his thumb at Winston and asked, "How're you caught up with this one?"

"We went to school together and now we're roommates," Nick responded.

"Yeah? You're new to DC?" Henderson asked.

"Yes, sir," Nick responded.

"We're glad you're here. I was born and raised here," Jackie said.

Nick surmised her to be in her mid-fifties. Her short stature, apple-like physique and firm tone made Nick think of one of his tougher college professors. Her blue eyes took everything in and missed nothing. "I noticed your Washington Capitals hat. Are you an ice hockey fan?"

"Oh yes. I was the only girl out of a bunch of us who used to play on a local pond in the winter. I wanted to play in high school, however, I was a girl and . . . well, I was told no." She shrugged.

Henderson broke the awkward silence. "Yes, welcome," he said. "I think you'll enjoy the city. I've lived here for over thirty years."

Henderson's kind brown eyes and a warm demeanor made Nick like him instantly. "Thanks. I'm excited to be here."

"My park, as I like to call it," Henderson laughed, "is only one of so many interesting places in our city." He turned to Winston. "Win, make sure you show Nick our newer museums, such as the African American Museum. Oh, and the Korean War Memorial is finally finished. That memorial and the Vietnam Memorial will take your breath away."

"Oh, and don't forget the World War Two Memorial. It's absolutely stunning and has sentimental meaning," Jackie said.

"I can't wait to see it and the others. Winston said he'd also show all the great bars and restaurants."

Henderson nodded. "Lucky for you, your choices of those are endless. I've seen lots of places come and go. But there are enough from the old days that are still around."

"I look forward to checking them out. Thanks for the recommendations," Nick said.

Henderson and Jackie sat back down into his golf cart. "Nice to see ya, fellas. Time to continue my rounds. I need to keep an eye on my park to make sure everyone is safe and enjoying themselves." He looked at Nick. "It was a pleasure. Hope to see you around."

"It was a pleasure meeting you two." Jackie smiled.

"Same here," Nick said.

They watched Henderson and Jackie drive out of sight toward the center of the park.

"How do you know Henderson?" Nick asked.

"From running here and from work," Winston replied.

"Work?"

"Besides working here, he also works part-time in the Cooper Building checking people's credentials."

Nick thought through what Winston had just said. "Wait a second. I'll see him when I start working there, right?"

Winston smacked himself on the head. "Duh! How could I be so dumb! Sorry, that connection didn't even dawn on me when I introduced you."

"Apparently not!" Nick laughed. "So, getting back to our earlier discussion. Who is this girl you're dating?"

"Her name is Jaida and we've been dating for four months."

"I can't wait to meet her. Maybe she has a cute friend."

"You'll meet her before long. And, yes, she does. Ready to head back?"

"I am. At a *slow* pace though!"

CHAPTER 11

Daisy arrived at work thirty minutes early and made small talk with Ira as she sliced limes, lemons, and oranges.

"I thought you weren't due in until four on Tuesdays," Ira questioned.

"You're right," Daisy said. "I was supposed to be at the dentist, but they rescheduled my appointment last minute, so here I am. How was lunch?"

"Pretty steady. The salad special was a hit. You should try it later." He let out a huge yawn. "God, I'm tired. I'm going home to crash out," he said.

"Yeah. You look tired."

"I didn't sleep so well last night. My puppy was up pretty much for hours on end, so I crawled into her cage to keep her company."

"Well, aren't you the dad of the year!"

"You know it! She finally settled down, only now I'm paying the price," he answered. "I'll see you later."

"Enjoy your nap!"

Daisy checked the cash register, restocked martini glasses, and checked the cleanliness of the bathrooms in anticipation of a busy night. Next on her to-do list was to create the drink of the day. *A special cocktail for happy hour sounds good. Something refreshing, not too sweet.* From underneath the bar, she pulled out a notebook that was divided into drink recipes based on the type of alcohol. Daisy flipped to the vodka section and found one that sounded delicious—chilled vodka, freshly squeezed lemon juice, club soda, and a splash of elderflower liqueur. She poured the ingredients into a cocktail shaker, shook, and drained the concoction into a martini glass. She dipped a straw into the glass for a taste. *Mmm, perfect. I can't wait to serve these later.*

From behind, she heard, "Drinkin' on the job I see!"

Daisy turned around to see Henderson approaching the bar. "Hey, Henderson! *Someone* has to do a taste test before serving," she joked. "How was your day?"

"I woke up, got out of bed, and went to work. It was good!" He sat on a stool at the end of the bar.

"Where did you work today, the park or Cooper?"

"I was at the park today. The weather gods blessed us with another perfect park day. I was happy to see so many people out there, especially on a Tuesday."

"I'm glad to hear the park was busy."

Henderson. That was the only name Daisy knew him by. He came into the Black LaSalle at least three times a week and always ordered the same thing—beer and chili. Every now and again, Jackie, his friend, joined him, but not tonight. They spoke easily about myriad topics and she appreciated his interest in her future career.

"Do you know what classes you'll take when school starts?"

"I have narrowed my choices down to three."

"How long do I have to wait until I see you sitting in the reporter's chair?" He laughed.

"A little over a year."

His rich voice and propensity for chuckling at his own jokes reminded Daisy of her old friend Hoot. His slow gait and grunts told Daisy Henderson was middle-aged.

Daisy placed a beer in front of Henderson and went to the kitchen for his chili. She returned with a large steamy bowl. Henderson inhaled deeply, savoring its spiciness.

"Enjoy!"

Daisy turned her attention to a group of four women who had just entered and plunked down at a high-top. The women were about the same age as Daisy. Two of them, blondes, sported professional bob haircuts, while one had long, silky black curls, and the fourth wore her dark brown hair in a twist. All wore minimal makeup, just enough to flatter. Daisy approached the women and heard one of them remark, "Yum, this lemon drink sounds good."

"It is. I made it myself," Daisy said and asked what they wanted to drink. She made a mental note of matching each woman's drink with their hair color.

"I'll try the lemon drink," blonde number one said.

"Chardonnay for me, please," blonde number two said.

"Gin and tonic for me, thanks," said silky black curls.

"I'll have a Stella, please," said brunette-with-a-twist.

Daisy brought their drinks and asked if they wanted to place a food order.

Blonde number two asked her friends, "Do you guys want to order any apps?"

"Sure," responded blonde number one. "I'm starving and too lazy to cook anything at home. Plus, a huge plate of nachos sounds damn good right about now."

"Let's get the nachos, jalapeño poppers and . . . what else?" brunette-with-a-twist said.

"How about something healthy? Lettuce wraps and hummus?" silky black curls asked.

The three others at the table nodded their agreement.

"Is that it?" Daisy asked.

"For now, yes," said blonde number one. "By the way, this drink is delicious."

Daisy smiled. "Thanks. I take pride in creating deliciousness!" She walked away to place their order and tend to other customers. Daisy kept her eye on the women. Experience told her they would want another round soon. When they gave the signal, Daisy asked if they wanted to order more food.

"If I eat any more, I won't fit into my pants!" moaned silky black curls.

"Yeah, but you work out. You'll burn it off," remarked blonde number two.

The woman with the black curls looked beyond Daisy and saw Erin behind the bar. "Hey Erin, it's me Jaida!"

Erin turned and looked at Jaida. She came over, big smile on her face. "Jaida! I haven't seen you in a few years—probably since playing volleyball."

"How long have you been working here?" Jaida asked.

"I've been the manager for three years. It's good to see you. Are you still playing volleyball?"

"Yes. I haven't been to the gym in like, forever. I need to start working out again because volleyball starts soon."

"I wish I could play, but this"—Erin patted her left hip—"won't let me."

"Oh, what a bummer," Jaida said.

"I know." Erin saw they were close to a second round and called to Daisy, "Daiz, please bring these ladies another round—on me!"

"Coming up!" Daisy said.

Jaida and her friends thanked Erin for the drinks. "Come back soon!" Erin replied.

Daisy placed the drinks on the table when Jaida remarked how nice it was for Erin to buy a round.

"Erin's the best. She's one of the most kind and generous people I've ever met. I love working for her."

"Lucky you!" one of the blondes said.

Daisy smiled and turned to Jaida. "Did I hear you talking about volleyball?"

"You did. My gym has a team. Do you play?"

"Not since high school," Daisy said. "Basketball was more my thing, though I really loved playing volleyball. Where do you play?"

"DC Fitness. It's not far from here. The team's coed if you're interested." Jaida added, "I'll bet you slammed the ball. I wish I were as tall as you."

"I'd love to play again," Daisy said.

"Well, we always need girls. If you want, I'll meet you there sometime and we can sign up for the leagues," Jaida told her.

"That'd be great. I moved here not long ago and I'm looking for fun things to do."

The woman's thick black curls tumbled over her shoulders. "Cool. I'm Jaida."

Daisy noticed Jaida's sapphire eyes and flawless mocha skin as they shook hands. "I'm Daisy. Thanks for the invite. I love your curls."

"Thank you."

Daisy said, "Check this out." She released her own red

curls from the ponytail holder.

Jaida laughed and said, "So you get what it's like to try to tame hair like ours!" Jaida high-fived her.

"You know it," Daisy said, and put her hair back up.

"Anyway, there are some hot guys who play too. I don't know if you have a boyfriend, but checking out cute guys was always one of my incentives!" Jaida laughed.

"I don't. I'll enjoy checking them out, though!" Daisy said. She pulled her phone from her pocket. "What's your number? I'll text you."

Jaida gave her number and Daisy texted her.

"Maybe we can go this weekend and sign up?"

Daisy checked her schedule. "Looks like I'm off on Sunday. How about then?"

"Sunday works. I'll text you on Saturday and we'll figure out a time."

"Perfect."

The women finished their drinks, paid, and thanked Daisy.

"Talk to you later," Jaida said.

"Sounds like a plan. Thanks, ladies! Enjoy your evening!" Daisy called after them.

CHAPTER 12

Beep! Beep! Beep! Zeke removed his sausage, egg, and cheese breakfast sandwich from the microwave and slathered it with salsa, his favorite topping for everything.

Rubi Lee sat at the tiny kitchen table and watched her brother with disgust. "How can you eat those things? They're so gross."

"They taste good and they're cheap. That's why," he answered her. "You should try one."

"No thanks." Rubi Lee checked the time on her phone. "It's four o'clock. Al and Teresa will be at the bar in half an hour, so we need to go."

"All right. Are the masks in here or are they in the van?" He flipped open the trashcan and tossed the plastic wrapper.

Rubi Lee flashed a menacing grin. "Right here." She pulled two ski masks from her bag.

"Excellent."

Zeke parked the van three blocks away from the Black LaSalle. The doors to the bar were open and music wafted down the street. Zeke noticed it first. "They're playing the Allman Brothers," he remarked. "I think I'm gonna like this place." Classic rock floated from the mounted speakers. Half-priced bottles were tough to turn away.

Uncle Vic was right, this place is popular, Rubi Lee

observed as she and Zeke approached the bar. Eyes darting, she scanned for Teresa and Al—no sign of them. A man whose nametag read IRA came to take their order.

"Two light beers please," Zeke ordered.

"Be right back."

"I didn't expect this place to be like this," Zeke remarked as he looked over the leather stools, shiny bar, and countless bottles of top-shelf alcohol. "The name made me think it was some dive."

"Good for you, if you like crowded, loud bars," Rubi Lee grumbled.

Zeke shook his head. "Sometimes you're a bitchy old lady."

"We're not here to have fun, remember?"

Fifteen minutes later, Al and Teresa showed up and sat at the other end of the bar. Teresa flung her bag over a third stool to save for Don.

"And there they are, at the other end of the bar." Rubi Lee tilted her head toward Teresa and Al.

Zeke studied them. "They're old. This'll be easy." He noticed Al's gray hair and glasses.

Rubi Lee sized them up. "Yeah they are. Her face looks like a prune."

They watched Al and Teresa order drinks and make small talk. The bartender placed a Manhattan in front of Teresa, a screwdriver for Al.

"I hope he gets here soon. I'm going to go broke paying for my own drinks!" Teresa said.

"It is expensive, isn't it?" Mumbles replied and shook the melted ice around in his glass. He signaled Ira for another round.

Teresa's phone jingled. She shoved her glasses up her nose and read it. "Don's not gonna make it tonight."

"What do you mean?" Al asked.

"All he said was he can't make it. Damn, I was looking forward to getting my doll."

"I'm sure he had a good reason. Tell him we'll take a raincheck. One more drink, then we'll go."

"Sure, if you're paying." Teresa cackled and texted Don back.

Al rolled his eyes. "Fine."

Don's phone buzzed in Rubi Lee's pocket. She and Zeke read it and decided to text her later, like tomorrow. "Now we wait."

Zeke and Rubi Lee kept watch and finished their beers. Teresa and Al rose from their seats or tried to stand up. Rubi Lee smirked at her brother. "Getting what we want from them won't be hard. She can hardly walk." Teresa teetered before Al took her arm.

Zeke and Rubi Lee waited two minutes before following. It was dark enough where if anyone saw them, identifying them would be difficult. Al steered them down the sidewalk into a parking lot. Zeke and Rubi Lee yanked on the ski masks, quickened their pace, and attacked their unsuspecting prey.

Al fumbled with his keys while Teresa dug into her giant handbag. Zeke slammed Al against the driver's door and laid his hand over Al's lips. Rubi Lee shoved Teresa into the passenger side door from behind, whirled her around, and clamped a hand across her mouth. She dragged Teresa to the other side of the car where Zeke held Al.

Rubi Lee pulled out her stiletto knife and flicked it

open—silver blade shiny, menacing. "See this? If either of you say *one word* when we take our hands away, I'll gut you like a fish. Got it?"

Wide, terrified eyes stared at her and Zeke. Al and Teresa were too scared to move.

"When I count to three, we'll take our hands away. You make *any* loud noise at all and you're dead." Rubi Lee nicked Teresa on her arm to prove the point. "One, two, three."

"Wha-what do you want?" Al asked, voice trembling. "Please don't hurt us, please!"

"Shut up. Tell us what you know about Don." Zeke pulled a gun from the waistband of his pants.

"Oh God, please no! Don't shoot us!" Teresa begged.

"D-D . . . Who?" Al sputtered.

"Don't play dumb. I'm warning you." Zeke cocked the gun and pushed it against Al's head.

"I . . . I'm not . . . sure . . . who, who you . . . you mean," Al stuttered. "Teresa, d-d-do you know?"

Rubi Lee sighed. "Jesus, you people are so damn *dumb*. DON. Don Gaylord, you drunken idiots."

Al frowned and swallowed hard. "Oh . . . you mean Donny . . . He . . . he's, um . . . our friend," he whispered.

"We were supposed to meet . . . him today at the bar. He has a present for me," Teresa stuttered.

"A *present?*" Rubi Lee sneered.

"Yes, a . . . doll he got me from his trip," Teresa answered.

"What trip?" Zeke asked.

"He said he was going to, um . . . Russia," Al murmured.

Zeke flicked his eyes to his sister. "What did he tell you about Russia?"

"Just that . . . he . . . had to go. Something . . . about part of his job," Al muttered.

"What job?" Rubi Lee pressed. "Did he tell you why he was going to Russia?"

"No . . . I . . . we swear, we don't know!"

"Are you *sure*?" Rubi Lee pressed the knife against Teresa's cheek.

"Yes. I'm sure. Please. Please stop. We don't know for sure, but it was something about imports."

"How do you know about imports?" Zeke asked.

"'Cause he liked to brag when he was drunk," Teresa said.

"What did he import?"

"We don't know!" Teresa cried. "We didn't care, as long as he bought drinks!"

"How long have you known him?" Zeke asked.

"A couple . . . a couple of years," Al said, faltering.

"Freakin' lushes, of course you don't know anything. You're always drunk." Zeke hauled off and punched Al in the face. Al fell like a dead soldier. Pavement scraped his face; blood seeped into the concrete. Glass crunched under Zeke's boot.

Teresa screamed and lunged for her friend. Rubi Lee yanked her back. "We're gonna be watchin' you. If you say one word, just one to the cops, you're dead. Understand?"

Teresa nodded.

Rubi Lee flashed her blade. "Don't forget, we know where to find you." Rubi Lee flung Teresa to the ground.

CHAPTER 13

Sunday rolled in with late summer gooey humidity. Daisy opened the glass doors to the gym and goosebumps popped out on her arms from the blast of air conditioning. She saw Jaida sitting in one of the chairs by the check-in desk.

"Hey girl, how are you?" Jaida greeted Daisy.

"I'm great. How are you?" Daisy took in the spacious, light-drenched gym. "This place is really nice."

"I know, I love how light and airy it feels. Plus, it's cheap!"

"Oh good."

One of the trainers greeted them. "Are you ready for your tour?"

"Yes, we are. Lead the way."

Thirty minutes later, Daisy was a member at DC Fitness. They thanked the trainer who gave them a tour and left.

"Are you hungry? I know a cheap, decent place with all kinds of brunch food," Jaida asked.

"Starving. I didn't eat much breakfast," Daisy replied.

Babe's Breakfast Buffet was the go-to place for a bargain brunch. If anyone left Babe's hungry, there was something wrong with them. Daisy and Jaida loaded their plates and settled into a blue vinyl booth.

"Did you grow up in DC? You seem like you did since you know the city so well," Daisy remarked.

"No—McLean, so not far. I've been here a few years though. How about you?" Jaida replied.

"Cab Station, opposite end of Virginia from where you grew up."

"I think I've been there, or through it. For years, we took a family vacation to the resort outside of there. It's where I fell in love skeet shooting."

Daisy picked up on the past tense. "Do you still go?"

The brightness in Jaida's face vanished. She took a sip of her juice. "Um, no. My dad died when I was eleven and Mom has dementia. She's in a home. She doesn't even know who I am."

"Oh Jaida, I'm so sorry. I can't imagine."

"Thanks, you didn't know. DC is my home now."

"Where do you live?" Daisy asked.

"Near the Hill. Not too far from work."

They continued eating, and their conversation flowed. Jaida asked Daisy about her family and laughed when Daisy told her how crazy it was to grow up with three brothers. And a father who was sheriff.

"But my mom kept the house running smoothly, even as a full-time teacher."

"I always wanted siblings, but it never happened." Jaida sighed.

"What did your parents do when they worked?" Daisy asked.

"My dad was a lawyer for the EPA and Mom was an architect."

"Did they travel a lot?" Daisy asked.

"Dad did more than Mom. I remember how he would always bring me back a postcard from wherever he traveled. I still have them all in a box under my bed."

"That's sweet," Daisy replied.

They talked about Jaida's career in the world of technology, Daisy's job at the Black LaSalle and her future career as a reporter.

"Oh boy, I'm stuffed," Jaida said.

"Me too. Everything was so good—especially the blueberry pancakes," Daisy answered. "This was fun."

"I agree. Let's get together soon."

They split the tab, walked to the parking lot, and made plans for Jaida to bring her friends to the Black LaSalle soon.

CHAPTER 14

August was the height of the golf season and Nick cleared close to eight hundred dollars a week in cash. He had Hoot, his friend from Cascades Golf Club, to thank for helping to land this job. The two had stayed in touch over the years, and when Nick called Hoot to tell him about the caddie job, he was thrilled.

Nick caddied at least once a day. The club was open six days a week and he arrived every morning by seven. Nick loved the quiet half-hour before the members and other caddies arrived. He used the time to fill buckets with range balls, read the tee sheet to see whose bags he would carry, and have a cup of coffee. The dew-covered, pristine fairways sparkled at this early hour. The undulating, wide layout of Carver's golf course reminded him of the Mill Course at Cascades Golf Club. Cascades was forever sacred to him because of one girl—Daisy Kathryn Taylor. Fearless, confident, lovely Daisy.

After caddying twice, he counted his cash: six hundred dollars—*Sweet!* Before leaving, Nick checked his phone: four emails and two texts. He grabbed his bike, hopped on, and rode down the long driveway of the club. He pedaled at an easy pace; the refreshing breeze cooled his sunburned face. Thoughts of riding around the streets of his bustling college town popped into his head. Nick enjoyed the social side of college a little too much. In his senior year, he had to take a freshman-level math course. Math 108 nearly kept him from graduating on time. After failing it a first time, he bribed an acquaintance to tutor him. The fifty dollars he spent on four cases of beer was the best investment he ever made.

He rested his bike against the side of the house, went inside, and flopped down on the couch. Weariness overcame him. He closed his eyes and drifted off.

Eventually he stirred when he heard voices.

"You alive, man? You didn't answer my texts," Winston called from the kitchen.

He rubbed his eyes and yawned. "What time is it?" Nick sat up and saw Winston with a stunning young woman.

"Eight thirty. Nick, this is Jaida. Jaida, meet Nick," Winston said. "This is the beautiful woman whom I've been dating. I told you about her the other day."

Nick jumped up and extended his hand. "Hey Jaida, nice to meet you. And yes, I remember, Win." He agreed with Win—Jaida was stunning.

"Sorry to wake you. It's nice to meet you too," she laughed.

"I'm glad you did. I didn't mean to sleep so long."

"Did you eat yet, Nick?" Winston said.

"No, I've been crashed out for a few hours. Did you guys eat?"

"Not yet and we're starving." Jaida glanced at Nick. "I'll go out on a limb and assume you like pizza?" Jaida asked.

"Sounds good."

"Jimmy's Pizza?" Winston suggested.

"I'll order," Nick said.

Over a large pepperoni pizza, Jaida told Nick she worked in the Cooper Building as a computer engineer.

"That's impressive. So, you test software and upload it?" Nick asked.

"Yup. I'm also responsible for executing upgrades and making sure no viruses attack our system," Jaida answered.

"I'm sure you don't get much time off, right?"

"No not really. The tech world is constantly evolving and it's my responsibility to stay ahead of developments. Even if that means a sixty-hour plus workweek."

Winston interjected, "Now you know why I'm so glad she works in the same building as I do, or I'd never see her!" Winston leaned over and kissed her on the cheek.

* * *

Before the five o'clock happy hour crowd, Daisy wiped down the bar in preparation for them. Pint glasses needed to be restocked as well as napkin dispensers. Tuesday was Trivia Night—one of the bar's most popular nights. At the end of the bar, she picked up the plastic-framed flyer advertising the annual golf outing which was in two days. The Black LaSalle was a devoted supporter of this outing because it was held in honor of Charlie Barone, a young man who disappeared one night. He worked there as a bar-back for several years, and his parents were the owners at the time of his disappearance. Each year, the outing was booked.

Daisy looked down at the young, handsome face staring back up at her: dark curly hair, smiling blue eyes, great smile. *He was cute. So sad about what happened.*

Teams showed up starting at six o'clock to secure seats. Daisy and Erin laughed at the names of some of the teams: Pickleface, The Simpletons, The Big O, and others. Daisy had just finished pouring a few beers when Officers Dunn and Norman entered, followed by Henderson's girlfriend, Jackie. Erin glanced at Jackie and gave Daisy a puzzled look.

"I don't know her. But I can tell you without a doubt she's a cop," Erin observed.

"How did you know?" Daisy was impressed.

"By the authoritative walk, the way she eyeballed the bar, and her clothes."

"She's a detective. Very perceptive of you!"

"One gift I have is to read people," Erin said. "It's been handy in my line of work!" Erin gazed at the stocky woman dressed in a somber gray pants suit. She wore her wavy salt and pepper hair cut short. Gold hoops dangled from her small ears.

"Hi Jackie and company. Can I help you?" Daisy asked.

"Evening Daisy, Erin. You may remember we were here before," Officer Dunn said.

"I remember," Daisy answered. "Erin, this is Detective Jackie Bishop."

"Hello, Daisy and Erin. I'm here to ask about Don Gaylord. Do either of you have a few minutes to answer some questions?"

"Yes, ma'am," Erin replied and turned to Daisy. "Daisy, why don't you talk to them and I'll cover the bar?"

"Are you sure?"

"Yes, I'm waiting for a few friends to come in anyway."

"All right. Do you mind if we use the office? It's quieter than out here."

"Go ahead. It's fairly clean."

Once settled, Jackie retrieved her notebook from her bag and began. "Officers Dunn and Norman relayed to me that you said Mr. Gaylord always paid in cash, correct?" Her tone of voice reminded Daisy of a school principal.

"Yes. He normally paid in cash for his drinks and others'," Daisy offered.

"I see. Did you ever see him use a credit card?"

Daisy pursed her lips together. "Not that I can remember. But he obviously did because you guys found a receipt from here in his pocket."

"Correct. Are you inclined to categorize him as a heavy drinker?"

"From what I saw, yes." Daisy continued, "He always paid with hundred-dollar bills and he loved buying rounds."

"Hundreds?"

"Yes, hundred-dollar bills. Nothing more, nothing less."

"Have you ever heard anything else about Don Gaylord? Family? Job?"

Daisy shook her head.

"Do you remember seeing Mr. Gaylord being here with people or by himself?"

"He knew a few of my regulars, yet I don't ever remember seeing him actually *come in* with someone."

Jackie scribbled in her book. "Did he ever refer to other people? Family? Colleagues? We're looking for any kind of background on him."

"No. I don't remember him talking about family or coworkers. I didn't engage in any real conversations with him."

Jackie wrote and talked at the same time. "Do you know

how long he's been frequenting your bar?"

"I've been here a short time. Unfortunately, I can't say for sure how long he's been coming in. Erin might, though. And no, I've never heard him mention any names either."

Jackie scribbled. "Okay. Did he ever indicate where he lives or what he does for a living?"

"I have no idea where he lives. But I think he travels for his job."

Jackie looked up from her notebook. "What makes you say that?"

"I remember hearing him on a couple of occasions talking loudly about traveling to Europe. Maybe he's a salesman?"

"What makes you think he's in sales?"

"I remember him saying something about an import business, so I assumed he imported things and sold them."

"Logical conclusion. Is there anything else along those lines you remember?" Jackie asked.

"Well, it seemed he always had a ton of money after those trips."

"Interesting. How long would he be gone?" Jackie frowned.

"Maybe a week? Longer? I'm not really sure. Why?"

"Because it *was* his body was found about five miles away from Reagan International."

Daisy's curiosity got the best of her. "What exactly happened?"

Jackie exhaled. "Unfortunately, it is a homicide—a hit and run."

"A homicide? How horrible," Daisy responded.

"Yes, it is." Jackie flipped her notebook shut.

"I'm sorry I wasn't more helpful. If I hear anything, I'll call you. I have to get back to work because we're busy." Daisy gracefully excused herself.

"I understand. Thank you for your help and we'll be in touch if need be. Have a good night."

CHAPTER 15

The calendar turned to September and slowly closed out the golden summer. It was time for Nick to exchange his caddie bib for work clothes.

His first day working for Senator Alexandra Boyd finally arrived. Before leaving the house, he tossed his phone, wallet, a pen, and other items into his cinch-bag and caught the seven thirty bus. He gulped coffee and listened to the hushed conversations of his fellow passengers.

He was jittery as he jogged up the marble stairs of his new home, the Cooper Building. He stopped at enormous double-glass doors and turned around to admire the immense cast-iron dome of the Capitol Building which reflected in the glass of the doors. The bright morning sun bounced off the building and spread warmth.

Tie straightened, he ran a hand through his hair and pulled open the doors. He walked through the metal detector to the reception desk to sign in.

He greeted the hunched-over receptionist sitting behind a desk, nose buried in book. "Morning, ma'am."

Annoyed eyes looked up at him. "Print your name on the left side of the sheet. Then sign it on the next line," she barked.

"Yes, ma'am."

She examined his signature through her half-moon

glasses. "Okay Nicholas, you must get your ID badge first. See him." She pointed to another desk where Nick saw a familiar face—Henderson.

"Thanks."

She grunted and buried herself back in her book.

Nick hustled over to Henderson. "Morning, Henderson. I'm glad to see a familiar face."

"Good morning to you. Nice to see you again, Nick. I have something important for you." He opened an envelope and handed Nick an ID badge. "Nicholas, you *must* wear this all the time while you are in government buildings. You will be asked to show it and it will be scanned each time you enter or exit. Understand?"

"Without this badge I get in nowhere?" Nick joked.

Henderson raised his eyebrow, leaned in, and whispered, "Let me tell you, son, if you are not wearin' this badge while you are in any of these buildings, expect the Secret Service fellas to teach you *how* to wear it. Got it?"

"That sounds pretty serious."

"Take my word for it. It is." Henderson pointed toward a set of steps. "Next step is the basement where you need to be fingerprinted. Go down those steps, turn right. Take this form with you and bring it back to me."

"Got it," Nick took the form and headed toward the basement.

"Ahem!" he heard from behind. He turned around to see Henderson shaking his head. From his finger dangled the all-important ID badge.

"Your *badge!*"

"Geez, not making a great impression, am I? Thanks," Nick said.

"It's okay, we've all been nervous on our first day. Just keep a cool head and an ear to the ground."

"I will," Nick replied and headed to the steps that took him down to the basement. He walked down and saw a security guard standing in front of an entryway to what looked like a tunnel. The man looked at him and said, "Fingerprints?"

"Yes sir."

"That way. And son, wear your badge so we can see it."

"Right." He re-clipped his badge to the pocket of his shirt and went to the office. Nick saw several women and men in line; three women looked to be about his age.

"This the line for prints?" he asked one of the women.

She turned and answered, "See the sign?"

A large sign emblazoned with FINGERPRINTS hung above his head.

"Ah, yeah." Nick's cheeks burned. "Sorry, first day."

Two of the women smiled politely. The third woman, who was on her phone, turned around. "I was wondering when I'd see you." It was Jaida. "Everything going okay so far?"

"Hi Jaida. Considering I haven't seen my official cubicle yet, things are going great," Nick replied.

"Good." She laughed. "Enjoy this calm while it lasts—it's rare. Today is upgrade day for me."

"Meaning a long day, right? I remember you mentioned that over pizza a few weeks ago," he replied.

"Oh yeah. Running around keeps my job fresh and I get my steps in!" Jaida joked.

"No doubt. I admire people like you who are experts in your field. What happens when systems crash?"

"I was trained to keep a level head in all situations. We do our best to avoid crashes and frequent upgrades help to ward them off."

"I'll bet. How long have you lived in DC?" Nick inquired.

"Four years. Hard to believe," Jaida said.

"I guess you like it here?"

"I love this city because of all the cultural things to do, and the restaurant and bar scene." Jaida remarked. "Plus, most people living here are a transplant."

"Yeah, I've heard there are a lot of us here and I fit right in since I'm from Philly."

"You definitely qualify!"

"Are you from DC originally?" Nick asked.

"No. I grew up in Virginia. My mom is still there though," Jaida said. "Did you grow up your whole life in Philadelphia?"

"Yes, I did. Born and bred."

"So, I guess you're a crazy, rabid Eagles fan?" Jaida teased. "You *do* know you're in Redskins territory, right?"

"I *bleed* green and white. And yes, I'm acutely aware of being in the enemy's territory."

"The Skins and Eagles play each other twice during football season. I suppose we'll have to watch it together and witness the Skins put a beatdown on the Birds."

"Sure. Bring your tissues though because the Eagles will put a serious smackdown on the Skins."

Jaida laughed. "We shall see!"

"Tyson! You're next!" a voice hollered.

Jaida heard her phone jingle. She looked at it—a notification of an urgent email. "I have to go. Good luck and enjoy your first day!"

"Thanks, see you later," Nick said.

* * *

Fortunately, her office was on the same floor. Jaida locked the door behind her and opened the computer on her desk. The sender of the email was her boss, Commissioner Knight. It was a short, encrypted message. Jaida took out the red book agents used to decode department-sent messages. Once deciphered, she read the message:

Urgent.
3 hot drop spots: Surge Coffee Shop, Black LaSalle bar, Blue Lagoon café.
One name—Victor Sykes
Coordinate with WW.
Check out and report back ASAP.

She memorized the message and shredded the paper she wrote it on. Jaida typed in several commands on her computer and the coded message disappeared. She shot Winston a text: *We need to meet for lunch. Red book info.*

Interesting. What time?

12:30 at Murray's.

See you then.

* * *

In the elevator, Nick unsuccessfully tried to wipe off the black ink from his fingers. The metal doors slid open and the minute he entered the frenzied office, the senator's private assistant was waiting for him.

He beamed at Nick. "I'm Jake Langley. Welcome."

"I'm Nick Tyson, the new one," he answered as they shook hands. Jake's flat front khakis and crisp pink shirt fit him as if they were tailor-made. Not a hair was out of place either.

"Yes, you are. Before I throw you to the wolves, I must give you the inside scoop on office life, especially since you're a newbie," Jake told him.

"All right," Nick responded.

"I'll begin with dress code. Casual dress is fine all week. Casual dress is defined as khakis of any color, and a collared shirt that must be tucked in. Jeans are permitted on Fridays. Cargo pants, flip flops, and baseball hats will *never* be worn. Ever. In the event of a press conference or photo op, you will be asked to wear a tie and jacket. Understand?" From Jake's bored tone, it was clear he had given this speech before.

"Yes."

"Good. The senator's schedule can fluctuate wildly, which means you need to be flexible during the day in case you are called to a meeting, or something of that nature. Always have your phone on."

"Easy enough."

"With regard to illness, Senator Boyd understands people get sick, have emergency situations, et cetera. If you are truly sick, she wants you to *stay home* for obvious reasons. But she expects you to have your phone and laptop at your side. Questions?"

"Who do I call if I'm sick or an emergency comes up and I can't work?"

"Please call or text me and I will tell her."

"Okay."

Jake continued, "The senator trusts every staff member to execute her or his job accurately and carefully. If you need help, you are to ask because someone here has an answer. Do not be shy or think you can get it done yourself. It's too hectic around here to play hero."

"I will, I promise."

"Any questions? I don't want you to get blindsided."

"I was kind of looking forward to getting blindsided." Nick tried a stab at humor.

Jake tilted his blond head and regarded Nick with an amused smile. "Oh, dear lad, you have no idea," he responded. "The senator is tied up at this moment. However, she will personally welcome you when she's available. For now, this pile is all yours." Jake handed Nick a stack of papers and a schedule.

Nick followed as Jake strolled through the noisy, cubicle-filled room and came to a stop toward the back. Inside an empty cubicle, Jake pointed to a gray desk with a phone on top of it. "Home sweet home!"

"Shall I start signing my life away now?"

"Please do. When you're finished, come back to my desk and we will finish the tour."

Nick spent fifteen minutes reading and signing the paperwork. He returned the papers to Jake.

"You will have your first meeting in that room over there." Jake pointed to a large glass-walled office. "The meeting starts at ten. Please be on time."

"I will be."

"If you need anything, I'll be here," Jake replied and glided back to his desk.

The morning was spent in various orientation meetings, setting up his laptop and other housekeeping duties. They broke for lunch and the entire afternoon was taken up with a rule and policy orientation meeting given by HR.

At his desk, Nick scanned through the schedule for the rest of the week and started reading through the manual. His eyelids were like stones; he felt his head bob and chin land on his chest. He looked around sheepishly, praying no one saw him fall asleep.

Nick and Winston had plans to go out later and Nick knew a pick-me-up was necessary. Winston could win a gold medal in partying. He hoisted himself out of his chair and headed to the staff room. *Hopefully, there's some coffee left.*

In the break room, he spotted an inch of something brownish in the bottom of the coffee pot. He held the opaque pot up to the light and promptly changed his mind.

"Looks like we need a new pot." Nick heard a woman's voice remark as he poured water into the slick new coffee maker.

"Yes, we do," he responded after the last bit of water trickled out. He turned around to see a tall, dark-haired woman. She was dressed in gray tailored pants complemented by a navy blouse. Against her collarbones lay a pearl necklace with a diamond-encrusted clasp. He looked at her and tried to keep his eyes from drifting to the long, thin white scar that ran from her right ear down her cheek to her strong jawline. Nick guessed she was in her late forties to early fifties.

The woman extended a well-manicured hand and introduced herself. "Hi there, I'm Alex Boyd." Her smile was warm and kind.

"Senator Boyd! It's an honor to meet you. I'm Nick Tyson, ma'am. And congratulations on winning a second term." He felt his armpits dampen.

"Thank you. One of many, I hope." She looked at him again. "You're new, correct?" She asked and tucked her hair behind her right ear. "Like I've told other new employees, please call me Senator. Ma'am sounds so old." She smiled.

"Yes, Senator. And yes, I just started today." The dribble of the water through the coffee machine broke the awkward silence. "And it's been a non-stop day."

"As it should be, right?"

"Of course."

"The coffee smells good. Thanks for making it. I'll come back in a little bit."

"You're welcome and I hope it's not too strong," Nick replied.

"The stronger the better. Thanks again." She smiled at him.

"You're welcome, Senator."

CHAPTER 16

Outside, Alex Boyd put her coffee cup on a ledge and took a long drag from her cigarette, inhaled deeply, and blew the smoke into the deep blue sky. She knew it was a horrible habit, and like her career, smoking was an addiction. She watched the young kids across the street, dressed in their maroon and white school uniforms, playing blissfully on the playground. Not a care in the world. A side door slammed open and out poured the older kids, relishing the end of the school day. She felt a stab of resentment from long ago as she watched the pretty girls sashay down the sidewalk, absorbed in their phones and tossing their shiny hair. She remembered those kinds of girls—girls who teased her about her clothes, her hair and lack of materialistic things. *Nasty bitches.* As a child, she wore threadbare hand-me-downs and was often mistaken for a boy, thanks to the bowl haircuts her mother gave her. She and her siblings waited turns in the kitchen for haircuts. Alex remembered the swish of the broom on the floor, pushing all the hair into one pile to be cleaned up before her father got home.

Her father labored long hours for little money in the paper mill where he worked since he was eighteen. The putrid smell of tree pulp stuck like glue on his clothes. Alex remembered holding her breath when he hugged her after a long day.

Alex immersed herself in school. Education was her ticket out of her hometown and destitute way of life. Books of all genres lined her small bookshelf in her room. A voracious reader, she acquired an impressive vocabulary that often left some of her teachers scrambling for a thesaurus or a dictionary. In junior high, she learned anyone could run for office, so she leveled her sights on being class president. Hours were spent writing a convincing and compelling speech.

"Allie honey, you sound a little flat and robotic. Try injecting a little emotion. People can relate to feelings," she recalled her mother saying after a rehearsal speech.

Alex took her mother's suggestion to heart. Every day after school Alex was glued to the *Oprah Winfrey Show*. She was fascinated with how Oprah reeled in her audience with her sincere and caring way of speaking and listening. Alex meticulously studied Oprah's body language as her guests poured their hearts out on national television.

Shut away in her room, she practiced her own speeches into a tape recorder. Practice paid off. She commanded the power of persuasive speaking and handily won presidential class elections year after year. Unlike her competition, Alex knew better than to promise unrealistic things—more recess or no homework—in her speeches. She focused on realistic goals for herself and her classmates.

At her high school graduation, Alex was voted as class speaker. The crowd of proud parents, siblings, and grandparents laughed when the principal introduced her as "the future first woman president of the United States." In college, Alex devoured each political science/government class she took, worked on campaigns, and at twenty-two started her career as a legislative aide. She thrived on the power, the favors, the secrets, and the control.

She glanced once more at all the school kids and flicked her cigarette butt in their direction. *They'll never know what it's like to wake up freezing and hungry.*

"Let me guess, cancer-stick break?" Jake asked when she returned to the office.

"I'm quitting soon. I promise," she replied.

"Oh really? And if I had a dollar every time you made that promise, I'd be wearing cashmere instead of rayon."

"Well, if anyone can make rayon look good, it's you, Jake."

"You're so right. Anyway, I put all the papers needing your signature on your desk. Oh, and your meeting for ten tomorrow is still a go."

"I hoped they may cancel—no such luck, though. And you need to get out of here if you're going to catch your train. Have fun in the Big Apple," Alex said and started toward her office.

"Ta ta, have a good weekend yourself," Jake answered and left to pack up.

Alex sighed as she watched Jake pack up and leave. *If I had been a mom, I'd have a child his age—late twenties.* As driven as she was to shatter the glass ceiling as a woman senator in a good ol' boy world, she could not ignore the question of what her life would like look had she been a parent. Growing up with siblings, motherhood was an automatic assumption. Yet after years of being married to Victor and miscarrying three times, she learned she was unable to carry a baby full term. This realization came after another doctor's appointment of endless poking and prodding. She sat out in her car, rain pouring down. Through her strangled sobs, she told Victor the devastating news—her body was unable to give them the children they longed to have. They discussed adoption at length. In their heart of hearts, they knew their careers could not warrant the time and energy to properly care for an infant. They achingly agreed to shut the door to parenthood forever.

CHAPTER 17

Daisy's assignment for school was to watch numerous clips of top news reporters and critique them. Her goal was to note how each one delivered the news, observe body language, and mimic their style. Eyes weary and blurred, she poured herself a glass of water and resumed her viewing. A rumbling stomach and slight headache needed attention.

In the kitchen, she opened the freezer and saw frozen dinners staring back at her. *I can't eat another one.* On a whim, she texted Jaida. *I know it's last minute . . . are u free for dinner?*

Jaida replied. *No can do, sorry . . . have to work late tonight. System problems.*

Ok . . . good luck. Talk to u later.

Starved, Daisy ordered a steak and veggie calzone for dinner.

She sat with Gussie who meowed and pawed at Daisy each time she took a bite of the cheesy calzone. "Sorry, Gussie. Calzones aren't good for kitties."

Daisy ate half and took the other half into the kitchen to wrap up and save for later. She cleaned up and did not hear her phone ring above the running water of the sink.

She flopped back down on the couch to watch television for a while before bed. As she sat down, her phone rang again. "Hey Momma, how are you?"

"Hi sweetheart . . ." Her voice sounded strange. "I know it's late, but I need to talk to you."

"Mom, what's wrong? You sound weird," Daisy said.

Her mother inhaled deeply and in a voice damp with tears she told Daisy, "Sweetheart, our dear Hoot died in his sleep a few nights ago. His brother James called and told us. Apparently, it was his heart. I'm so sorry to call with such sad news."

Daisy was numb. *Dead? Hoot? What?* The room felt like all the air was sucked out of it. Her mouth felt like a desert.

"Oh my God." A fist squeezed Daisy's heart. Her eyes burned with hot tears as they trickled down her face. "I can't wrap my head around this, Mom."

"I know, honey. Your dad and I are so sad."

"Hoot was like another grandfather. I loved him." Daisy wiped her eyes and tried to focus. "When is his funeral?"

"It's on Saturday at St. Matthew's. Why don't you come home tomorrow, Friday?"

"I will. When I book my train, I'll let you know when I get in."

"All right. I can't wait to see you, honey. I love you."

"I love you too. See you on Friday."

Daisy dropped her phone and stared at the wall. *Hoot gone. I can't believe it.* Gussie's head became damp from the tears that fell as Daisy clutched her close.

* * *

Across town, Nick and Winston sat on the back patio grilling hot dogs and burgers when he felt his phone buzz.

"Hey Dad, what's going on? Isn't Thursday golf night?"

His father inhaled deeply. "Hi son, I'm afraid I have some bad news for you." His voice caught in his throat. "I'm so sorry to tell you this, but Hoot passed away."

"*What?*" Nick felt the blood roar through his ears. Shock silenced him for a moment.

"Son, are you there?"

"Yeah, yeah. Oh my God. What happened? When?"

Winston looked at him and mouthed, "Is everything okay?"

Nick shook his head, walked into the kitchen, and sat heavily in a chair at the table.

His father continued, "Two nights ago. It was his heart and he died in his sleep. It was a blessing. After all, he was getting up there in age."

Nick's eyes welled up. He cleared his throat. "When's the service?"

"This Saturday at ten o'clock at St. Matthew's."

Nick steadied his voice. "I'll catch a train to Cab Station."

"Good, we'll all be there. As you well know, he meant a lot to your grandfather and I know how influential he was in your life."

Nick blinked away the tears. "I can't believe this. I just talked to him a few weeks ago. He sounded fine. I'm crushed."

"I know, son. I am too and so is your grandfather."

Nick finished the conversation with his father. "Okay, I'll see you next Friday." He blinked his eyes and rubbed them. He fought to process what he just learned about his dear friend, Hoot. Hoot, the man who coached him to three junior club golf championships, the friend who listened to him vent about his parents' divorce when it was fresh and raw, and the man who helped to uncover the murderers of his great Uncle Clay.

Winston walked into the kitchen and asked, "Are you okay? I almost burned the dogs and burgers."

Nick sat in the chair; he was silent.

Winston sat down. "Hey man, you look like you lost your best friend."

He looked at Winston. "I kinda did."

"What's going on?"

Nick told Winston all about Hoot and his summers in Cab Station. "I used to hang out in the caddie shack all the time too. My grandmother would have killed me if she had known that. I talked to Hoot about everything."

"I'm so sorry, Nick. I wish I had known him. Is there anything I can do for you?"

"A beer please."

Over dinner, Nick continued talking about Hoot. "You would have loved him. He listened to me vent when my parents got divorced. He was so smart and knew how to talk about anything."

"Like what?"

"Sports, movies, girls. One of my favorite memories is talking about *The Old Man and the Sea*. He and I read it together when I was fourteen."

"One of my favorite books," Winston said, trying to change to a less painful subject.

"I remember telling Hoot how I felt like Santiago because I really wanted to win a golf tournament just like Santiago wanted to haul in the big fish. Remember?" Nick reminisced.

Winston tried to comfort his friend. "I sure do. You're lucky, though—you have that memory and others."

"I know." Sadness dug in and lingered in the chambers of Nick's heart.

"He sounds like he was a great guy. When is the funeral?"

"This Saturday." Nick sighed and stared at the wall opposite him. Winston said nothing and let him talk. "He was the best. And like I told you, he helped me get the caddie job at Carver. I just talked to him like a month ago."

"This is rough, Nick. I remember when my favorite uncle died. I was shattered. It took a while for me to learn to live with it."

"I'm really sorry. How old were you?"

"Fourteen, and he was only forty-six."

"Yikes, that's young. Another cool thing about Hoot is how he helped us solve the cold case murder of my great uncle, Clay Tyson. When you said uncle, it reminded me of that."

Winston was stunned. "Cold case murder? You were part of solving a cold case murder when you were fourteen? Very impressive."

"Come to think of it, it really was."

"I'll say." Winston took a swig of beer. "Are you taking the train?"

"Yup. I'll make a reservation after I clean up."

"No, no. I got this. Make your reservation."

"Thanks."

In his room later, Nick absentmindedly pulled clothes from his dresser and tossed them into a bag. *I can't believe Hoot is gone.* His thoughts turned to Cab Station and he wondered how it had changed in the last seven years. His only suit hung in the closet. He put that and a colorful tie into a hanging bag.

Winston knocked on Nick's door. "Hey Nick? I've been called into work. I'm not sure when I'll be back. Have a safe trip if I don't see you."

Nick opened his door. "Work now? It's late."

"Yeah, something about a new security system at the airport. Since our department has the contract, I'm part of the team to fix it. Could be an all-nighter." Winston sighed and tightened the straps of his backpack.

Thanks, I'll let you know when I'm coming back."

Winston squeezed his friend on the shoulder. "Again, I'm really sorry about Hoot."

"Thanks man. Good luck tonight."

CHAPTER 18

Winston headed out the door. He walked the three blocks to a waiting SUV. He sat in the back seat next to Jaida and asked, "What do you have for me?"

"We got something good here." Jaida shifted in her seat to turn her laptop toward Winston. "Take a look at what we intercepted."

Winston scanned the screen and saw three incoming flights that had been red-flagged for potentially carrying contraband.

"Damn. These guys spread their web far and wide, didn't they?" Winston said.

"Very much so. Commissioner Knight directed us to cross-check passenger lists from the past two months for certain names appearing repeatedly—especially from flights originating in Moscow. We need to get to the airport so I can check the lists on the airport's system."

"I'll call the deputy there and tell him we're on our way."

"No need. Commissioner Knight already did," Jaida said.

On the way to the airport, they discussed their plan again once they were inside.

The SUV came to an abrupt halt outside the airport. Jaida and Winston entered through a side door where a security guard was posted. They showed their ID badges and proceeded up the stairs to the office of Joel Silver,

Deputy Director of Reagan International Airport.

"Welcome, Agent Campbell and Agent Wang. I'm Joel Silver, Deputy Director." He offered his moist hand to Jaida and Winston. "Please, follow me." He showed them to a large office that reminded Jaida of HQ's war room: a space filled with computers and communication devices.

"We have complied with the request from Commissioner Knight. Please, do what you need to do," Silver said.

"Thank you. We will let you know if we find anything. I'll warn you—this may take most of the night," Winston informed him.

"No need. We will all be in communication. You can control everything from this office. I'll leave you to it."

"Thank you again. You've been very cooperative. We think it best for you and your security detail to circulate through the airport and wait for any word," Jaida told Silver.

"As you wish." Silver quickly exited the room.

Jaida started in on the long task of entering data into her computer while Winston was charting all incoming flights from Europe, Asia, and Africa including passenger lists and the gates to which the planes arrived.

Down the hall and out of earshot of the agents, Silver called Victor.

"Hello Joel. I'm not sure I like hearing from you, especially this late."

"I'm not thrilled about having to call you either," Silver said. "However, you need to know that all incoming flights from Paris, Moscow, London, and Johannesburg are under surveillance. Two agents from US Customs are here."

Victor ground his teeth. "For Christ's sake, what options

do we have?"

"I'll have the London flight diverted by a controller to another gate right as it lands—kind of last minute. I will also . . . shall I say *edit* . . . the passenger list. I know one controller who won't say no to some extra cash. Is that amenable?"

"Yes, it is. I'll ensure that controller won't ever speak again."

"Fine, but it's going to cost you. I'm thinking a thousand in cash will do it."

Silver's brazenness irritated Victor. "A *grand*? Shit! You pay him and I'll reimburse you tomorrow."

* * *

Frustration grew in Jaida and Winston as they ran through all the data on the flights. "Damnit. Do you think the intel we received about tonight's flights was accurate?" Jaida asked wearily.

"I'm starting to wonder that too." Winston removed his glasses and rubbed his eyes. "I just checked passenger list for the last inbound plane—no red flags."

"We've been here for six hours, and nothing," Jaida groaned. "Knight needs to know. I'll call her so she can inform our European office." Jaida picked up her phone.

They packed up their equipment and headed out of the office. Winston called Silver and informed him of their status.

"Thank you for your help. Our search proved fruitless," Winston said.

"Oh, I'm sorry to hear that. I'll keep you abreast of any

strange goings-on, Agent Wang." Silver hung up, a smug smile on his vulpine face.

Along with Winston and Jaida, several airport employees exited through the doors after long overnight shifts. The chill in the dark early morning air was biting. Jaida ducked her shoulder under Winston's arm, and he gave it squeeze. "Don't worry, we're gonna find these guys," he said to her.

"I know, but I'm getting impatient," Jaida responded.

"I understand, trust me."

A few yards away, a white van sat idling—Rubi Lee in the driver's seat, Zeke in the passenger seat.

Rubi Lee said, "Uncle Vic said to grab this Benson guy. He's short, fat and has a beard. Keep your eyes on the door."

They watched the parade of people come out of the airport. Rubi Lee looked again at the screen shot of the air traffic controller Victor sent her. "There he is!" Rubi Lee pointed at their unsuspecting quarry.

Zeke asked, "Why are we grabbing this guy?"

"Because Uncle Vic said to. This guy had something to do with diverting a plane with illegal stuff on it. Uncle Vic doesn't want him around."

Zeke shrugged as he rolled down the window and yelled, "Hey, Benson! Over here!"

Head in his phone, Benson did not look up. Zeke yelled louder. Benson looked up and frowned.

Jaida and Winston stopped and turned sharply at the sound. "Did you hear that?" Winston asked her.

"Yes. It sounded like they said Winston, didn't it? It came from that direction." She pointed toward the van.

Zeke yelled again, "Benson!"

Jaida and Winston watched as a man wearing an airport ID badge shuffle toward the idling van.

Zeke hopped out of the van as Benson neared it. A quiet conversation turned loud and angry. Zeke suddenly grabbed Benson by the shoulders and threw him against the van.

"What in the hell are you doing? Help! Someone please help!" Benson yelled.

"Shut up!" Zeke yelled and squeezed Benson's throat. "Get in the van!"

"Hey! Hey stop! Stop!" Winston yelled and sprinted toward the van.

"Are you crazy! Get back here!" Jaida yelled.

"Stop! Stop!" Winston hollered.

Zeke snapped his head toward a charging Winston. Benson struggled in his grip until Zeke pounded his into fist into Benson's solar plexus. He dropped like a sack of flour.

Zeke bent over to load Benson into the van, but Winston jumped at him. He caught Winston by the front of the shirt and hurled him into the side of the van. Winston felt like his ribcage shattered. He could not breathe. He tried to stand up, but Zeke kicked him in the side and the face.

"Winston!" Jaida screamed and sprinted toward her partner. She stopped short when she saw, with horror, a masked woman standing over Winston—a gun pointed at his head.

"Stop or I *swear* I'll kill him," Rubi Lee said.

Jaida's stomach turned. Her instincts prickled and she knew to listen. "Okay, okay. Just let him go."

"Not one more step. Or *bang*. Got it?" Rubi Lee said. Next to her, Zeke loaded an unconscious Benson into the van.

"Yes. Let him go. Please."

Rubi Lee looked disgustedly at Winston. "Don't stand up. I want you to crawl back to your girlfriend like a dog. I don't want to see your ugly face." She watched him on all fours crawl toward Jaida. "Good boy." Rubi Lee backed away, gun pointed at them and got back into the driver's seat. She revved the van and peeled away.

"Win! Win! Are you all right?" Jaida squatted down.

Winston groaned and held his head. Blood trickled from a nasty abrasion on his head. "Oh man, that hurt. I feel okay, except my face and side *kill*." He groaned, moving his extremities.

"You have a nasty cut over your left eye and your cheek and lip are swelling. Stay on the ground until our ride comes."

Winston sat up slowly and shook his head. "Did you get the license plate?"

Jaida shook her head. "There *was* no plate. But I did see the driver's side mirror was duct-taped."

Minutes later a SUV pulled into the lot and stopped next to Winston and Jaida. Two men got out and assisted them into the car.

"When we get back to the office, we'll debrief this whole long night," Winston said, holding his head.

"Only after you get patched up properly," Jaida said.

CHAPTER 19

Daisy boarded a late morning train for Cab Station and settled in for the three-hour ride. Once the train chugged out of the station, she texted Jaida to remind her to feed Gussie.

Sure thing . . . Gussie won't starve! I'll be thinking about you. Love you.

Love, Daisy replied.

She gazed down at her bag and sighed. Inside it was her laptop loaded with unfinished schoolwork. She thought, *I just don't have the focus. Schoolwork is not gonna happen.* She dug in her bag for the magazine she bought. She opened Spotify on her phone, stuck in her ear buds, and lost herself in the warm, velvety sounds of the Grateful Dead and Bob Marley and in the pages of *People* magazine.

Two cars back, Nick squeezed into a middle seat between a middle-aged man and woman. Immediately, the man pulled out his laptop and earphones—the universal sign: *I don't want to talk.* The woman began eating the minute the train pulled out. She looked at him and said, "I'm a nervous traveler and food soothes me."

"I see." Nick took out his copy of *The Old Man and the Sea*—an homage to Hoot. He ran his hand over the faded cover and reminisced about the conversations he and Hoot had about this book. Nick's most fond memory was the summer-long debate whether Santiago was a skilled or lucky fisherman. Twenty-three pages in, his eyes felt heavy. He laid his head back and closed his eyes. The slow rock of the train worked its magic. Within ten minutes, Nick slept.

He was jolted awake by the overwhelming odor of tuna fish. He fought to hide the look of revulsion as he turned to the woman next to him.

"I told you I was a nervous eater." She laughed shrilly as she dug into a pack of tuna with her fingers.

Get up before you gag! He rocketed from his seat and headed toward the lounge car. Nick was grateful to see the few leather chairs were empty. He settled into the plush seat and stretched out his long legs and looked at his phone. *Another hour and a half. Scrabble sounds like a good idea.* He was so engrossed in the game he did not notice the lounge car began to fill up. Laughter and chatter bounced around. Nick looked up and saw two older women sitting in chairs opposite him. Both were smiling at him.

"You certainly look comfortable," one of them said.

"Yes I am. Those seats are tight back there," Nick replied.

"I would imagine a tall handsome young man like you needs lots of leg room, especially on a long trip to Chicago," the other said.

Nick felt his cheeks burn. "Actually, I'm headed to Cab Station, not Chicago."

She clucked her tongue. "Pity for us. We were hoping you were headed to the flower arranging convention too."

He chuckled. "No ma'am. I'm headed to Virginia for the funeral of an old friend."

"Oh no. You poor thing. We're so sorry. Please let us buy you a drink!" she said and stood up. "What would you like?"

He knew saying no was not an option. "A light beer please."

"Be right back." She walked to the bar.

Soon the three were chatting about jobs, family, and traveling. Nick took the last sip of beer and through the glass, he saw a flash of gorgeous, curly red hair. He almost spit out that last sip. He knew only one person with hair that noticeable. Goosebumps dotted his skin from head to toe. He did a double-take, but she was obscured by a man wearing a large hat.

"Excuse me ladies. I think I see a friend," Nick said. His heart pounded in his throat as he approached the woman. Her soft curls bounced as she spoke animatedly on the phone. She tossed back her head and laughed heartily, showing her beautiful profile. Nick was sucked in by her beauty. He stared at her and felt his stomach flip. *Oh my God, it's Daisy.*

Suddenly she turned in her seat and her gaze landed on him. At first, she only glanced at him and looked away. Not for long though. Still on the phone, she returned his stare with an expression of unbridled joy and disbelief. Nick heard her say, "Erin, I, ah . . . um, I have to call you back." Her phone fell onto the chair. "*NT?* Oh, my goodness! What're you *doing* here?" She leaped out of her chair and they hugged tightly. "It's *so good* to see you!"

At the touch of their bodies, electricity coursed through them from head to toe. He squeezed her hard and said, "Daisy Kathryn Taylor. Fancy meeting you on a train." They released each other and gawked at one another for a bit until he asked how long it had been since they saw each other.

"Six years? Somewhere in there," she replied.

"Sounds about right. You look great by the way, all grown up." He stared at her. Remnants of the girl were still there in the few freckles peppering her perfect nose.

"You do too." She saw the fullness in his face was gone, replaced by cheekbones which gave his face stunning contours. "I can't believe we ran into each other—on a train no less!"

"I know. Where are you going?" he asked.

"To Cab Station for . . ." She didn't finish.

"Hoot's funeral, right?" He knew by her tone.

She gaped at him. "Yes, how did you know?"

"Because I'm going to the same funeral and I could tell by your sad voice. My dad called me the other night and told me."

Daisy's mind whirled. "But wait. *Where* did you get on the train?"

"In DC. I live there now," he answered.

"You do?" Her eyebrows shot up. "So do I."

"Seriously? For how long?"

"A few months—how crazy is this?" she said.

"Very. How about we catch up over a drink?"

"Lead the way," she said.

For thirty minutes, they caught up on the past six years and both admitted to ghosting on each other and promised to spend more time together in their new city. The bartender called out last call. "Bar's closing, folks!"

Nick lamented to Daisy about returning to the cramped seat and the lady who chowed down on tuna.

"That's so gross and rude. Come sit with me."

His heart leaped. "I'd love to."

115

When seated, they talked about Hoot, their summers with him and how sad they each felt at the loss of their dearest, oldest friend.

The light beer buzz coupled with the lolling of the train was hypnotic. Soon they both were yawning.

"Time for a nap," Daisy said. "We don't get in for another forty minutes."

"Sounds good. Don't snore too loudly," Nick joked.

Daisy laid her head against the window and watched the blur of red, gold, and orange-leafed trees whiz by. The blending of those brilliant colors reminded her of mixing finger paints when she was little.

Soon she felt her eyes close and she succumbed to a dream-filled nap. In it, Hoot was standing on a green of a golf course, holding a putter, big smile on his handsome face, waving to her. He looked so alive, silhouetted against the vibrant pink and lavender sunset. As Daisy ran to him, he faded away as the sun sunk behind the green.

A cramp in her neck woke her. She did not realize she had eventually fallen asleep on Nick's shoulder. His hand lay palm up on her thigh. She rubbed her neck and listened to his even breathing and felt the warmth of his body next to hers. A contented smile crossed her face as she closed her eyes and relished finding her friend again.

* * *

Hoot's funeral was held at St. Matthew's church. A warm breeze carried the scent of fall on the clear October day. Most of the denizens of the small southern town turned out for one of their favorite lifelong residents. Mourners sat shoulder to shoulder in the gothic church. Tears, laughs and love were shared by all those in attendance.

After the beautiful, moving service, Nick stood in the parking lot chatting with his parents and grandparents. He kept an eye on the enormous wooden doors to see when Daisy came out. He soon saw her, flanked by her mother and father—her three brothers trailed behind. He watched her look around . . . for what he hoped was him. He called her name and waved. Soon, the Taylor and Tyson families stood in the emptying parking lot talking and reminiscing about their friend, Hoot.

"Are you headed back today or tomorrow?" Nick asked her.

"Tomorrow. How about you?"

"Same, but I'm not sure of what time." He pulled out his phone and checked. "I'm on the 11:14."

Daisy consulted her phone. "It looks like I'm on the two o'clock train."

Damn. "Maybe you could change it to earlier so we could ride home together?" he suggested. *I hope I don't sound too desperate.*

She turned sideways and gave him a smile, thinking, *I'd love that.* "Sure, I'll check." After a few seconds, she told him, "You're in luck. Give me your number and we can meet at the station, okay?"

"Sure, here." Nick texted her.

"Great, thanks. See you tomorrow. Fingers crossed we don't sit with someone eating tuna."

* * *

The train rumbled to a stop and exhaled loudly. Daisy looked over at a sleeping Nick and sighed. *I wonder if he wants to get together again. I don't want to seem like I'm pushy or smothering him if I say something.* Softly, she nudged him with her elbow.

"We're here?" He blinked and rubbed his face.

"Yup, sleepyhead. We're here."

Nick and Daisy gathered their belongings and deboarded. They weaved their way around the people milling about the station.

"So, are you headed home?" Nick asked when they walked out of the station.

"Yes. Uber will be here soon."

"Oh okay." Nick tried to hide his disappointment.

Daisy noticed his tone. "I really need to get some schoolwork done and see Gussie," Daisy replied.

"Gussie?"

"My cat. You'll have to meet her."

"I'd love to," Nick replied. "So, when do you want to hang out again?"

Daisy smiled inwardly at his question. "I'm not sure. I'll text you when I see what my week looks like, okay?"

"Sounds good. It was great to see you," Nick said.

"You too." She turned at the sound of a car. "Well, my ride is here." The wind kicked up, swirling her hair around.

He gently moved a curly tress out of her face. "See you soon."

"Yes, you will."

* * *

Winston was watching TV when Nick walked in. He dropped his bags and sat down. "What the hell happened to your forehead?" Nick pointed at the ugly red abrasion. "What, were you in some kind of fight?"

Shit! My head! Winston forgot Nick had not seen the parting gift Zeke gave him at the airport. Thinking quickly, he lied, "Oh this. I tripped on the bathroom rug after too many beers. Good thing I didn't knock myself out."

"I'll say."

Quickly, Winston asked about Hoot's funeral. He did not want Nick to ask anything more about his head.

"It was sad, but he lived a successful and happy life. I'll always miss him though. I saw a lot of people I haven't seen in a long time," Nick responded, thinking of Daisy first. He'd be a fool to not admit he hadn't stopped thinking of her. "Get this, Win. One of the people I reconnected with is a girl named Daisy. We used to hang out during the summers when we were kids and I haven't seen her since we were seventeen."

Win dug further. "And?"

"Well, she's in DC too. Neither of us knew the other was here. Pretty cool, huh?"

"Oh really? That is cool." His eyes were glued to the television.

"And she tends bar." Winston's head snapped around.

"Where?"

"The Black LaSalle."

"That's like one of *the* bars to be seen in. What does she look like?"

"She's tall, red curly hair?"

"I think I know who she is. Jaida and I go there. She's

hot," Win said. "No wonder why you're psyched she's here!"

"Easy man, we're friends." Nick rolled his eyes. "How're things with you and Jaida?"

"Great, that is *when* I see her. Tomorrow is computer upgrade day. She hates it because it takes forever. People don't remember to restart occasionally or back stuff up. Drives her nuts. So, make sure to do that."

"I will," Nick promised.

CHAPTER 20

Jaida gobbled down a sandwich and washed it down with a swig of iced tea. She checked her schedule and remembered she and Win were meeting after work—something they tried to do on Mondays. Before that, though, she was due on the third floor to upgrade computers. She tossed the bottle into the recycling bin and headed toward the elevator.

Jaida loved her undercover job as a computer engineer, especially the troubleshooting aspect. It was never boring. She worked in the Cooper Building where she was known as "The Codebreaker"—a nickname she appreciated. Engineering suited her because it was constant, challenging and it allowed her to know everyone in the building.

The doors slid open and Francine passed by the elevator and stopped abruptly. "God, the *boots!*" She pointed at Jaida's newest pair of boots. "Is the favorite code breaker here to expose all of the deep, dark secrets buried in our computers? Or to show off her *fabulous* footwear?" Jaida had on her latest acquisition: scarlet red cowboy boots with black embroidery.

"Both, of course." Jaida frowned and glanced around. "Seems a little empty in here."

Francie shrugged. "Well, it *is* Monday." She looked around the spacious office. "Although I do know a handful of aides are here, so you can get theirs done. Oh, and Victor

Sykes."

Victor Sykes. Jaida had never formally met him; however, she knew about him, thanks to the intel from the agency. Jaida knew he was ex-military and a temperamental perfectionist.

Twenty minutes later, Jaida finished the other computers. She found Francie. "Time for me to upgrade Victor's computer. What's he like? I've never met him."

"Well . . ." Francie pursed her lips together. "He's quite intelligent, serious, and polite."

"I see."

"Here, I'll introduce you. Anything to get me away from this desk." Francie pushed herself away from her desk and rose.

Francie knocked on Victor's door. "Knock, knock. It's Francie with Jaida, from IT."

"Please enter." Victor looked up from his computer and quickly swiped right across his touch pad. He stood and assessed Jaida with his beady, light blue eyes. Jaida locked eyes with him and they nodded curtly at one another. He reminded Jaida of a high school football coach: average height, built like a barrel with close-cropped gray hair. He maintained his perfect military posture as he brushed off imaginary dust from his expensive suit. Too much sun left lines around his eyes. Jaida guessed his age to be in the late fifties to early sixties.

"Jaida, this is Victor Sykes. Victor, this is Jaida Campbell. She's here to upgrade your computer, sir." Francie made the introduction.

He and Jaida shook hands. "That certainly is an impressive handshake," he said to Jaida.

"Thank you," Jaida replied. "As Francie said, I am here to upgrade your computer."

"I see. I was working on something of the utmost importance. Can this wait? I imagine it will take some time to run an upgrade."

Jaida's instincts tingled. *He's trying to dodge it.* "I'm afraid it can't wait. I can get it done in about thirty minutes," she told him.

He tossed this over. "Thirty minutes? Why so long?"

"I need to run diagnostic tests, scan for viruses, clean out the dust, and see if your hard drive is up to date." Jaida rambled, banking on the fact that he had no idea what she meant.

"Fine. My machine is a bit slow. Can you help?"

"Yes. I will check the hard drive." Something about him alerted Jaida's radar. "Often they are obsolete and need to be replaced."

"All right, fine. Are you sure this is going to take only thirty minutes? That doesn't seem like much time for you to properly execute this process."

"It's plenty of time, trust me."

"If you say so." Victor glared at her.

"Yes, I say so," Jaida shot back. "Please close out any running programs and log off too. Thank you."

Hesitantly, he surrendered it and she put the machine in her black bag and started to walk out of his office.

"Thank you."

"When will this be returned, young lady?" he asked.

She turned on her heel. "Like I said, within thirty minutes. And my *name* is Jaida."

Jaida found an empty room and opened Victor's

computer. She went to his settings and upgraded with the latest security and antivirus software. While she waited for the software to load, she wondered why Victor was so hesitant to give her his laptop. After it loaded, she popped open the back of his computer. Lots of dust hid in the crevices. She cleaned it out and removed the hard drive. She replaced it with a new one and put the old one in her bag. She closed Victor's machine and turned it back on. *I can't wait to look at what's on this.* She ran through a few more diagnostics before she was satisfied. Since Victor was a perfectionist, she was not going to give him an inch to criticize her. Thirty minutes later she was back up to Victor's office and knocked on the door.

The door flew open, as if he was waiting behind it. "Oh good, you're finished." He reached out for his computer.

"Yes I am. I did exactly what I said I was going to do. Your machine will run much more effectively now with the new security upgrade and new hard drive."

"New hard drive?"

"Yes. I took the old slow one out and replaced it," Jaida said.

Victor started to tap his fingertips together. "Interesting. What do you IT people do with the old hard drives?"

His rapid speech and nervous finger tapping told Jaida he was hiding something. "We *IT people* can do a variety of things. We can recycle it, reuse it, give it away, or destroy it."

"Ah, I see that I have choices. I feel destroying the old hard drive is the best course of action. Agreed?" It was more of a command.

"I agree. No one needs an old hard drive. Plus, it's part

of my job to destroy anything not reusable." Jaida noticed he was rubbing his hands together.

"Thank you for giving me your *word* on that. Now if you'll excuse me, I have work to do."

"And so do I," Jaida replied and turned to leave.

His voice sounded like it slid out from under a slimy rock. "Oh, Miss Campbell, I *do* have your word you'll destroy the old hard drive, correct?"

Jaida turned around. "Of course." She walked out, leaving the door open on purpose.

"Everything go okay with him?" Francie said.

"Yes. He's an interesting one—kind of robotic," Jaida said.

"Are you finished with the upgrades?"

"I have one more. Senator Boyd is last. Thanks for your help."

"Don't mention it, see you soon."

"Yes, you will."

Right on time, Jake dropped off the senator's laptop. "Hello Jaida, how long for you to run your magic?" he asked Jaida.

"Not long—twenty minutes, thirty max," Jaida responded.

"Perfect. I haven't eaten the entire day. Busy, busy, busy!"

"Go grab something, take a break and come back. It'll be done."

"Thank you, you're an angel." Jake left.

Jaida yawned, rubbed her eyes and opened Senator Boyd's laptop. *Wake up, girl.* Jaida shook her head and stretched. Innumerable files, documents, and other sensitive material were Jaida's responsibility to protect. She ran a diagnostic check and updated the security and anti-virus software. Jaida scrolled through her phone as the program ran. No new emails, or other notifications. Twenty minutes later, the update was complete.

"Boy, did I need that little pick-me-up!" Jake announced sipping an enormous drink with a puff of whipped cream on top.

"Late lunch?" Jaida asked.

"Sure, if you consider lunch three almond biscotti and this sugary cup of sweetness!" Jake responded. "Everything fine?"

"You bet. It's all yours."

"Thank you. See you soon."

Jaida texted Winston that she would meet him in twenty minutes.

* * *

"How was your day?" he asked when she dropped into the chair.

"Eventful, but long," she answered. "Wait till you see this though." She scooted her chair over and pulled out Victor's old hard drive from her bag.

"What do you have here?" Winston asked.

"This is the old hard drive from Sykes's computer," Jaida smirked. "I replaced it today and he didn't like it. He was like a caged animal—all nervous. To me, it's obvious he's in deep with the smuggling."

"And his name was the one from the red book." Winston stroked his chin.

"You got it. Let's see what made him so nervous." Jaida loaded Victor's hard drive.

They combed through every piece of data and opened every file until they landed on it.

"Holy crap, look at this." Jaida pointed at the screen. "Those are *not* names of veterans. These names look Russian, which potentially means two things: Sykes is the ringleader and his connections are international."

"Yes, they do. And these names here"—Winston pointed—"are names of senators."

"And these," Jaida added, pointing, "are dates without question. And the numbers in this column look like the amount of contraband being delivered."

"Yup. And this date is last week," Winston said. "The *exact* night we went to the airport."

"Win, these are definitely the people we've been hunting."

"Yes, they are. Like Commissioner Knight said, we will proceed slowly."

Jaida sighed and stretched her arms over her head. "I don't know about you, but I could use a stiff drink."

"Black LaSalle?" he suggested. "I'll text Nick to see if he wants to meet us."

"Sure," she responded.

At the bar, Winston grabbed Jaida's hand and wound their way through the crowd to the bar. Daisy was at the other end, cashing out other customers. She glanced down their way and waved.

"Hey guys, what's up?" Daisy asked when they sat down. "You must be Winston."

"And you must be Daisy," Win said.

"I forgot you guys haven't met! Sorry," Jaida said.

"It's great to finally meet you," Daisy responded and asked what they were drinking.

"I'll have a Peroni," Jaida answered. "And an order of fries, please."

"A gin and tonic with Bombay Sapphire is calling my name," Winston replied. On the bar, his phone lit up. "Nick'll be here soon."

When Daisy returned with their drinks, Winston noticed Daisy looking past them, a happy grin on her face. Winston turned around and saw Nick approaching the bar.

"Hey man, glad you're here," Winston said.

"Hi all, what's going on?" he asked as his eyes lingered on Daisy.

Jaida noticed the look and gave Winston a kick under the bar. He looked at her and she subtly nodded at Nick. Winston raised his eyebrows and nodded in understanding.

"Hey NT. How are you?" Daisy greeted him. "What can I get you?"

"Hi Daiz. I'm doing well. What's new on draught I'd like?"

"Hmm, the new IPA is really good. It's not too hoppy— try it."

"I'll have one of those, please."

"Be right back," Daisy said.

"NT? Who's NT?" Jaida joked.

"It's a childhood nickname," Nick replied.

"What does the T stand for?"

"Tucker—my middle name. Daisy, my parents, and others call me NT. Kind of a hangover from being a kid."

"Hmm, NT. It's kind of cute—if you're a kid. I think I'll

stick with Nick," Jaida laughed.

"Fine by me." Nick took a slug of beer. "Daisy knows her stuff. This is really good."

Daisy returned and asked Nick, "You like it?"

"It's delicious. You know what I like."

Daisy leaned forward toward him. "I'm certainly learning."

"Yes, you are."

Even Winston felt the heat between them. He glanced at Jaida, who cocked her right eyebrow.

"If that wasn't obvious flirting, I don't know what is!" Jaida exclaimed. Both she and Winston stared at Nick.

He felt their eyes burning into him. "*What?*"

"Oh, come on! You know what! You two are so hot for each other!" Jaida said.

"Daisy and I are *just friends*." He glared at them.

Jaida cut right to it. "Nicholas, come on. Really? Really? You guys have known each other forever."

"I know. But that doesn't mean we'd be a good couple."

"Oh really? That little conversation y'all just had about learning what each other likes is pushing past the boundaries of friendship."

"Jaid, it was a conversation about *beer*. Not feelings." Nick shook his head and took a sip.

Jaida continued, "Practically every guy who comes in here drools all over her, it's so obvious. And *that* doesn't bother you?"

Nick sipped his beer and studied Daisy, who chatted with customers. "Maybe a little. If some creep were bothering her, yeah, I'd do something. She's tough, though. She grew up with three older brothers."

From the other end of the bar, Daisy noticed his empty glass. "Another round?" she asked.

"Sure, why not?" Winston said.

"Looks like you guys are going to be busy for a few hours," Nick said, observing the crowded bar.

"Yes, we will," Daisy said. "More money in the bank for me!" Daisy flitted off to serve other people.

"So, you guys have dated a few months Win told me," Nick said.

"Actually, it's been *a little over a year*." Jaida turned and shot daggers at Winston.

"A year? Win said a couple of months," Nick countered.

Winston realized his blunder. "Um, yeah. A year is twelve months, so that counts, right?" He tried.

"Sure. Whatever you say." Jaida's tone chilled the whole bar.

"This is probably a good time for me to use the bathroom." Nick left his seat.

"Did you actually tell him a *few months*?" Jaida glowered at Win.

"Yea, whoops," Win answered.

"Win, we *can't slip up.* We can't give an ounce away of who we are, right?"

"Yes. I'm sorry. I'll be more careful."

Nick returned and asked if they were ready to go.

"Yup. It's a school night," Jaida said.

"Unfortunately," Nick added.

Winston, Jaida, and Nick finished their drinks and said good night to Daisy and left.

CHAPTER 21

An hour later, Rubi Lee and Zeke walked into the Black LaSalle and sat at a table in the back. Before they left their apartment, Zeke packed the sweatshirt in a backpack.

"Uncle Vic said to look for the hooks in the back room, near the back door." She pointed behind her brother as their server appeared.

"Hi guys, what are you drinking?"

"Ya got some Yukon Jack?" Zeke asked.

"We do."

"Gimme a double," Zeke ordered.

The server turned to Rubi Lee. "You?"

"Wild Turkey, double too," Rubi Lee answered.

"Be right back."

"Good," Zeke said.

Their server returned and placed the drinks on the table. "You need anything else? Any food?"

"Another round, and an order of nachos," Zeke said and ran his eyes over the server. "My, you do have beautiful skin. Anyone ever tell you that?"

"I've heard it all my life," she responded as she left.

"Nice try. You really think she'd fall for your crap?" Rubi Lee said.

"Can't blame a guy for tryin'."

"Kind of like in high school how you tried to date those

girls totally out of your reach."

Zeke cut his eyes to his sister. "I'll have you know I *did* date one of them—Michelle Hart. Joke's on you, Rube," Zeke laughed.

"Michelle *Hart*? Isn't she the one who got pregnant senior year?" Rubi Lee stared at her brother.

"Yep." Zeke felt his sister's eyes bore into him. "For shit's sake, Rube, don't worry—that kid wasn't mine."

"Thank God for that."

Zeke shrugged. "Yeah. I couldn't imagine being a teen dad. When we were younger, I thought I'd play pro baseball for a few years. Remember when those scouts came to watch me pitch?"

Rubi Lee nodded.

"But that fell through, thanks to Dad who drank away the money set aside for me to travel to Florida for Triple-A spring training. What an asshole." He threw back his drink. "Anyway, I thought I'd get married and have a family. But after the crap we've been through—marriage and kids? Not happening."

"Yeah, the thought of having kids means having a relationship with someone. No thanks." Rubi Lee stuffed a loaded nacho chip into her mouth. "I'd rather do what we're doing for the money we're earning."

"Yup, and we'll always have each other. Cheers to that." Zeke clinked his glass against his sister's.

When they finished, Zeke removed the sweatshirt and hung it on the hook as directed. They left the bar as Henderson and Jackie walked in. Rubi Lee bumped into him.

"Pardon me," Henderson said.

"Whatever, old man," Rubi Lee responded.

"Excuse you!" Jackie reprimanded them.

Rubi Lee and Zeke kept walking, and ignored Jackie.

"You okay? Henderson, you look agitated," Daisy told him.

"Two young people were leaving as we entered, and they plowed right into me!"

"That's so rude," she responded. "I was hoping you all would come in." She placed a draft beer in front of him. "What are you drinking Jackie?"

"Woodford with Ginger beer please," Jackie said.

"Tasty combo. I'll be right back," Daisy said.

Jackie and Henderson talked about the British comedy they saw earlier that day.

"I have loved British comedies since I was a kid," Jackie laughed. "Thank you for indulging me."

"You're welcome. I'll warm up to them someday. The actors are just so damn hard to understand 'cause they talk too fast!" Henderson sipped his beer. "How did you get hooked on them?"

Jackie chuckled. "I had a nana who loved Monty Python. When my older brother and I spent the night at her house, we watched those movies. It was such a treat. She made us promise not to tell our parents. The secrecy made it all that much more fun. It's kind of like how you feel about Westerns."

"Understandable. My daddy loved his Westerns—especially John Wayne. When I was young, I remember asking him if he wanted to be a cowboy when he was little. Wanna know what he said?" Henderson asked.

"Sure," Jackie answered.

"He laughed and said, 'Son, I'd have loved it. But where

I grew up, black cowboys just didn't exist,'" Henderson said.

"Good point." Jackie clinked his glass and heard her phone ring.

Henderson knew from her abrupt answers she had to leave.

"Let me guess, duty calls? I thought you were off all day and night." He rubbed her back.

"I did too. I can't ignore this. I'm so sorry. Rain check, okay?" She rose from her seat and slung her bag over her arm. "I'll talk to you later." She gave him a kiss on the cheek.

"Okay, see you later." Henderson sighed and tugged at his beer.

Daisy returned and asked where Jackie went. He explained that duty called.

"Bummer. But now that I have your undivided attention, we haven't chatted in a while and it's your turn to pick the topic du jour."

"Okay, let me think," he said and glanced around. "Good crowd tonight."

"It is. The Redskins are on, so I'll make some good cash tonight. Are you ready for your chili? It's so good. Ira made it earlier today."

"You bet. Chili is good stuff on a cold night like this."

Daisy brought him a steaming bowl with shredded cheese on top.

He took a bite and sighed contentedly. "Since you mentioned football, let's tackle that subject. No pun intended!" His belly jiggled.

"You got it. Where do you want to start?"

"Since the NFC division is tight, I'd like to discuss who will finish first in the NFC East." Henderson put a loaded spoonful into his mouth.

"Sure thing," she said.

Daisy chose the Philadelphia Eagles; Henderson chose his beloved yet weak Cowboys to win the division.

He frowned at her. "The *Eagles*?"

"Yes, the *Philadelphia* Eagles."

"Why them?" Henderson stirred his chili.

"One, they beat the Patriots in the Super Bowl. Two, I love their uniforms, and three, Philadelphia gave birth to freedom."

Henderson rubbed his chin. "Okay, okay. I get you."

Daisy pulled at the taps, filled two glasses. "Why do you like Dallas so much?"

"My daddy loved 'em and their toughness. My favorite player, Tony Dorsett, was one of the best running backs of all time."

"Never heard of him. He must be really old by now!" Daisy teased.

"Ha ha. Google him—you'll see." Henderson glanced at his phone. "Time for an old man to hit the hay. As always, a pleasure, Daisy." He crumpled his napkin and put it in the empty bowl.

"Good night, my friend. See you soon."

"Indeed."

"Go Eagles!" she yelled after him; he waved back at her.

She wiped down the bar where he sat, closed out her cash drawer, and got ready to leave. Erin materialized from the office and asked Daisy how the night went.

"Very well. Did you get the books done?"

"Yes, I did. I still see numbers swimming in front of me!" Erin replied. "Where's Ira?"

"Ira, where are you?" Daisy called.

"Down here. I'll be right there!" His voice echoed up from the basement.

"It's time for you guys to head out," Erin said.

Ira trotted up the steps. "Ready Daisy?"

"Yup. See you later, Er." Daisy looked at her friend.

"See you guys. Have a good rest of the night."

"You too," Ira said.

A cold nip of air hit Daisy when she opened the door. "Brr, it's freezing!"

"Feels good to me," Ira said.

"I'm always cold and I'll freeze on the way home. I didn't bring a jacket or anything."

"Do you want to borrow something off one of the hooks? I think I saw a sweatshirt or two hanging up. People forget they hang stuff up and just leave," Ira said.

"I'll return it." She grabbed a red Washington Wizards sweatshirt off a hook and the two of them headed home into the dark, chilly night.

CHAPTER 22

Rubi Lee and Zeke sat in the van a few blocks away from the Black LaSalle. She took a long drag from her cigarette and dialed.

It was answered in one ring. "Well?"

"Yeah Uncle Vic, the sweatshirt is on the middle hook in the back of the bar. Right where you said to leave it," she said.

"Good work. I'm out of town now. I'll retrieve it when I return."

"You'll call when you have it, right?"

"Yes. That will be either tomorrow night or the next day."

"Okay."

The phone went dead.

Zeke started the engine, scanned the area, and pulled out. He paid little attention to the two people leaving the bar—until he saw one of them wearing the sweatshirt he hung on the hook. He did a double-take. "Oh no! Oh *shit!*" he yelled.

"What?" Rubi Lee looked up from her phone.

"That!" He pointed. "She has on the damn sweatshirt! That redhead! Look!" Spit flecked the windshield.

"How do you know?"

"Because I just saw the W of *Washington* lit up by the

streetlights when they walked under it!"

Zeke threw the van into park and got out. He yelled at Daisy and Ira, "Hey! Hey! Stop!" They did not hear him.

Zeke ran toward them, yelling loudly and waving his arms. His attempt was futile. "Damnit!" he yelled and ran back to the van. He fired up the engine and sped after the redhead and her male friend.

"Son of a bitch! We're gonna lose 'em!" Zeke punched the gas and raced down the narrow side street.

The van roared behind Daisy and Ira with the high beams lasered on their backs. Daisy turned around and saw the white van barreling down on top of them.

"What the hell?" She waved her arms to stop them and screamed, "Slow down!" But the van kept coming at them.

"Run, Ira!" Daisy and Ira sped to the next cross street twenty yards ahead. "Go down there!" Daisy screamed.

They raced down where she pointed, yet they were no match for the van. Terrified, they heard the roar of the engine grow louder.

"Quick, turn here!" Ira grabbed her hand and pivoted at a ninety-degree angle down a different street. The van shot past them and whipped around with such viciousness it teetered on two tires for a split second. It righted itself and continued the chase. Only fifty yards sat between the van and its prey.

"Run!" Ira grabbed Daisy's hand and they raced down the opposite direction of the street toward a usually busy intersection. Since it was late, very few cars were on the streets.

"Keep running!"

Tires screeched and red brake lights lit up the dark

street. The van snapped a U-turn, the driver stepped on the gas and it barreled toward them again.

Daisy and Ira sprinted toward the intersection and saw the orange glow of the SAFE TO CROSS sign ticking down from ten seconds—*nine, eight, seven.* Ira looked left and right and saw a handful of cars waiting at the red light. *Six, five, four.* By this time, Daisy dropped his hand and sprinted toward the intersection. *Three, two.* Daisy and Ira raced across the wide white lines on Pennsylvania Avenue just as the orange seconds ticked down and the light changed.

"Oh my God, I might puke," Ira said when they slowed down.

"Ira, look!" Daisy shrieked as she watched the white van barrel through the intersection toward them. Horns honked, brakes screeched, yet the van continued its relentless chase like a hungry lion chasing a sickly zebra.

"Keep running!" Daisy yelled. Up ahead, she saw the black square pole with a glowing white *M* at the top. *Thank God.* "The Metroline! Go!"

Before plummeting down the steps, Ira turned and saw the van door fly open and a man leap out.

"Hurry Daisy! He's following us!"

They leaped down the steps, two at a time, dashed to the platform and prayed for a train to arrive soon. In the tunnel, they saw a train light bouncing off the walls.

"Hurry up! Oh my God!" Daisy yelled.

The train stopped and its doors squealed open. They jumped in, panting like dogs. Passengers stared at them.

"Where're we going?" Daisy was breathless.

"We'll take this to the next stop and get off. It's a lot safer than hanging out down there," Ira said.

When they caught their breath and sat down, Daisy asked, "What was *that* about? Think they were trying to hit us?"

"It sure seems that way," Ira wheezed.

"This is not cool, Ira. What if the saw us get on here and are waiting at the next stop?"

Ira answered. "I doubt they followed us all the way down here."

Daisy sat and took several deep breaths. I've never seen that van before in my life." Daisy's heart still raced. "Have you?"

"Never." They rode in silence to try to calm down. When the metro came to a stop, Ira rose from his seat. Daisy stopped him.

"I think we need to get off at the next stop. What if they figured we were getting off here and they're waiting out there?"

"Okay." He took his phone from his pocket. "I'll get an Uber to pick us up at the next stop, so we aren't wandering around on the street, okay?"

"Thanks, Ira."

At the next stop, they scanned the area and were relieved to see the van was nowhere in sight. The Uber was waiting.

* * *

Zeke parked the van on a side street. He pounded the steering wheel. "Son of a bitch! How could this happen? Uncle Vic is gonna freak the *fuck* out when he goes to get the sweatshirt!" Zeke yelled. "Gimme a goddamn cigarette!"

He almost smoked the entire thing in one drag. "I can't believe this! Who is she? And why is she wearing the sweatshirt?"

"I don't know."

He lit another cigarette. "What do we do now?"

Rubi Lee chewed her fingernail and spit it out. "Call Uncle Vic. We have no choice."

Zeke threw the cigarette butt out the window and called. He explained what happened and hung up, face ashen.

"What'd he say?"

"He's pissed. He told us to get back to the bar early tomorrow morning, wait for her to get there, grab her and bring her to him."

"Hopefully between now and then that bitch won't find the diamonds." Rubi Lee gnawed on another nail.

"Shit, I didn't even think of that."

"Uncle Vic wants us to *kidnap* her? How does he know she's going to be there?"

"Yes. *Kidnap.* He said his other people have watching the place for a while, and said the redhead gets there early."

"All right, then we go tomorrow morning. Sounds fun."

* * *

Daisy waved good night to Ira, unlocked her door and was instantly calmed by Gussie's meow.

Gussie weaved in and out of Daisy's steps. "Easy girl, I was almost run over by a van."

Gussie followed Daisy into her room and leaped up onto the bed. Daisy sat and took a few deep breaths. *What just happened?* She could not shake the notion that someone tried to kill her and Ira. Her stomach turned at the thought. Too wired for sleep, Daisy played over the events of the night. It had been a normal night at the bar. No customers were unruly. She and Ira walked home together like they often do. Then out of nowhere, a van tried to run them down. *What the hell?* Gussie's loud meow broke Daisy's reverie. "You win." She got up and went to the kitchen to feed the cat.

I need a glass of wine—badly. She helped herself to a healthy pour and dropped onto the couch. After a few sips, she decided to call Nick. Sleep was out of the question; she had to tell someone what happened earlier that night.

He answered on the fifth ring. "Hullo." His voice was thick.

"What took you so long to answer?" she said.

"Daisy, are you okay?" he rasped.

"Yeah, I am. Sorry, I know it's late. But I have to tell you what happened tonight." Her voice caught in her throat.

Suddenly, Nick was wide awake. "What the hell happened?"

She poured out the story.

"That's *nuts*! You guys are okay though, right? I can come over if you'd like."

Daisy's heart skipped a beat. *I'd love that, but it doesn't feel right—yet.* She pondered what to do. Part of her said yes, the other said no.

"Daiz? You there?"

"Um, yes. Thanks for your offer, but I'm okay, and plus, it's so late." She heard him sigh. "Wait, how about lunch tomorrow? If you're free?" *Please say yes.*

"I think I'm free. If not, I'll clear an hour for you."

"Thanks, NT. I'm really sorry for waking you up."

"Don't apologize. I'm so glad you're okay—Ira too."

"Text me tomorrow morning about where and when to meet."

"I will. Get some sleep, Daisy."

"Night, NT."

"Night Daiz, see you tomorrow."

After talking to him, she felt less amped up. She changed and put the sweatshirt on a chair and got ready for bed. Gussie was already nestled into the blue, puffy quilt. Daisy fell into bed and slept soundly.

CHAPTER 23

"You got everything?" Rubi Lee asked her brother on the way out of their dingy apartment. It was the early hours of the morning.

"What do you think?" he said, referring to two pairs of gloves, zip ties, ski masks, a crowbar, and a lock pick. "Got it all."

They listened to the cheery morning DJ greet her five a.m. listeners. "Good morning, early birds! And what do you hope to accomplish today?"

Rubi Lee glanced at the radio and responded, "Accomplish? Gee, how about breaking into a bar and kidnapping some bartender without being caught?"

"Relax. How many times have you broken into somewhere?" Zeke asked.

"I know, but there's a lot at stake here if you weren't aware."

"You're a real pain in the ass in the morning, you know that?"

"Shut up and drive."

Zeke killed the headlights and steered the van into a spot on the street behind the bar. Rubi Lee tossed him a ski mask, which he pulled over his head.

"I'll text you when I have her."

"Don't forget to kill the cameras."

Rubi Lee saw his breath puff above his head as he jogged toward the back door. It was dark—not a soul in sight.

Zeke noticed it was an older lock. *No sweat.* Without a great deal of effort, he worked his magic and the lock yielded easily to the pick. *No damage for them to investigate.* He stuffed the crowbar back into the bag. Next stop was the office. Its locked yielded easily too. He saw the antiquated security for the cameras. With one yank, the system was disarmed and he hustled to the front. Zeke melted into the darkest area where he could clearly see the front door.

An hour and a half went by before he heard it—the jangle of keys followed by the scraping of the front door across the floor. Cold air swirled in when Erin opened and closed the door behind her.

Zeke's heart shifted into overdrive as he watched Erin remove her coat and fill the coffee maker with water. She opened a drawer and fumbled around in it. "Crap, no coffee up here," he heard her say. She flicked on the light leading into the dank basement. Like a cat, he darted over to open the basement door and hid behind it. He counted the number of steps she descended—twelve. A powerful rush of adrenaline surged through him. In the basement, Erin found a packet of coffee and headed back upstairs.

Zeke counted her steps, which helped control his breathing. As he got to twelve, Erin turned off the light and shut the door. He wasted no time. He grabbed her from behind with one arm around her neck and the other around her waist. Erin screamed and stomped on his foot with her thick boot heel. "Bitch!" He howled in pain.

Erin sprinted toward the dimly lit kitchen and grabbed a heavy copper pan from the rack above the stove. She ducked around the wall and crouched behind the food prep counter. She heard the squeak of his shoes come closer. Her heart pounded in her throat and she tried to keep her breathing quiet. Erin took her phone out of her pocket and attempted to dial 911, but her hand shook so violently she dropped it. The squeaking stopped, then came toward her. *Oh my God!* Retrieving it was out of the question. She stood slowly, pan held over her head.

Squeak, squeak, squeak. Louder the sound became. Erin knew her timing had to be perfect.

"I know you're in here. You can't hide," he said, his tone melodic.

Her attacker skulked around the side of the wall. Erin swung with all her might. *Whack!* She got him in the side of his head.

"Son of a bitch!" he roared.

Erin ran toward the front door and pulled on the handle. It did not budge. *Oh no! I locked it! Get out! Get out!* She raced toward the back door, but was too late. Her attacker regained his senses and grabbed her again. "No! Stop! Let me go!" Erin pounded his head. She managed to rip off his ski mask and scratch his face.

He slammed her against the wall and whispered, "Now you've done it!"

He popped Erin in the jaw and knocked her out cold. From his pocket he took out a syringe Victor gave him and injected Erin in the arm.

"Sleep tight," he said.

Zeke looked around and quickly cleaned up any evidence, including retrieving Erin's phone. He texted Rubi Lee, *Get in here n bring the blanket.*

They wrapped Erin like a mummy and carried her to the van, where they laid her down in the back. Zeke drove through the dark streets to meet Victor. The sun was struggling to rise against a thick wall of clouds.

* * *

Zeke and Rubi Lee carried Erin into the house where they dropped her on a small bed.

"Good work." Victor's voice emanated from a corner of the room.

"We have a problem though. She um . . . she . . . saw me." Zeke's voice quavered.

"How did that happen?" Victor appeared out of the shadowy corner.

"She ripped off the mask."

Ice would not survive his steaming glare. "You do understand what this means, correct?"

Zeke and Rubi Lee stood in silence.

"We cannot take a risk. I will take care of that situation later. Please leave now."

Victor returned to the corner and watched Erin, who opened her eyes again only to discover her vision was blurry. She stirred slightly.

What is going on? How did I get here? Where am I? Erin willed herself to try to remember what happened. Flashes of the bar's kitchen and a man wearing a ski mask flashed in her brain. Her mouth was a block of salt and her tongue a slab of lead. She shook her head to try to rid the syrup oozing around in her brain. She squinted at the four gray walls and tried to swallow the rising panic.

"Aw, poor thing. You're groggy, aren't you?" The unfamiliar voice came from beyond the bed. "Well then, it should be easy to get what I want from you."

A shadow emerged from the corner of the room. A man stood at the foot of the bed to which she was chained. The panic she tried to swallow burst to the surface. She screamed and thrashed until the metal cuffs bit into her wrists. He laughed as he watched her.

"You are going nowhere. Get used to it." She felt his weight at the bottom of the bed when he sat down. Shadows obscured his face. "Well my dear, you have something I want."

Erin struggled to sit up. "I . . . don't know . . . what you mean. Please." She fell back into the pillow.

"The drug will wear off soon and you'll be able to speak. Yet, if you choose not to, I have means of forcing you to tell me what I want to know. Not pleasant ones, mind you, but effective. Now, again, are you going to cooperate?" His voice slithered like a snake from his mouth.

She sat up and moved her arms a few inches until the chains yanked. She looked up at her captor and wretched at what stared back at her.

He rose from the foot of the bed, walked toward her, bent down and whispered, "Now, what did you do with the sweatshirt?"

She shook her head. *Sweatshirt?* Memories of the bar and the man started to come back in sharper focus. "Who are you? Where am I? What are you talking about?" she whispered.

"The sweatshirt—with my diamonds in it."

Clammy chills crawled on her skin. She mumbled, "I

swear I don't know what you're talking about!"

He grabbed her face in a vise-like grip. "You're lying."

"I'm not lying!" Her jaw felt crushed. She thrashed in the bed and he just laughed at her through the vile, leather mask which looked like melted flesh. The eyes were slits and the mouth a sick, smiling gash.

"Did you think I was going to let you get up and walk away with *millions* of dollars in diamonds? Come now, you're making this more difficult than need be. Just tell me where it is."

"I don't know anything about a sweatshirt or diamonds! Please, you have to believe me!" Sweat streamed down her scalp into a thin river down her back.

Victor took a syringe from a bag. "I will give you some time to think this over. Meanwhile, you look tired. I'll give you something to help you sleep. He pricked her arm. "If I don't get out of you what I want, you will force me to do some awfully bad things. I do hope it doesn't come to that," he said as he brushed her hair away from her face and then slowly ran his finger down her cheek, her neck, and her breastbone. Vomit sloshed in her stomach.

"I'll be back. Don't go anywhere—not that you can." Victor turned and walked into the shadows. Erin's tears flowed as the darkness enveloped her.

CHAPTER 24

Ira thought it was strange Erin was not at the Black LaSalle when he arrived later that morning. *I guess she's just late.* After he stocked the fridge and filled the glass holders, she still had not shown up. He looked at his phone—eleven o'clock. *Weird. I wonder where she is? She's always here on Wednesdays.* He double-checked the schedule and saw her name written down along with his and four servers. He asked his coworkers if they knew anything; they did not.

"Did you call or text her?" one asked.

"Not yet. I figured I'd ask you guys first." Ira called her; the call immediately went to voicemail. He left a message and continued to prep for the lunch shift.

Lunch was steady until the bar emptied in the mid-afternoon. Ira seized on the lull to call Daisy.

"Yes, it is very strange for her not to show up. She could have had an appointment," Daisy said.

"Maybe. Seems weird for her not to at least call."

"That's true. I'll call her too. Let's not panic, all right?"

"Okay, talk soon."

Daisy called Erin and it went to voicemail. She left a message and focused on her assignment due for her Journalism Ethics class. To her, the name of this course was contradictory, given all the purported fake news infiltrating peoples' lives reported by less-than-ethical media outlets.

Gussie jumped up onto the couch and nestled down beside her. Two hours later, Daisy checked her silenced phone and saw five notifications—nothing from Erin. She called Ira back and asked if he had heard from her; he heard nothing.

"Wait a second. I remember her telling me she has a grandmother who is very old, so maybe something happened to her," Daisy said.

"Okay, we'll give it another day, and if we don't hear from her, I'll go to her house."

"Good idea."

* * *

Still good for lunch? Nick's text said.

Daisy's response was immediate. *Yes. When & where?*

Brasserie on 11th . . . noonish?

Sounds good . . . Cya then.

Brasserie was hustling with diners. Nick arrived first and sat at a high-top table close to the door. The server placed two menus and two glasses of water on the table. As Nick scanned a menu, his stomach rumbled.

"Look at you in a tie!" Nick heard from a few feet away.

He stood and smiled broadly. "We had a photo op this morning, so we had to look professional."

Daisy lifted the tie from his chest. "I love the colors. And you look very handsome."

"Thank you. I'm not used to wearing one. I sort of like it, though."

They sat and scoured the menu and placed their order.

"What's going on with you? How are things in the

senator's office?" Daisy asked him.

"Busy, busy, busy. I'm working my butt off. I like the pace and energy. Each day is a little different because things change all the time."

"Especially in the political world. Do your coworkers work as hard as you do?"

"Overall, I'd say yes. Some are incredibly lazy though and think others will do their work for them. Not me," Nick answered.

"Do you see Jaida and Winston often?"

"I see Winston more because she's always pulled in a thousand different directions putting out tech fires."

"I could never do what she does. I can't imagine being in control of an entire network system," Daisy said.

"I know," he said.

Daisy took a bite and sighed in contented pleasure. "This is so delicious. How's yours?"

"Really good." He swallowed and remarked, "You were really upset the other night when you called me. Did you tell the cops?"

"No. If I do, they may think I'm nuts."

He put down his sandwich and looked at her. "If you tell them, Daiz, they'll have it on record. It can't hurt."

"You're right on both points. I'll think about telling them."

Between bites, they talked about Jaida and Winston, life in DC, and her classes.

"Delicious." Nick wiped his face and checked the time. "I have to get going."

"Okay." Daisy glanced at her phone and saw an email marked urgent. She read it and inhaled sharply. "Are you *serious*? This can't be happening!"

"What?" She handed him her phone. His eyes widened in disbelief. "They're selling your building and you have to be out in *fourteen days*?"

"I can't believe this! I *love* my place and now I have to leave?" Her face crumbled.

Daisy's dejected face stabbed him in the heart. "Daiz, I'll help you look around for a place. I'd say you're welcome to stay with me, but I can only offer you a corduroy couch," Nick offered. "And you'd have to share a bathroom with me and Win." He chuckled, trying to lighten the mood.

Daisy glared at him. "Thanks, but no. You're sweet to offer, though." She jabbed at the ice in her empty cup. "What am I going to do? Finding affordable housing is so hard."

"Like I said, I'll help you. I'm sure Jaida will too."

"I know. I'm going to call these people later and get to the bottom of it." She scrunched up her napkin and tossed it on the table. "Let's go."

Stomachs full, they decided a walk was in order. Side by side, they ambled around other people and absorbed the brilliant late autumn day. The bite of chill in the air was noticeable, yet not uncomfortable.

"Thanks for lunch. My treat next time," Daisy said.

"Deal. I'll make sure it's an expensive steakhouse!" Nick joked and bumped her shoulder.

"You're hilarious. Glad your sense of humor hasn't changed!"

They walked in silence until she commented, "This was nice."

"Yes, it was. If you let me know in enough time, I can free up my lunch hour when you're not working."

"I'll check my schedule and let you know. Maybe we could look at apartments too?"

He cocked his head and looked at her. "You're asking me to move in after one lunch together? Who needs speed-dating?" He laughed.

"Sure, why not? We've known each other for ten years. Winston'll understand if you move out," she deadpanned. "Plus, I'm much cuter." She batted her eyelashes.

For a split second, Nick was unsure if she was serious. "Very funny, and yes, you *are* much cuter than Win." He gazed down at her; affection filled his eyes. "Daisy?"

"Hmm?" She turned to him and his look made her stomach flutter.

"I'm glad you moved here, and we reconnected." He put his arm around her shoulder and pulled her to him.

"So am I." She wrapped her arm around his waist and squeezed him before leaving.

* * *

Daisy strolled to Margaux Ford Park. She pondered these unexpected, but not unwelcome feelings for Nick. *He and I have always been just friends. Friends.* Lying to herself was out of the question; his arm around her shoulder felt *good.*

Red, yellow, and orange leaves dangled from branches in magnificent contrast to the blue sky. There was a smattering of people enjoying the day too. Senior citizens played solitaire, college kids lounged under trees, and shrieking children chased each other.

She plunked down on an iron bench, tilted her head back, and warmed her face. *This is nice.* She sat with her eyes closed, relishing in the sun's rays when she heard his voice.

"Fancy seeing you here," Henderson said from behind.

She opened her eyes and greeted her friend. "Hi Henderson. I was wondering if you were working today."

"Well, here I am." He hoisted himself from the cart and sat with her.

"You really enjoy keeping watch, don't you?"

"I do. Makes me feel like I'm on the beat again," he said. "Plus, working outside on a day like this really isn't working!"

"I agree," she said. "What made you want to be a cop?"

Henderson smiled. "Henry Peters. He's the man responsible for my career in law enforcement."

"Who's he?"

"Henry Peters was the father of my best childhood friend, Jason Peters. I spent a lot of time in their house and loved hearing his stories of bustin' the bad guys. He was so very proud of his shiny badge and of serving the community. As a little kid, I wanted to protect and do good for my community. But I really wanted to have a shiny badge and carry a gun too." Henderson chuckled. "I guess lots of little kids do."

"How did he influence you to be an officer?" Daisy asked.

"Officer Pete, as I called him, was one of the bravest men I ever knew-aside from my own pop. Anyway, one night, Jason and I were eavesdropping on the adults talking and I heard him telling Mrs. Peters how he helped a distraught man from leaping off a bridge into the raging river fifty feet below. Officer Pete hated water, but we heard him tell his wife how he climbed out onto the trestle. Four hours later, Officer Pete and the man were back on solid ground. And from then on, I knew what I wanted to do with my life."

"Great story Henderson. He sounds like a wonderful man."

"He was, until cancer got him. That's one bad guy he caught too late."

"I'm so sorry." She reached over and squeezed his hand. "I don't think I ever told you that my dad was sheriff of Cab Station for years."

Henderson tilted his head. "Is that so?"

"Yep."

"Then I guess that makes us part of a big family, right?"

"Yes, it does. And, I wouldn't have it any other way. Since we're family now, what do you think of this?" She relayed the night she and Ira were chased.

"Daisy, that's very odd. What did this van look like? Did you see who was driving it?" He furrowed his brow.

"No, it was dark. It was an older white van—like countless others."

He removed his hat and rubbed his head. "It's possible someone was out on a joy ride and you two happened to be their targets. Maybe kids?"

"Maybe. Except I can't shake the feeling they were trying to kill us because the van *flew* through red lights and crosswalks. And one of them tried to chase us into the Metroline."

Henderson turned sharply to her. "Oh really? Male or female?"

"Male. It was so damn scary."

"Can you remember anything else about that van?"

"Old, loud . . ." Daisy scowled.

He put his arm around her. "If it happens again, or

anything else along those lines, you better tell me. I don't want anything to happen to my favorite bartender."

"I promise I'll tell you."

Henderson glanced at his watch. "Time to continue my rounds. Stay safe."

"I will. And thanks for the talk, Henderson."

"You bet." She watched him drive away and stayed a while longer until the drop in the temperature told her it was time to go.

CHAPTER 25

After a long day of being pulled in a thousand directions, Jaida was relieved to spend the late afternoon in her small office down in the sprawling data center of the Cooper Building. She thought of it as her own private, comfortable sanctuary. The calming hum and purr of the enormous servers washed over her like an exquisite piece of classical music.

Jaida was jarred by something rarely heard in this area—voices. She rose from her chair and quietly moved to the door. She opened it a crack.

"Make this quick. My order was to be filled today. I've received nothing."

Jaida did not recognize the voice. She wanted to get a look at this faceless person. She kicked off her clickety heels and slipped out. The voices came from around the dark corner.

"Senator, my computer was just upgraded and I'm still encrypting the appropriate file of all inventory. It does take time, you know." Jaida felt her pulse quicken at that voice—Victor Sykes.

"I don't give a *damn* about your computer. I have other people who have paid me *significant* amounts of money for their merchandise. And they're expecting it."

Jaida pressed herself against the wall and peered

around the corner. Victor and the other man stood roughly fifty feet away from her. Jaida stared at the man's profile. She did not recognize him. She noted he and Victor were close in height. Light bounced off his carefully styled black hair. A gold signet ring glinted in the light as he gestured. Jaida reached for her cell phone to record the conversation, but her pocket was empty. *Crap! It's on my desk.*

"I don't care about who's breathing down your skinny neck. I have lots of cash invested too!" Victor retorted.

"Listen to me. My neck is on the line here. My clients don't like to wait, and they for sure don't give a rat's ass about your computer and other problems. I want what I paid for!"

Jaida gasped when Victor jacked the man up against the wall by his jaw.

Victor laughed. "How dare you *threaten* me. I can—and will—kill you right here, right now with one hand if I wanted. You'll get your *precious* shipment when I have it ready! Tell your clients they're going to have to wait." Victor increased the pressure on the man's jaw.

He sputtered. "Jesus, Sykes, let me go!"

Victor released his grip and the man coughed and sucked in air. Quick as a cobra, he swung at Victor and landed a punch to the side of Victor's head. Incensed, Victor drove his fist into the man's stomach. He crumpled to the floor, gasping. Victor drove home his point with a sharp kick to his side. The man groaned and begged him to stop.

Jaida was nauseous as she watched Victor kneel and wrench the man's head by his hair. "Don't screw around with me! I don't care who you are. You will suffer greatly if you threaten me again or try to intervene. As a senator, you are an exceptionally good liar. Invent a plausible story to tell your people that will make them get off your back." He took a breath. "Got it, *Senator?*" He kicked him once more in the side. Victor stepped over him, straightened his tie, and headed up the steps.

The man lay on the floor, coughed several times, and rose to his knees. He wiped his brow with his hand and saw a little blood. He shook his head. "Son of a bitch." He stood shakily and slowly headed up the steps.

Jaida remained where she was until she heard the door close. She exhaled slowly and tried to settle her racing heart.

Back in her office she called Winston and left a message. To be safe, she sent him a text asking him to call her ASAP. *I need to write down everything I just saw.* She noted every word she remembered from the heated conversation. She heard her phone ding. *Oh good, it's Winston.*

The text was Daisy inviting her for dinner. Jaida replied yes and Daisy came back with *Great. I have news—7ish?* Jaida sent a thumb's up emoji.

Jaida stared at her phone. *Staring at your phone won't help. Get some work done.* Jaida ran security checks until her phone rang. It was Winston.

"Are you sitting down?" she asked, "'Cause I have a good one for you."

"I am now. Shoot."

Jaida relayed every detail of the encounter she witnessed.

"You witnessed *all* of that?" Winston whistled.

"Sure did."

Winston asked, "Did you get a look at the senator?"

"Not really. Tallish, dark hair, but not a full facial shot.

Sykes was the aggressor; I'd bet my life savings he's the ringleader—especially after we saw what was on his hard drive and his name was the only one mentioned by our intel."

"Sounds to me like he's pulling the strings. But we have no concrete proof that he's the leader," Winston said.

"I know. I have a feeling we will sooner than later," Jaida replied. "I need to go. Daisy invited me for dinner and if I don't leave now, I'll be late."

CHAPTER 26

Before Jaida arrived, Daisy called Erin again, and it went right to voicemail. She texted Ira to see if he had heard anything from her. He had not.

But I did call the police . . . and they said we need to wait 48 hrs to file a report, Ira's text read.

Oh geez . . . not good. I guess we have to wait. I feel nervous tho, Daisy replied.

Same . . . hopefully we won't need to file one, Ira said.

I know . . . got to go.

Jaida and Daisy sat on the couch and savored a red Zinfandel. Gussie purred happily between them. The aroma of baked ziti wafted through the apartment.

"Smells so good in here!" Jaida said.

"Thanks," Daisy replied. "This will be one of my last dinners in this kitchen."

Jaida put her glass down. "What do you mean?"

Daisy filled her in about having to move.

Jaida rubbed her arm. "I'm sorry, Daisy. I'll keep my ears open at work in case someone is looking for a roommate."

"Thanks for your help. I may have a place though."

"Oh really? Where?"

"Above the Black LaSalle. Erin asked the owner if I could move up there. And she said yes."

"Oh good. That was nice of Erin to go to bat for you," Jaida said.

"Speaking of Erin, she didn't show up for work and no one has heard from her."

Jaida scowled at her. "Is that out of the ordinary for her?"

"Very much so. I called and texted, so did Ira. I'm very worried."

"I don't blame you."

"Ira called the police and they told him he had to wait forty-eight hours."

"That's a start. Maybe there was a family emergency?"

"I thought the same thing, but still."

They heard the kitchen timer beep. Daisy rose from the couch. "Dinner!"

"I'll help."

Jaida set the table in the kitchen while Daisy doled out steaming baked pasta onto plates and brought them to the table.

"I have another strange story to tell you," Daisy said.

Jaida lowered her fork and peered at Daisy. "Do tell."

Daisy relayed the story of being chased by the white van and escaping via the Metroline.

Jaida stopped mid-bite, her spider-sense tingling. "Did you see who was driving it?"

"No, but at the metro, a big guy got out and ran after us."

Jaida thought, *I wonder if it's the same van from the night at the airport.* "What do you mean by a big guy? Fat?"

"No, more like a football player big."

"What did the van look like?" Jaida asked.

"It was white. It was dark, so I couldn't really see much."

163

Jaida pushed, "If you see the van again, do you think you'd recognize it?"

Daisy frowned. "Maybe. I'm not sure."

"If you do see it again, get your phone and try to take a picture of it and the license plate."

"That whole chase reminded me of a Stephen King movie. The one where that car was possessed. I can't remember the name though." Daisy swirled her wine around her glass.

"*Christine*! My dad was a huge Stephen King fan."

"That's it!" Daisy said.

After dinner, Daisy washed the ziti pan while Jaida rinsed and loaded the dishes.

"You're an NBA fan?" She indicated with her chin at Daisy's sweatshirt.

"What do you mean?"

"You're wearing a Washington Wizards sweatshirt. I didn't take you for a fan."

"Oh, this." Daisy looked down. "I grabbed it from a hook at work and wore it home the other night. It was freezing." Daisy dried her hands on a dish towel. "Do you mind if we watch the news?"

"Not at all."

Daisy turned on the television and the broadcaster began with a feel-good story. "In tonight's feel-good news, a ten-year-old boy called 911, but not for an emergency. He was having trouble with his math homework and called the emergency service line for help."

"Aw, that is so cute," Jaida said.

"I know. If I had done that, my parents would not have been happy, especially since my dad was a sheriff," Daisy laughed.

Daisy tucked her hands into the front pocket of the sweatshirt and discovered what felt like another pocket sewn on the inside. She ran her index finger across it. It felt like something was in there. It felt puffy, so she squeezed it and they both heard it at the same time: a crackling, crunching, papery sound.

"What was that?" Jaida asked.

"I don't know, it feels like there's another pocket sewn onto this one," Daisy answered. She pulled it over her head and squeezed the pocket. Again, the sound and she felt something. "There's something in here. Feel this."

"Strange. What's in here, paper?" Jaida asked.

"I have no clue. Let's cut it open!" Daisy offered.

"Are you sure you want to tear it open?"

"Sure. I can stitch it back up as good as new."

"Wait, you know how to sew?!" Jaida teased.

"Yup, thanks to Miss Duncan's eighth grade home-ec class. I'll get the scissors."

Jaida held out the sweatshirt for Daisy to cut into the inside pocket.

"Anything in there?" Jaida said.

"Yeah, what is this?" Daisy pulled at the hidden object. "There's paper in here. I need tweezers, hold on."

She guided the tweezers into the pocket. A folded piece of paper, roughly an inch by three inches, was tucked inside. She pulled it out and saw it was folded into a perfect rectangle. Indents dotted the outside. She pulled out another two and stared at them.

"What the . . ." Jaida stared at the paper rectangles.

Daisy felt something small and solid in the bottom of

them. She gingerly unfolded one and peered into the crease of paper. She frowned. "What in the world? Jaida, look at this."

Jaida looked down at the small, glittery objects. She blinked several times and looked up at Daisy. "Holy crap!"

"*Diamonds?* I wonder if they're real?" Daisy said.

"They sure look like diamonds. If they're fake, what's the reason for them to be stitched into the pocket?" She almost fainted at what was in her hand. At least twenty-five BB-size diamonds sparkled and shimmered up at her.

"Something is very bizarre here, Jaida." Daisy unfolded the paper. "Look, there are numbers written on the inside of these papers."

"Numbers?" Jaida ran her eyes over the papers.

"Yes." Daisy stared at the stones. "Something is definitely not right."

They sat and gaped at the discovery.

Daisy broke the silence. "Why are there diamonds sewn into this sweatshirt?"

Jaida swallowed. "I have no clue. We need to put them back exactly how we found them and get this back to the bar."

Daisy put the delicate packages on the table and got up. "I agree. I'll go get my sewing stuff."

Jaida swallowed her excitement. She picked up one of the packages and gently shook several of the clear, brilliant stones into her palm. *Unbelievable, right into my hand.* Jaida pocketed four of them and returned the others.

Daisy returned, and cautiously stitched the packages back inside the secret pocket. Jaida was impressed with Daisy's tailoring skills.

"Perfect. No one will know," Jaida warned.

"I know. We need to put it back tonight. This is making me nervous."

They tossed theories about the sweatshirt back and forth.

"I'll Google it," Daisy said.

She typed in *diamonds + clothes.* Numerous unhelpful articles popped up.

Jaida looked at her. "Try something like *hiding diamonds.*"

"Wow. Look at this."

She handed Jaida her phone, who skimmed the top articles Daisy found. "Looks like people transport—or smuggle—gems sewn into clothes," Jaida read. "Interesting."

"Do you think this is what's going on? Oh God, did I take a sweatshirt that someone is using to *smuggle* diamonds?" She paced the living room. "This may sound nuts, but what if the people in the van chased us because of this sweatshirt? After all, I had it on that night!"

"Hey, calm down. That is a little crazy, but we don't know anything at this point. Try again to remember exactly what that van looked like," Jaida said.

Daisy thought. "It was old and beaten-up looking. I'm pretty sure there were no windows on the sides, and it sounded like the transmission was going to fall out."

Jaida tried to be nonchalant. "Anything else? Like bumper stickers, decals?"

"Not that I remember and besides, we weren't about to get any closer, trust me." Daisy said.

"I understand. I think it needs to be returned. No doubt

someone is going to be looking for it."

"Uh oh. I didn't even think of that."

Ding! Daisy looked at her phone and smiled.

"Nick, right?" Jaida pointed out and smirked.

"How'd you know it was him?"

"By the happy, adorable smile on your face. You *like* him."

"Yes, I do. He's kind of like another brother since I've known him for so long. We're having lunch tomorrow."

"Have you ever considered taking things *past* the friendship level?"

"Stop." Daisy laughed. "He's great, but he's my friend. *If,* just *if* we ended up as more than friends someday . . ." A Cheshire cat grin spanned her face. "You and Winston, though, are really good together."

Jaida looked at her like she had four eyes. "Seriously?"

"Yeah, you guys seem so comfortable with each other."

"I guess we are. We've known each other for a long time." Jaida shot Daisy a look. "Kind of like you and Nick."

Daisy cocked her eye at Jaida. "I see where you're trying to go with this, but we have more important things to do."

"Do you want to come with me to return it?" Daisy asked, pulling the sweatshirt over her head.

"Yes. I don't want you going alone. Besides, the van could still be out there." Jaida thought, *The Black LaSalle is definitely the drop spot.*

At the bar, Daisy took the sweatshirt out of the plastic shopping bag and made sure to hang it exactly as she had found it.

"Not our problem anymore, right?" She turned and looked at Jaida.

"You got it, girl."

They walked halfway to Daisy's when Jaida said, "I think I'll get an Uber home from here. I don't feel like walking anymore."

"Okay. I'll wait with you." They sat down on a bench near a bus stop and waited for the Uber.

"This sweatshirt thing has me intrigued," Daisy confessed. "And little uptight."

Jaida shifted on the bench. "Oh, me too, trust me. I think we're smart to let it go, though."

"Wait a minute!" Daisy's voice crackled with energy. "There're cameras in the bar! When I can, I'll check them."

"Good plan," Jaida said. "In fact, that's an *excellent* plan."

"Thanks." She redid her ponytail. "I may tell Nick. Are you going to mention it to Win?"

Jaida hesitated. "I might. After all, it's a pretty wild story." She saw headlights sweep across the intersection. Jaida's Uber idled in front of them. "Time for me to go home and get some sleep. Thanks for dinner and the adventure!" Jaida wrapped her arms around Daisy and held her tightly. "Daiz. I'm so glad we're friends."

"Me too. See you or talk soon."

In the car, Jaida looked in disbelief at the stones in her hand. She snapped a picture and sent it to Winston with a smiley face emoji.

Winston's text arrived quickly. *Wow! How did that happen? Is that what I think it is?*

Yep, she texted back. *Can't talk. Breakfast tomorrow? 8:00 at Molly's to discuss next step.*

Yes . . . see you then.

A satisfied smile played across her pretty face.

CHAPTER 27

Jaida and Winston sat in a back booth of Molly's Kitchen where they kept an eye on who came and went.

"Coffee?" the server asked.

They both said yes as their server sloshed coffee into the cups and onto the saucer.

"Do you know what you want?" The server yawned and snapped her gum. Jaida ordered fried eggs with home fries; Winston ordered French toast and extra bacon.

"Check this out." Jaida carefully handed the small package to Winston. She explained how it all happened.

Winston tilted the folded paper over his open palm and looked down. He shook his head. "I can't believe this happened." He admired the stones. "These look good. Shiny, hot, and expensive."

"Hot ice is *always* expensive."

"There's a lot at stake here—not just millions of dollars. This is the break we've been looking for. We now know the Black LaSalle is the prime drop spot." Winston finished his breakfast and laid his fork on the plate.

"As we thought earlier. When should we inform Commissioner Knight?" Jaida asked.

"Soon, not yet. We need to gather more evidence first before talking to her. You know how concrete she is." Winston laughed. "How did you play this with Daisy?"

"I didn't have to play because I was as surprised as she was," Jaida answered. "But get this." Jaida swigged her last sip of coffee. "She also told me she was chased by a beat-up white van the night she wore the sweatshirt home. Win, I'd bet a million bucks it's the same van we saw at the airport."

Winston rubbed the scab on his head. "So you believe the van that chased Daisy is the same one we saw?"

"Yes, I do. My instincts are screaming they're one and the same. She said it looked old, no side windows. No way it's a coincidence."

Winston nodded. "I'm inclined to agree. We need to keep an eye out."

The server came by and asked if they cared for anything else.

"No thanks. A bill please," Winston said.

"And chances are she'll tell Nick, right?"

"I'd say more yes than no." He scrutinized the bill and threw some cash on the table. "You understand that Daisy may be suspected of taking these, right?"

Jaida lowered her eyes. "I know. She's a great person and I feel close to her. As you well know, sometimes there's collateral damage in what we do. We can deal with what's thrown at us."

Winston scowled and exhaled. "I know. We never expected it to turn this way. Considering the Black LaSalle is the drop spot, it will be easy for you or both of us to stay in close contact with Daisy," Winston said and stood.

"Good point."

* * *

On the way to the Spy Museum to meet Nick, Daisy picked up some sandwiches, chips, and drinks. He was waiting for her on a bench outside the museum.

She plopped down and handed him his lunch.

"You found my favorite chips! Thanks, Daiz," he said digging in the bag.

"You're welcome. I remembered you loved these when we were kids. I think you ate at least five bags a week when we were kids!"

"Well, maybe not five, probably more like seven," Nick joked.

They enjoyed their lunch in the warm sun. People scurried past, faces buried in their phones.

"Ouch!" They turned to see a man rubbing his knee. He had walked smack into a bench across from where they sat.

"Careful, you may want to look up once in a while!" Daisy called out.

"Huh? Yeah, whatever. Sorry." Face in phone, he walked off.

"I wonder if people ever look up from their phones and see the beautiful world around them? I sometimes hate being so reliant on mine," she said.

"I do too, and we're all trapped. There are people at work whose heads would blow up if their phone were out of reach. We're all guilty of it, although I do take breaks."

"Same with me." She crumpled up her sandwich wrapper and asked Nick, "You finished?" She extended her hand for his trash.

"I am, thanks."

Inside the museum, a life-size carboard cutout of Sean Connery greeted them. *Fifty years of James Bond Villains* was the featured exhibit. Daisy ogled the cutout, admiring Sean Connery's gorgeous looks—especially in a white dinner jacket. "Wow," she said aloud.

"What?" Nick asked.

"Oh nothing. Ready to learn about our favorite spy's enemies?"

"Yup. This exhibit makes me think of Mrs. Walker's cat—Mr. Bond. Do you remember him?" Nick asked.

"Yup. He was a cool cat. Nowhere near as cool as my Gussie, though."

Very few people were in the museum. Nick and Daisy took their time and weaved in and out of the iconic villain exhibit. Each placard relayed interesting facts and anecdotes about some of Hollywood's most popular yet evil miscreants.

Nick stood a few feet ahead of her, reading about Goldfinger. "I think Goldfinger is my favorite bad guy," Nick commented. "Especially since Bond caught him cheating at golf."

He turned to look at her, but she had stopped a few feet behind him and was entrenched in reading about Dr. No. He loved the way she gently tucked her curly hair behind her ear, exposing her soft cheek and strong jawline.

Daisy laughed. "Dr. No was a horrible villain too. Since we're talking about bad people, I have something sort of related to bad guys to tell you." She relayed the entire story of she and Jaida finding the diamonds.

He stopped walking. "Are you *sure* they were diamonds?"

"They sure looked it, but I don't know if they were *real* diamonds. They could've been cubic zirconias."

"What did Jaida say about it?"

"She was shocked too. And she agreed about how strange it was finding them. We googled it and apparently diamonds are smuggled in clothing, hats, and other things."

"Are you thinking you found *smuggled* diamonds?" Nick stopped and looked at her.

"I don't know, maybe. And the night Ira and I were chased by the van, I wore that sweatshirt home."

"Do you think those two things are connected?" Nick asked.

"I can't help but think they are, NT. I have no proof though."

"Where's the sweatshirt now?" Nick asked her.

"We returned it."

Something stirred in Nick—a profound feeling of protection. "Daisy, you really should think about talking to the cops. Or better yet, I know a guy who is a retired cop who works in my building. I'll talk to him if you'd like."

Daisy grinned. "Any chance his name is Henderson?"

He glanced at her and shook his head. "Obviously you know him."

She rubbed his arm. "Sorry! I feel like I spoiled a surprise. But yes, I know him. He comes into the bar a couple times a week. Sometimes his girlfriend, Jackie, comes with him."

"Next time he's in, you should talk to him. Without a doubt, he'd have the right idea of what to do."

Daisy pushed open the glass door. Outside, the sun poked in and out of fluffy clouds.

Nick inhaled the outdoor air and exhaled loudly. "Lucky me, I get to go back and finish researching a bill for the senator."

"Sounds exciting. At least it's almost the weekend. Do you have any plans?"

"Who knows. I plan on sleeping, but if you want to do something, text me."

"Or *you* can come over and help me pack my stuff, right?"

His body suddenly warmed up. "I certainly will. What time?"

Daisy kept her excitement in check. "Come over around nine and we can pack."

He liked her use of *we.* "I look forward to it. See you Saturday."

"Thanks, NT. I'll cook dinner when I'm all moved in."

CHAPTER 28

Victor ducked out of the rain into the Black LaSalle. He removed his hat, shook off the water, and pulled it tight on his head. There was only smattering of customers at the bar and only one bartender, oblivious to Victor. *Slow day— good*, he thought. As he walked toward the back of the bar he saw a sweatshirt hanging—the white W of *Washington Wizards* stood out against the red material.

Well done, Rubi Lee and Zeke. He took a plastic shopping bag from his pocket and placed the sweatshirt inside. His fingers itched to open the bag to admire his latest acquisition.

Victor was so focused on his mission that he did not hear the door to his left open, but he felt it smack into his arm. He was knocked to the side. "Damnit! Watch where you're going!" he yelled at the woman.

"Oh! I'm so sorry! I didn't see you!" Daisy apologized. "Are you okay?"

"Just be more careful!" Victor spat as he brushed past her.

Victor laid the sweatshirt on the passenger seat and cautiously cut open the secret pocket. *This is like performing surgery.* He removed a set of tweezers from the glove compartment and steadily extracted the paper packages. Victor slid the stones into his palm from their paper home.

His breath quickened as he admired the miniature stars sitting in his palm. Something looked off. He counted them: twenty-one. He counted again. *Why are there four missing? Jesus Christ!*

Once his breathing was under control, he made a call.

"Hey Uncle Vic," Zeke mumbled.

"I just picked up the sweatshirt." No hello in his cold voice.

Zeke muted the phone and whispered to Rubi Lee what Victor said. She raised her arms in a *Score!* gesture.

"Is everything okay with it?" Zeke asked, putting him on speaker phone.

"No, goddammit! Four diamonds are missing!" Victor balled his phone-free hand into a fist so tight it turned purple.

"Do you have any idea how this happened, Zeke?" Victor asked.

Zeke exhaled and looked at his sister, who shrugged. "No. We followed your directions. That girl we grabbed— maybe she's the one who took 'em, right? She wore the sweatshirt home."

"There's one way to find out. Be at the house in thirty minutes and we can *ask* her."

Zeke dropped his phone on the table and stared at Rubi Lee. "Oh man, how the eff did the sweatshirt end up *back at the bar* after we saw the redhead wearing it?" He grabbed a cigarette.

Rubi Lee returned her brother's stare. "Obviously she returned it. But that could be any Washington Wizards sweatshirt, right?" She walked over to the refrigerator, yanked open the door, and took out a bottle of Jägermeister.

"He's pissed. I need a drink to deal with him."

"Pour me one too," Zeke said.

* * *

Erin had no idea how long she had been held captive. Her head felt like a stretched balloon and her stomach churned sour acid. She yanked at the tight restraints. She heard a succession of footsteps before the door was pushed open. Light filtered in behind three figures as they entered the room.

"Is she awake?" a female voice asked.

They walked over to the bed and looked down. Erin was hovering somewhere in a fog of consciousness. Through the haze, she saw three figures.

"What do you want?" Erin croaked.

"You have something that belongs to me." Victor looked down at her.

Please God, let Ira, Daisy, and others be looking for me, please. "I don't know what you're talking about. Please just let me go."

"I don't have to believe anything you say. Now, again, you were seen wearing a sweatshirt when you left the bar the other night. There was something in it that is mine. Diamonds, to be exact."

Erin lay deadly still in the bed. Her mind raced as she tried to process his words.

"I asked you a question."

Erin squeezed her eyes shut. "I promise I don't have a *clue* what you're talking about." She froze when she felt a gloved hand on her thigh.

"I'll walk you through it. Some nights ago, you left the bar with another person and you were wearing a sweatshirt..."

Erin reeled through her memory bank until it clicked. *Oh God! He thinks I'm Daisy!* "NO! No, I wasn't the one wearing it! I swear to God. It was another bartender—we look alike!"

"Another bartender?" He laughed.

"Yes! She was cold, so she wore it home!"

Victor rose from the bed and motioned for Rubi Lee and Zeke to follow. In the hallway, he asked them if there was another bartender there who resembled Erin.

"I'm not sure, Uncle Vic. We haven't been there a lot," Zeke answered.

Sweat poured down Erin's back when the three re-entered the room. *Please God, let them believe me. Help me.* "I'll get back whatever it is you're missing and won't tell anyone about this. Please!"

Uncle Vic sighed. "Where are my diamonds?" He squeezed her thigh with all his strength.

Erin shrieked in pain. "I don't know! I don't have them!" Erin tried to stop crying. "Please let me go!"

He held out his hand to Zeke and asked for Erin's phone. "Here's what's going to happen. You're going to give me the name of the other bartender whom *I* will text using *your* phone. Following that, we will work out a deal. Understand? Now, tell me her name."

Erin remained silent. She closed her eyes and silently asked for forgiveness. She gave him the information as he scrolled through Erin's contacts and found it. "Ah, Daisy. She must be concerned about you—look at all these texts." He waved her phone around and laughed. "Oh, and Ira? Who's he? He certainly is worried about you too."

"I'm begging you. Please don't hurt them," Erin whimpered.

Victor pulled up a chair and sat down next to the bed. "Here's how we're going to calm your friends' worries. *We* are going to text them something concise and *plausible* to explain your absence."

Erin's heart skipped a beat. "Like what?" Panic muddled her thinking.

"Oh, please. You strike me as reasonably intelligent. Think of something—or else."

Erin breathed deeply; she knew her life or her friends' lives depended on this. "I have a grandmother who is very old and not doing well."

Victor nodded. "Perfect! I'll inform them that your poor granny is close to death and you had to be there. Now, how would you phrase it to sound like you?"

Erin inhaled deeply. "Um, I would say, 'Hey guys! Sorry ... had to leave town really quick to see my sick grandmother. Be back soon.'"

"Do you text in all lower case, upper case or a mix?" Victor asked.

"*What?*" Erin spat.

"You heard me."

"A ... a mix I guess."

Victor turned the phone for Erin to read before he hit send. "It's fine," she said.

He hit send and tossed her phone to the foot of the bed. "Now, where does Daisy live and when does she work?"

Erin shrank back into the thin mattress.

Victor leaned over and whispered, "*Tell me where she lives.*"

Tears ran down her face. "Um, it's an apartment building, walking distance to the bar. Like, six blocks west. I don't remember the exact name of it."

"You've been cooperative and helpful. For that, you will be rewarded."

"I promise I won't go to the authorities. Just please let me go, please!"

"Oh, I will eventually." He held the syringe out. She screamed when she saw the full syringe coming at her.

Erin twisted and screamed, "No, please no! Oh God, no!"

With a smile, he plunged the needle and watched as twenty-five ccs of GHB flowed into Erin's arm. "This will make it painless." He smiled when her head drooped like an unwatered flower. He removed the mask, hoisted her limp body from the bed, and carried her over to the top landing.

Victor peered down the steps. "I need to calculate *just* the right angle." He peeled Erin from his shoulder, held her up at the top of the flight of stairs, and tossed her like a discarded doll.

Zeke and Rubi Lee watched Erin bounce off the walls and freefall down the wooden steps.

"Done." Victor wiped his hands together as if dusting off filth. They stood in stunned silence until Rubi Lee spoke.

"Looks like ya killed her, Uncle Vic," Rubi Lee said. "Good job."

Zeke stood frozen to the floor and glanced at the lifeless body. Erin's head was tilted at an unnatural angle and a ribbon of blood snaked from the corner of her mouth. He did not notice his knuckles were sheet white from gripping the stair railing.

"Go check to see if she's breathing," Victor ordered Rubi Lee and Zeke. "Put these on first." He threw two pairs of gloves at them.

Rubi Lee placed her finger on Erin's warm neck. "She's dead all right." Blood seeped into the dirty rug beneath her.

"Now what?" Zeke fought to keep his voice steady.

"Zeke, grab her under the arms—I'll get her legs. We'll take her out to the van. Rubi Lee, yank the rug out from under her when we lift her. Got it?"

"Yes sir," Rubi Lee replied as Zeke and her uncle removed Erin's body and carried her outside to the van.

When they returned, Victor ordered them to roll up the rug, and find a place to burn it. "When you're finished, you will dump her body."

"Yes, Uncle Vic. Except I'm a little nervous. I've, well . . . *we've* never, um, dumped a dead body," Zeke confessed. "Where do we dump her?"

"Somewhere far from here. One of the older parks with thick woods. Don't be nervous. The authorities will think she's just another junkie with all those needle marks on her."

"Okay, we'll find the right spot. Don't worry." Rubi Lee grinned ear to ear.

CHAPTER 29

That evening, Daisy bought packing boxes and other items for her move. Earlier in the week, Daisy lamented to Nick that she detested the thought of placing Gussie in one of those hateful plastic pet carriers. Nick surprised her by sending her a duffle-like cat carrier. It zipped on a diagonal with mesh on either side for Gussie to peer out and breathe. Daisy placed it on the floor and after a sniff, Gussie nestled right in.

Daisy Facetimed him later that night. "I love how I can just sling the strap over my shoulder and have her right up against me! Watch this." She put it on the floor and Gussie climbed right in. "See? She loves it!" Daisy exclaimed. "Thanks, NT. You're so thoughtful."

"I'm happy to help. See you tomorrow morning."

Nick showed up at nine with two large steaming cups of coffee. "I took a shot with the coffee."

Daisy took a grateful sip. "And you succeeded. Thank you. You're the best." She gave him a hug.

"You're not so bad yourself," Nick loved the warmth of her body.

She lingered in his arms for a few minutes until she pulled herself away. "Time to get packing for my move!"

After two hours of up and down steps, Nick came in with the last box and dropped it on the floor. "Last one. Man, my legs are shot." Nick flopped down on the couch. Daisy sat down next to him and looked around at her new apartment.

"You know, my new place is warm, cozy, and clean."

"You're right, and you don't need to walk to work anymore—or worry about cooking."

"I know. Speaking of food, are you hungry?"

"I'm starving. What's for dinner?"

"I *did* offer to cook except I have nothing to make. Will you take a rain check?"

"Of course. You can always pick up the check tonight though!" He teased.

"As long as you don't mind if we go downstairs for dinner," Daisy said.

"Not at all. Oh, I hear there's a really hot redhead who tends bar there. Do you know her?" A sly grin crept across his face.

"I think I *do* know her. She's not only scorching hot, but she's a hell of a bartender!" She giggled. "Sadly for you though, I don't think she's working tonight. Apparently, she just moved."

"Yes, she did," Nick said.

* * *

Early Monday morning, Gussie was perched on her new lookout spot—the windowsill. Bird and squirrel watching kept her busy for hours. The window looked down onto a wide street that hummed with action.

As Daisy was getting ready to head to school, her phone dinged. Relief washed over her when she saw it was a text from Erin telling her she was sorry she left town so quickly.

But she was fine and would see her soon. Daisy immediately shot back, *I'm sooo happy to hear from u!*

During class, Daisy's mind wandered away from the lecturer to the sweatshirt and the cameras at the bar. The diamonds lingered in her mind. On her laptop she googled *methods of smuggling diamonds*. Lots of articles came back. Daisy learned gems can be transported by being sewn into belts, hats, jacket lapels, and more. *So why not a sweatshirt? They're thick and bulky.*

After what seemed like centuries, class ended. Daisy raced to the bar and saw the hook was empty. The sweatshirt was gone. She looked up and saw the camera located above that area. *Yes!* Daisy went back to the office, anxious to see the video screen. Hopes were dashed when she saw the video screen was blank. Upon further investigation, she saw it was unplugged. *Shit!*

Daisy walked back toward the bar. "Hey Ira, did you know the video system was unplugged?"

He frowned, "No, I didn't. I checked last month and the system was working."

"Okay, thanks." Daisy started to walk away. "I'll catch ya later."

"Hey, I heard from Erin. She just said she had to leave town really quick," Ira said. "Something about her grandmother?"

Daisy pivoted around. "You did? I did too. I'm so relieved. I had a feeling it was her grandmother. I know they're really close."

"True. She didn't say when she'd be back," Ira said. "Hey, it's kinda slow right now. Any chance you can hang out?"

"If it was earlier, I would. But it's already five and I have hours of schoolwork—probably an all-nighter. Sorry," she said.

"No worries. I'll catch you later," Ira responded.

At home, Daisy fixed a sandwich, and tackled her work. At nine o'clock she took a break. *I wonder what NT is up to?* She called him, but he didn't answer. She left him a short message, finding it strange he didn't pick up. Daisy felt a foreign emotion surge through her—jealousy. *Stop it. It's not like you're dating. He's allowed to do what he wants. Get back to your work.*

Her head bobbed one last time until it lightly knocked the window pane next to where she sat at her desk. Startled awake, she saw it was past three in the morning. She stood up and shook her head and stretched her arms, hoping to break out of the fog. She glanced down at her laptop. Five more pages. She put on a pot of strong coffee. When the machine beeped, she poured a mug and sat back down and sighed. *I have to get this paper finished.*

Daisy gazed out the window and noticed a van parked half a block down from her apartment. Soon, an SUV came to a stop across the street. Her attention snapped back to the van. *No way! It reminds me of the van that chased me and Ira!* The van doors opened, and two people exited—one petite and one tall. Both had on dark pants and hoodies. Daisy knew by their builds that the small one was a woman and the other was a large man. They moved furtively toward the SUV.

The passenger side window of the SUV came down and Daisy heard voices mumbling indistinctly. She slowly slid the window open a few more inches to capture some of the conversation. Phone in hand, Daisy tried to video the scene.

Ears straining, Daisy heard bits of their conversation.

"We dumped . . . body . . ."

Daisy heard a hiss from the SUV. "Shhh!"

"Sorry. We followed what . . . and . . . all clean . . ."

The hushed conversation continued briefly until a hand, clenching a brown envelope, stretched from the window of the SUV. Immediately, it was snatched by the woman from the van.

Suddenly, Gussie leaped onto the windowsill, nearly giving Daisy a heart attack. "Jeez, Gussie!" she yelled and picked up the cat.

Daisy's voice carried down to the street. The man from the van looked up sharply at the sound.

"Oh shit!" Daisy moved out of their line of vision. Cold tendrils of fear snaked over her skin. On her hands and knees, she crawled to the other window and gazed down. The man took a drag of his cigarette and tossed it. As he did, his eyes landed on Daisy's apartment. He pointed out Daisy's window to the woman. They stared. Daisy realized the glow from her computer was visible from the outside. She crouched down. *Oh my God, did they see me?* She was wide awake now, heart hammering.

She heard the van sputter to life. Suddenly she was dragged back in time. *That's the same sound of the van that chased me and Ira.* She looked at the video on her phone. She could distinguish nothing. It was total blackness.

CHAPTER 30

Rubi Lee and Zeke sat in the kitchen the next morning, drinking coffee and smoking. Rubi Lee blew out a puff from the side of her mouth. "Do you think whoever was in the window last night heard anything?"

"I doubt it. We were pretty far away," Zeke answered.

"I hope not." She tamped out her cigarette. "Or else we're in deep shit."

"Rube, Uncle Vic and Alex wouldn't let anything happen to us."

"He won't, but Alex?" Rubi Lee spit out a laugh. "She doesn't give two shits about us as people."

"Maybe, but I think we're fine."

Rubi Lee's phone rang. "Uncle Vic, we were just talking about you. What's up?"

"You and your brother need to meet me ASAP."

"You sound pissed," she said and flicked her eyes to Zeke.

"We have a problem. Meet me at Big D's on H Street. It has a small blue awning over the front door. I will see you in twenty minutes."

Rubi Lee hung up. "Sounds like we're in trouble."

"What do you mean?"

"He sounded really pissed."

Zeke rolled his eyes. "Did he say why?"

"No. He wants us to meet him at some restaurant called Big D's on H Street in twenty minutes."

Victor arrived ahead of Zeke and Rubi Lee. He chose a booth in the back and ordered a Manhattan. They soon joined him and ordered beers.

"Hey Uncle V, what's up?" Zeke slid his long body into the cramped booth. Rubi Lee sat across from them.

"Here's what's up." Victor told them he had spoken to Alex. "We are all in agreement that the top priority is to recover the missing diamonds. I have clients who paid for them and want them."

"The girl who was killed said there was another redheaded bartender. Do you think she has them?" Zeke asked.

"So, what's the plan?" Rubi Lee asked. "Do you want us to grab her too?"

Victor sipped his drink. "No. My intel advised us to steer clear of the bar because of Gaylord's murder as well as the disappearance of the other bartender."

"What do you want us to do?" Zeke asked.

"I found out she lives above the bar. I'll figure out how you two can gain access and ransack her apartment and locate the diamonds."

"Wait, hang on. I think we saw her in her window the other night. That makes it easier for us," Zeke said.

"I'll go to the bar tonight to scout out the upstairs area. You will wait outside in the van and I'll call you when it's safe. It will be your job to upend her entire apartment until you find the missing stones. Understood?" Victor instructed.

"And if we don't?" Zeke asked.

Victor sat silently for a moment. He lifted his near-empty glass to his thin lips. Zeke and Rubi Lee tried to read the expression in his faraway eyes. "We will find them, one way or another," he whispered.

* * *

Several hours later, Victor sat in the Black LaSalle and ordered a Manhattan. He swirled the heavy glass and admired the glowing amber whiskey. Manhattans were his drink of choice ever since he tasted his first one at Ophelia Lounge, an upscale New York city bar. Always fastidious, Victor requested his drink with only one dash of bitters, not two. One sip of this magical cocktail always eased his clouded soul. He glanced around but did not see Daisy anywhere—until a door slammed open from behind a corner of the bar. Arms full of napkins and coasters, Daisy appeared and kicked the door shut.

Over his glass, he studied the meticulous way she mixed drinks, and ease with which she handled her many customers. *She does resemble the dead girl.*

He admired how Daisy squatted down and easily picked up a box full of six large bottles of vodka. He emptied his glass, threw a few bills on the bar, and headed to the restroom in the back. He paused, scanned the area, and quickly jogged up the narrow staircase to the second floor. He tugged on a pair of gloves and sized up the four doors in the hallway. His instincts told him they were all locked and he was correct except for one, a storage closet. He turned on the flashlight on his phone, got down on all fours, and peered under the space under the second door. The light did not spread far underneath. Victor took a pen from his pocket and poked it under the door. It hit something solid. *Most likely more storage.*

His knees ached from being on the floor and his back seized. *Christ, here we go again.* Begrudgingly, Victor crawled on all fours and peered under the other doors. Light was visible under one of them. Pen in hand, he stuck it under the door and heard a sound. He scratched the door and heard the sound loudly this time—a meow. He ran the pen under the door and was pleased to see a little paw shoot out from underneath, trying to capture his pen. Victor smiled triumphantly and disappeared down the staircase.

Outside in his car, he called Rubi Lee. "The stairs to the second floor are next to the bathroom. She lives up there in number 3C. The door is locked, so you'll need to pick it cleanly and get in. You and Zeke will leave no stone unturned. Look through everything—pillows, cabinets, cracker boxes. Got it?"

"Yes sir. How do you know it's 3C?" Rubi Lee asked.

"Because I heard a cat meowing behind that one. And the others are storage rooms."

"Zeke hates cats."

"Who cares? Now make it quick." Victor dabbed at his brow.

"We will." Rubi Lee stubbed her cigarette out on the dashboard.

"I'll wait around the corner. Call when you're finished."

Zeke moved the van to a darker area around the corner. He yanked his hood up and Rubi Lee pulled on a beanie.

It was close to ten o'clock when Rubi Lee and Zeke entered the bar. Music pumped loudly through the speakers mounted on the ceiling. Ira and Daisy were busy with customers. *Perfect*, Rubi Lee thought. She and her brother headed to the stairs and up they went.

Zeke charged into the living room and quietly flipped over Daisy's sofa and chairs. Rubi Lee plunged her stiletto into cushions and pillows and ripped them open. Feathers flew out all over the floor. "Nothing," she said. They tossed the pillows to the floor like angry children. Drawers were emptied onto the carpet. Still no stones. Behind the television was only a wall, and the small desk in the corner yielded nothing. Zeke snatched two paintings from their walls and looked behind the frames—no gems. A small, modern light fixture hung above the coffee table. They searched it. Nothing.

That's when they heard it—a hiss.

"What the hell was that?" Zeke stopped and listened, heart racing.

Rubi Lee walked into the kitchen. "It must be her cat." She pointed to Gussie's bowl on the floor. "And there it is." She nodded toward the living room where Gussie squeezed herself under a toppled chair, flicked her tail and hissed.

"What should we do with it?" he asked.

"Leave it alone. It ain't gonna bite you, you big baby."

In the kitchen, they rifled through every drawer, every cabinet. They searched the oven, stove, fridge, and freezer. No gems were hidden anywhere in the appliances. The two of them went through cereal boxes, cracker boxes, and even the coffee maker. Nothing. They even dumped the trash and recycling. Empty.

"Bedroom." Zeke pointed.

All drawers were open, clothes snatched out, bed torn apart. It was as if a cyclone tore through it. Clothes, pillows, sheets, books thrown everywhere. Nothing was left untouched.

"Where the hell are they?" Zeke yelled.

"They've got to be here somewhere."

They stood in the middle of the destroyed apartment and looked around. Zeke looked at his phone and saw they'd been there for close to fifteen minutes. "We better get outta here."

"Son of a bitch! We're leaving here with nothing. You know how pissed he'll be?" Rubi Lee yelled.

"I know, but tough shit. What else can we do?"

Rubi Lee sighed, yanked on her hat, and headed out the door.

* * *

Downstairs, Live Music Night finally wound down at ten thirty. Usually the entertainment was decent, but not this night. The bone-thin, whiny singer reminded Daisy of a greasy-haired middle school kid who had not gone through puberty.

As Ira wiped down the bar, Daisy counted the cash in the tip jar. "Not too shabby for tonight—especially with that crappy singing."

"Thank God he stopped," Ira remarked.

"That noise isn't even singing," she replied. "Whining is more like it."

"Good call. Well, I cashed out, dishwasher is on, lights are out. Ready to go?"

"I'm so ready."

"Luckily for you, you only have to walk up a flight of

steps. Night, Daiz."

"Night, Ira," she called after him. "Stay warm on your way home!"

She opened the door to her dark apartment and the smell hit her first. *Ew, that trash stinks.* The distressed meow of Gussie set off alarm bells. Daisy stepped inside the apartment, flicked on a light, and froze. A wave of nauseous fear engulfed over her as she took in the destruction of her once-tidy apartment. Gussie darted out from underneath the chair and leaped into Daisy's arms. "Oh Gussie, you're okay!" She held Gussie to her chest and surveyed the ruin of her living room. The devastation led down the hall toward her bedroom. She knew not to touch anything and backed out into the hall.

She called Nick. "Someone broke in and trashed my apartment!" Daisy began to cry. "My place is destroyed!"

"*What?* Are you okay? Is there anyone in there?" he asked.

"I . . . I don't think so, but I'm not going back in there. Can you please come over?"

"I'm on my way. Please call the cops and stay put until I get there, okay?"

Daisy called the police, and within ten minutes she opened the door to two officers not much older than Daisy—one female, one male. "Are you Daisy Taylor?" the female officer asked.

"Yes ma'am."

"I'm Officer Hefner and this is Officer McGrath." They tipped their hats. "We understand you had a break-in?" she asked.

"Yes ma'am. My apartment is upstairs. Follow me."

After the officers gauged the damage, Officer McGrath asked Daisy if she touched anything.

"No sir."

"We're going to secure the area," Officer Hefner said.

Daisy watched them carefully step into her apartment and spread the yellow crime scene tape around. "Officer Hefner, can you please hand me that purple canvas bag?" Daisy pointed at Gussie's bag on the floor.

"Here you go, Miss Taylor."

"Thank you." Daisy slipped Gussie into the bag and slung it over her shoulder. Daisy's phone buzzed—Nick arrived. She ran down the steps and unlocked the door. He opened his arms and she threw herself into them and cried.

"What exactly happened?" he asked and stroked her hair.

Her words gushed like an opened fire hydrant. "Someone broke in and trashed my place. I feel sick. I've never had anything like this happen before! And I was *working right downstairs.*" She wiped her face.

He gently put his hands on her shoulders and looked into her puffy eyes. "Daiz, you're okay. That's all that matters."

She turned and walked up the steps. "I know, I know. Wait until you see my place. It's beyond . . . I can barely think straight."

"I saw the cop car."

"Yes. They're inside now looking at it. It's totally trashed. And I *just* moved in!" Her voice quavered.

Nick glanced into the apartment and his jaw dropped. Daisy was correct—her apartment was destroyed. His blood ran hot, and anger seethed through him as he absorbed the destruction. *Jesus, what if she'd been here when this happened? I'd kill whoever did this to her.* White-hot fury pulsed through him at thought of Daisy being home when this happened. *But she wasn't, Nick. She's with you now.*

"Miss Taylor, do you have somewhere you can stay for a night or possibly longer? We need to get our fingerprint team in here to sweep," Officer Hefner said.

"Yes. She can stay with me," Nick said.

"Did you find anything that might tell you who did this?" Daisy asked.

"Not yet, but we'd like to ask you some questions about tonight, okay?" Officer Hefner asked.

"Yes, ma'am."

"Where were you this evening?"

"I was at work downstairs."

"What time did you get there?" the officer asked.

Daisy rubbed her head. "Around four thirty."

"Where were you before work?"

"I had class, came home, and changed," Daisy answered.

"Was everything normal during your shift? Did anyone give you a hard time? Were any of the customers inebriated?" She made notes.

"It was Live Music Night. Ira and I were really busy. And no. No one was staggering drunk."

"Ira?"

Daisy shook her head. "Yeah, Ira. He's another bartender."

"What time did you finish?"

"We closed the bar around eleven or so."

"Do remember if you saw anyone hanging around the premises after you closed?" Officer McGrath asked.

Daisy frowned and shook her head. "No, sir. Everyone pretty much cleared out after last call."

"We need you to see what, if any, valuables were taken. Officer McGrath, please go down to the bar to see if there are cameras that may have caught the crowd."

Inside her room, Daisy saw her personal laptop was on the shelf in her closet. No jewelry had been taken and her full tip jar was untouched. Her school-issued laptop lay on the floor.

"My tip jar is still full. I wonder why they didn't take that money?"

"If they were in a hurry, they may not have seen it," Officer Hefner replied.

"Maybe. What happens next?" Daisy asked.

"We will file a report. It does seem strange that nothing of value was taken, specifically since both laptops were out in the open. My feeling is the perpetrators were after something specific."

"Like what?" Daisy said.

Daisy did not expect her response. "Like drugs. Drugs are quite often the reason for a break-in and ransack," she replied.

This hung in the air for a while.

"*Drugs?* Seriously?" Daisy found it difficult to hide her indignation. She scowled at the officer. "I don't do drugs."

"I'm sorry. We have to ask. If not you, do you think your friend or anyone else may have stashed something here?" The officer nodded her head toward Nick.

"No way. He doesn't do drugs."

"Can you think of anything else they were after?"

"No, I have no idea why my apartment was targeted. I'm

so flustered, it's hard to think."

"I understand. But please try to. I think we're through here for the night. You are going to a friend's, correct?" Officer Hefner asked.

"Yes ma'am. How long until I can return to my place?" Daisy asked.

"We need to file this report and a technician needs to check for prints. Someone will be here tomorrow. As far as returning home, it'll probably be a day or two. We will let you know when you can return permanently."

Officer McGrath returned. "There are cameras, but they weren't working."

"Of course not," Nick said.

Daisy looked at the kitchen. "Can we at least pick up the trash and recycling?" she asked.

Officer Hefner nodded. "Yes, we looked through it for any evidence."

"Thank you. I really appreciate your help. I feel so violated." Daisy's eyes filled with tears.

Officer Hefner rubbed Daisy's arm. "I know you do. I'm sorry this happened. We'll work hard to try figure out who did this."

Daisy packed a bag and returned to the kitchen. "I can't imagine how expensive it will be to replace all my stuff." She pointed to the broken plates, torn pillows, and other damaged things. "I can't afford to buy a new bed or anything else." Tears slid down her face.

Nick put his arm around her. "We'll figure things out. Let's clean this crap up before we go."

CHAPTER 31

Winston was waiting for them. "Thank God you're okay! Nick called ahead and told me what happened!"

"Thanks . . . My place is destroyed." Daisy put the cat carrier on the ground. "Do you mind if I let her out?"

"No. Do you have any idea who did this? Maybe some creep or stalker from the bar?" Winston asked.

She shook her head. "I'm so rattled I can't think straight. Sorry."

"I understand. Can I get you something?"

"No thanks. I'm fine." Daisy dropped onto the couch next to Nick. Winston perched on the edge of a chair across from them, elbows on knees, and listened raptly to Daisy.

"What did the cops say?" Winston asked.

"They think the perps were looking for something specific. They asked if I or any of my friends kept *drugs* at my place."

"Drugs? What? Why do they think the perps were looking for something specific?" Winston asked.

"Because not one of my personal things was taken—*not one.* My tip jar included. I have to admit, the cops would know about the specific thing."

"I wonder what?" Winston asked.

"Who knows. The police will file the report, get a fingerprint technician to dust for prints, and then they'll let me back in."

"I'm really sorry for you. Luckily, you're okay and you're welcome to stay for as long as you want. I'll sleep on the couch so you can have my bed," Nick said.

"Thanks. It'll be only a day or two," she responded and patted his shoulder. "I hope you don't mind Gussie . . ."

The front door swung open and Jaida came rushing in. Daisy hopped off the couch and hugged her.

"Daisy!" Jaida enveloped her tightly. "I saw Win's message and rushed over as soon as possible!" She looked at her friend's drawn face and knew it was not time to ask questions. Jaida quickly added, "Where are you staying tonight?"

"I'm going to stay here until I'm allowed back into my place."

Jaida looked around the living room and shook her head.

"She's welcome here for as long as she wants," Nick interjected.

"No. And no. You come stay with me," Jaida demanded.

"I can't put you out like that," Daisy answered.

"Daisy, we're *friends* and that's what friends do for each other. Besides—no offense, boys—my place is a *little* neater than this. And I have plenty of room."

Daisy looked at Nick's glum face and she knew he wanted her to stay at his house. "I think for everyone's sake of comfort, I'll stay with Jaida."

"Are you sure?" Nick asked. "I can try to be neater!"

She turned and faced him. The look of earnest on his face melted her. "I think it makes more sense for me to go to Jaida's."

Nick nodded in defeat.

Daisy turned to Jaida. "Okay, Jaida. I'm all yours until I get back on my feet."

"Daisy, you can stay with me for as long as you want. With my ridiculous work hours, I come and go at various times. I'd love to have someone there on a regular basis."

"I can't thank you enough," Daisy said.

"It's twelve thirty and I have a long day tomorrow. Time to go, okay?" Jaida announced.

Daisy and Jaida said goodnight to Win and Nick and headed to Jaida's apartment.

Jaida's apartment building stopped Daisy in her tracks. She counted—ten stories. Red brick was inlaid with enormous green-tinted windows, which absorbed hours of gorgeous sunlight. Under the marble porte-cochère, a doorman stood at attention. Daisy noted their long navy coats and shiny black shoes.

"Hello, Miss Campbell. How are you this evening?" asked a doorman whose nametag read STANLEY.

"Hi Stanley. I am doing quite well. How are you?" Jaida responded.

"No complaints!" Stanley laughed.

Jaida introduced Daisy. "She'll be staying with me for an indefinite period of time, so please watch out for her, okay?"

"Yes ma'am." Stanley opened the door into the tastefully decorated lobby. The sumptuous velvet furniture, elegant lighting, and marble floor made Daisy feel as if she just entered a castle.

"Jaida, it's stunning here! And it's pet-friendly." Daisy absorbed the magnificence around her. They walked to the elevator. Jaida hit the up button.

"I know. I was sucked in the minute I opened the lobby door. Rent is expensive. I've put myself on a strict budget. Lots of soup for me!" Jaida laughed.

Daisy issued the ultimatum she decided upon earlier. "Speaking of budgets, I have every intention of helping with rent and food, so don't even try to say no. Got it?"

Jaida smiled and put her hands up in mock surrender. "If you say so!" They laughed and stepped out onto the tenth floor and walked down the carpeted hallway to a door with a shiny brass placard—*1010*.

"Welcome home!" Jaida opened the door to Daisy's temporary home.

Daisy walked a few steps inside, dropped her bag on the floor, and unzipped Gussie's bag. Her eyes grew wide at the view across the room. Three floor-to-ceiling windows captured the life of the city from ten stories above. Daisy walked over, reached out her hand, and ran it slowly down the glass; Jaida heard her sigh.

"I know, it's mind-blowing, isn't it?" Jaida remarked. "I love seeing all the lights and energy of the city."

"Jaid, my God. This view is truly incredible." Daisy clutched her hands to her chest. "I could stare at this all night."

"Sometimes I do. This view always mesmerizes me."

"I'll say." Daisy remained in place for several minutes.

Jaida joined her, two glasses of wine in hand. "Even though it's late, I thought you may need this. Cheers!"

"Oh, I do. Cheers."

"Ready to see your room?"

Jaida led Daisy through the open-floor plan apartment. The white-walled kitchen was bright and cheery. Cherry cabinets complemented the stainless-steel appliances. Three stools were neatly tucked under a granite island in the middle of the kitchen. In the living area, a gray love seat and matching chairs formed a welcoming seating area. A glass topped table served as centerpiece. Behind the seating area, a royal blue sofa faced a gas fireplace. A television sat in the corner.

Daisy was mesmerized by the striking beauty and refinement of the place. "How did you manage to get on the *top* floor?" she asked Jaida.

Jaida hesitated and shrugged. "Right place, right time, I guess. Follow me."

"I'll say." *How does she afford this?* Gussie followed them down the carpeted hallway to a door on Jaida's left.

"This is your bedroom. I hope you like it," Jaida said and opened the door.

Daisy entered the lavender bedroom. "This is lovely and calming." Gussie trotted in and immediately jumped onto the queen-size bed covered in a purple and white duvet cover.

"Someone looks comfortable!" Jaida laughed at Gussie.

Daisy ran her hand over the bed. *This duvet costs more than my entire bed!* Two nightstands flanked the bed. Tasteful gray lamps adorned them. A large six-drawered bureau sat across from the bed with another lamp on top.

Jaida pointed to the bathroom across the hall from Daisy's new room. "Let me go grab some towels."

Daisy opened the bathroom door and inhaled the delightful smell of eucalyptus. A small closet was built in behind a walk-in shower. Looking around, Daisy suddenly felt overwhelmed. Tears sprang to her eyes.

Jaida returned with the towels. "Are you okay?"

"I'm just overwhelmed with everything. I'll never be able to thank you enough." Daisy wiped her tears.

Jaida embraced Daisy. "I'm so happy I can help you out. Believe me, I love having you here."

"And I love being here." Daisy yawned. "God, I'm so tired."

"I know. You need your rest. Good night, roomie." Jaida left the room.

"Night, Jaida. Thank you again."

Daisy tossed and turned. Something nibbled the back of her mind. *What if there's a connection between being chased, those diamonds, and my apartment ransacked? All those things happened pretty close to each other. Coincidence? Maybe, maybe not.* She lay awake for a few hours until sleep took her into its warm embrace.

CHAPTER 32

Old Man Winter soon cloaked the city in a frigid coat nobody wanted to wear.

Henderson detested cold weather. Hated it. He sat at his desk in the small office of Margaux Ford Park. Despite its old age and boring beige walls, the office held heat and was a second home for Henderson. A refrigerator hummed in the corner to the right of the cramped bathroom. A small closet to the left of his desk held his coat. Above his desk hung a calendar that showcased twelve of the country's most beautiful parks. He scrolled through the fifteen-day forecast. "Man, it's gonna be *this* cold for two weeks?"

He sipped on his coffee as he finished organizing the week's schedule. "All right, old man, time for the drive through." Henderson turned off the heater, stood, and stretched his legs. He yanked his heavy coat off the hanger in the closet, slipped on gloves, and wrapped his neck with a thick scarf. The red wool hat he clamped on his head was a must. He looked at the current temperature on his phone: thirty-eight degrees. But with the wind, the "real feel" was thirty-three degrees. *Real feel? Real feel is I'm gettin' too old for this crap. Maybe next winter, Jackie and I'll go to Florida. Ha—like we can afford that.*

Henderson turned off the computer and the lights and headed to the garage where his golf cart awaited him. He hoped the battery died—no such luck. After his drive through, he was going to head to the Black LaSalle to meet Jackie. She had been busy lately, so he looked forward to their date.

The flimsy plastic zip-up siding attached to the cart tried to protect him from the cold, but it failed miserably. Henderson drove the cart into the dark, desolate park. He dodged the small piles of gray, filthy snow dotting the path. Not a soul was around, as he expected. In his mind, there was no rhyme or reason why people voluntarily exercised outside in the freezing cold. *Fools.* He drove the cart out of the north end down the lighted path to the southern end. The wind kicked up and rattled the sides of the plastic covering. Henderson rolled his eyes and turned left down the path that led to the west side of the park. The small head lights swept across the brown landscape flecked with more gray mounds of snow. No one there.

He bumped his way toward the south end of the park— his favorite end. He loved the statues of the freedom fighters, the red and purple tulips that popped up in the spring, and the life-size chess board. The headlights of the cart started to flicker. *Aw, come on. Not now!* The darkness limited his ability to see further ahead. *Damnit.* He sighed, unzipped the plastic cover, and got out. The statues looked down at him. He looked up at Susan B. Anthony and said, "I'm freezing my tail off too, Ms. Anthony." He clicked on his high-powered flashlight and swept it around the area. The light reflected off the cold benches in front of brown skeletal bushes. Henderson cast the light across the broad lawn toward thick rows of pine trees when something caught his eye. He walked over and saw it was a yellow piece of wool, like a sweater. Brown stains leaped out in contrast. *What is this?* He assumed the stains were mud. He flashed the light closer and saw that the stains were not mud, but blood. Dried blood. *Oh man.*

His cop instincts kicked in and he ventured further past the row of dense trees. He no longer felt the cold wind biting through his coat. A few steps more and then he saw it—a foot sticking out from under a second row of thick pine trees. *Ah Jesus!* He plodded over.

In between the trees, the body of a woman clad in a torn yellow sweater and jeans lay on the ground. Blood caked the back of the sweater. She was lying on her side, right knee bent over her left leg. His heart banged in his chest. Henderson shone the light onto the back of her head. Blood and winter debris mingled in red curly hair. *Daisy! Oh no! NO! NO! NO! Not HER!* He cautiously approached the body. *I have to see if it's her.* His heart was a hammer battering against his chest. Sweat ran down from under his hat. He swallowed hard. The flashlight shook in his hand as he shone the light on the woman.

"Please Jesus, give me strength."

His eyes followed the beam. His whole body sagged with relief. It was not Daisy. It was Erin. "Oh God, no!" He yanked his phone from his pocket and called 911. He then called Jackie.

"I'll be right there!" she told him.

He shook as he glanced again at the lovely and dead face of Erin.

Within minutes, several patrol cars appeared at the

park.

Henderson ran through the entire story with Jackie, who stroked his arm and murmured how sorry she was. She told him the coroner was on her way.

CHAPTER 33

After a long day of work, talking to the police, and arguing with the insurance company about the break-in, Daisy was spent. She took a long steaming shower after dinner. She wrapped her hair up in one of the plush towels and found Jaida working on her laptop.

"I'm exhausted, so it's bedtime for me."

Jaida looked up from her work. "I'll be up a little longer. Do you have everything you need?"

"Thanks to you, I do."

"Good. Sleep tight, Daiz. I'll see you sometime tomorrow."

"Same to you. Night, Jaida."

Daisy fell into the soft warm bed and said a prayer of thanks. She was deep in the ocean of sleep when something woke her. A dream? A sound? She looked at her phone—3:17 a.m. She lay there and the same thoughts from before floated through her head: being chased by a van, finding diamonds in a sweatshirt, having her apartment destroyed. *Maybe DC isn't the place for me. Seems like the universe is trying to send me a message.* The more she thought about it, the harder it was to believe all those things were coincidental. Her heart started to beat. She took calming breaths. *Please God, let me sleep.* Gussie leaped up on her bed and purred until she lulled Daisy back to sleep.

* * *

Daisy's brain felt like the consistency of a bowl of oatmeal as she prepared for the lunch shift. Ira joined her in pouring salt into the shakers and organizing silverware.

"You okay?" Ira asked.

"Yeah, just really tired."

"Do you have any idea when Erin will be back?"

"Her text said a few days, right?" Daisy answered and reread Erin's text. "This says she had to leave town quickly but will return soon."

"Okay." He opened the door to the basement.

"I'm afraid she won't be retuning." The subdued voice came from behind her. She recognized it as Henderson's, but he sounded off.

She turned around. He stood near the bar with a grave look on his face, fidgeting with the hat in his hand. Jackie was with him.

"Hey guys. Henderson, what do you mean?" she asked and flicked her eyes to Jackie.

He cleared his throat and looked at Jackie. "I don't know how to tell you this, Daisy. But Erin is gone," he told her in a whisper.

She stared at them. "Gone? Henderson, what're you talking about?"

"Daisy, I found Erin's body in Margaux Ford Park. I believe she was murdered."

Daisy's throat constricted as she blinked at Henderson. The room spun. "What are you saying? No, no. This must be a horrible mistake!" She shook her head. "No! Henderson, no!"

"I'm afraid it's true," Jackie said. "I'm so sorry, Daisy." She sighed and told Daisy scant detail about finding Erin.

Daisy sank down to her knees and felt her breakfast roiling in her stomach.

"What's going on here?" Ira glanced around at the stricken faces.

Jackie broke the grim news.

He gaped at them. "Erin dead? What? What are you *talking* about?"

Daisy felt like an icicle. She tried to process what she learned. *Erin ... dead ... dead ... no.*

"We have started an investigation. I can't tell you both how sorry I am. We will find who did this," Jackie promised.

"I can't believe this. What exactly happened?" Ira asked.

"We have reason to believe she was murdered. Her injuries are suggestive of one."

"This can't be real," Ira whispered.

"You have my deepest condolences," Jackie said. "I know this is a terrible shock to you both. However, if you are comfortable with answering a few questions at this time, it may help to find who did this to your friend."

Jackie's last two words—"your friend"—tore into Daisy. "Oh God, give me a minute!" Her vision blurred as she ran to the ladies' room and promptly threw up. She stood up slowly from the floor in front of the toilet and pushed open the stall door. Cold water ran from the faucet into her cupped hands. She splashed her face and washed her hands.

When she returned, Ira asked her, "You okay?" and squeezed her shoulder. "You're really pale."

"Yea, I'm fine. I'm ready."

"This can wait, Daisy," Jackie said.

"No, it can't. She was my *friend*."

"All right then. How long have you and Daisy known her?" Jackie asked.

"I've known her for close to two years," Ira answered.

"I just met her earlier this summer and I considered her a sister—a ginger sister, to be exact."

"Ginger sisters?" Jackie asked.

"She's a redhead and so am I. People often confused us for each other," Daisy explained.

Jackie hesitated at Daisy's response. "I see. She was your boss, correct?"

Daisy nodded as Ira added that Erin was the manager.

"Did you know her to do drugs?" Jackie asked.

Daisy and Ira exchanged stunned glances. "Are you crazy? Erin? No way," Ira responded. "Why?"

"Routine question. We'll know more when we get the ME's report."

"Like exactly how she died?" Daisy asked.

"Yes," Jackie said. She continued, "There was bruising on her right arm and neck, which is why I asked about drugs." Jackie looked at them.

Daisy leveled her eyes at Jackie. "Erin *did not* do drugs."

Jackie stared right back. "We have to explore every option. Eventually, I will need to ask you more questions about when you last saw Erin and things of that nature." She softened her tone when she added, "I know you've been dealt a horrible blow. Why don't we reschedule for a day or two from now?" Jackie's bracelets jangled as she rubbed Daisy's arm.

Suddenly Daisy remembered the text she got from Erin.

"Wait! Jackie, wait! Ira and I got a text from her saying she had to leave town quickly! Look!" Daisy shakily scrolled through her text messages. She found it and showed it to Henderson and Jackie.

Ira showed them the same one.

"Thank you for this. It's possible her killer or killers made her text people saying she was fine. Especially since the messages read the same and were sent simultaneously," Jackie said. "We will—" Her phone buzzed in her pocket. "I have to take this, sorry. I'll catch you all later. Please make a time to come to the station for questioning, okay?"

"I just can't believe this. It's surreal," Daisy said.

"How about we all take a seat for a bit?" Henderson suggested.

They sat down at a table and stared into space. "What do we do now?" Ira asked.

Henderson gazed at Ira. "Like Jackie said, she will need your assistance to help solve this. Write down whatever you can remember about the last time you saw her. Even if it seems mundane. If possible, please include anyone who came into the bar who may have stalked her, or someone who stayed too long at the bar, things of that nature."

"What else?" Ira asked.

"You can tell Jackie what Erin's routine was outside of work, provided you know what she did for fun. Tell her about any family, relationships outside of work, hobbies, et cetera."

"My head is spinning. I don't know how to even *start* thinking about what you just said," Daisy admitted.

"I understand. Remember, *anything* you can tell Jackie may be helpful."

Sadness hovered over them until the phone behind the bar rang. Ira jumped up to answer it and Henderson reached across the table and placed his hand over Daisy's.

"Oh Daisy. I don't know how to tell you how sorry I am."

Daisy's eyes welled up. "I am too. Who would want to *do* this to her? Why? Erin is a beautiful person." She grabbed a napkin and loudly blew her nose.

"There are horrible people out there, Daisy. People do unspeakable things to others. Usually murders occur because of greed, money, or sex."

"I guess you know that from being a cop."

"Oh, I do. Believe me."

"And to make matters worse, someone broke in and trashed my apartment."

Henderson stared at her in disbelief. "*What?* When?"

"Just a few nights ago."

"What did they take?"

"Nothing, aside from my feeling of being safe. Not. One. Thing."

Henderson tapped his fingers on the table. "You're sure?"

"Yes. The cops said it was obvious the perps were looking for something in particular."

"It sure sounds it. Do you have any idea who did it?"

"Well, no one I can name. What's eating at me, though, is how it happened so soon after Ira and I were chased . . ." Daisy's voice caught in her throat. "And now Erin." She wiped her eyes.

"I can't ignore the timing of all this either," Henderson said.

"What would you do if you were me?" Daisy asked.

"You did the right thing contacting the police. Second, stay vigilant about your surroundings. And third, keep an eye out for that van. If you see it again, take a picture."

"I will. Thanks, Henderson." Daisy sighed and looked down at her hands. "It's just not going to be the same around here, Henderson. Erin was the sister I never had."

"I know, sweetheart, and I am terribly sorry. "We'll find out who did this." He squeezed her hand. "I promise."

"Thanks, Henderson. I should try to get back to work. Maybe it'll keep my mind off Erin."

"I understand." They stood; he hugged her and left.

CHAPTER 34

For the rest of her shift, Daisy felt like she was floating outside her own body, watching herself from above. A palpable darkness shrouded the bar even though sunlight poured in. Daisy's thoughts were jumbled to the point where she served the wrong lunch, twice. She could not stop thinking about Erin. *Please God, let this day end so I can go home, hug Gussie, and sleep.* Dread filled her when she thought about telling Nick, Jaida, and Winston. They had to know. Before she left, she he texted them and asked to meet at her at Jaida's place that night.

Daisy needed the few hours to herself when she got home. A hot shower was first on the list followed by a nap. At home, she stripped quickly out of her black work outfit, showered, and put on less somber clothes. She collapsed onto the couch. Gussie was only too happy to join her. She flipped on the television and realized the only decent shows on at that time of day were murder shows. *No thanks.* She settled on a silly but feel-good movie about a family who adopted an older pony no longer used for rides at his barn. Soon her eyes were closed, and she slept.

The rustling of keys startled Daisy out of her nap. The apartment was dark, save for the glow of the television. *I must've slept forever.* She picked up her phone from the table and saw it was almost six thirty. *Wow, a two-hour nap.*

She sat up, stretched, and put Gussie on the floor.

"Daiz? You here?" Jaida called.

"Yup, on the couch," Daisy answered with a yawn.

Jaida walked in and plopped down next to her.

"What's up?" Jaida asked, her blue eyes cheery.

"Not a whole lot. I just woke up actually." Daisy rubbed her face.

"Rough day? You don't look so good."

"Yes, pretty awful. I need to tell you something when the guys come over."

Jaida rubbed her back. "Win texted me about it. What's up?"

"If you don't mind, I'd rather wait until they get here. I don't think I can tell it twice. I'm going to freshen up."

"Sure, of course. You're worrying me, though."

"I'll be okay." Daisy got up.

Jaida rose from the couch. "I've been wearing these clothes all day. Time to change."

Nick and Winston showed up a few minutes later. Nick walked in and gaped at the view of the city. "Jaida, this is unbelievable. How'd you land this place?"

"Right time, right place—with a touch of luck."

"I'll say. This view is incredible." He looked around some more and saw Daisy coming down the hall. "Hi Daiz, what's up?"

"Hi guys. I need to talk to you. Let's go sit in the living room."

"Daiz, you okay?" Win asked her.

"Um, not really." Daisy inhaled and, through new tears, haltingly continued, "Henderson and Jackie came to work today and told me that, um, Erin was, oh God . . . Erin was murdered." Pain etched her face as her tears flowed.

Shock silenced Jaida, Winston, and Nick. Three pairs of eyes pinged back and forth until Jaida jumped out of her chair. "Oh no Daisy, I'm so sorry!" She hugged her and wiped Daisy's tears away.

"Oh no, I ruined your blouse!"

"Stop. No, you didn't," Jaida responded.

Nick took Daisy's hand. "Oh, Daisy, I'm so sorry. This is shocking. Wow, shocking." His heart ached for her. He longed to hold her and tell her everything would be okay.

"*Dead?* God, we just saw her not long ago at the bar," Winston remarked.

Daisy shook her head. "She didn't show up on Wednesday. Ira and I thought it was so unlike her not to come in to work."

"Did you try to get ahold of her?" Winston asked.

"Yes. Ira and I called and texted her." Daisy sank back on the couch. Eventually, she texted us later that she had to leave town suddenly."

"Did you tell Henderson and Jackie she didn't come to work on Wednesday?" Jaida asked.

"Yes. We also showed them the text."

"And?" Winston asked.

"Jackie said it was possible the murderer or murderers *made* her text me and Ira to make it look like she was fine."

"I see," Winston said.

Jaida added, "Sounds premeditated to me as well."

Nick rose and stood behind Daisy's chair and gently rubbed her shoulders. "You've had it rough, Daisy."

The epiphany crackled through Daisy like a bolt of lightning. She shot from her seat and began to pace. "What if the person who killed Erin was after *me*? What if they thought *Erin* was *me*!"

They all stared at her. Nick asked, "Daisy, what do you mean?"

"Think about it. Ever since I moved here to DC, weird things have happened to me. First, Ira and I were chased by a van on *the same night* I wore home a sweatshirt with *diamonds* sewn in it. What if they thought *Erin* wore it home? Second, my apartment gets destroyed. And third, Erin is *dead*. Dead."

Something imperceptible changed the atmosphere in the living room.

"I have to admit, what you just told us does seem very strange," Nick said.

"Yes, it does. But why would *you* be targeted?" Winston asked.

Daisy shrugged and sighed. "The only thing I can think of is that sweatshirt. But we returned it with all of the diamonds in it, right Jaida?" She glanced at Jaida, who gave a tiny nod.

Winston cut his eyes to Jaida. Her face gave away nothing.

Daisy stood up. "I really need a beer. Anyone else?"

"Sure. I'll help you." Nick followed her into the kitchen.

Winston pivoted in his seat. "Jaida, we're this close"— he held up his thumb and index finger—"to busting this smuggling ring *wide* open. But we have a problem: Daisy thinks all the diamonds were replaced, which means—" He was interrupted by a cold beer placed in front of him. "Oh, thanks Nick. Daisy, I want to hear more about the night the van chased you," Winston said.

"Ira and I closed that night. It was cold, so I grabbed a sweatshirt from the back. On the way home, a white van came out of nowhere and came after us—or seemed to, at least. It flew through red lights, intersections and..." She took a swig and almost spit it out. "I forgot to tell you this."

Nick scowled at her. "Forgot what?"

"A few nights ago, I was up late doing schoolwork, sitting by my window. I looked out and saw a van—I couldn't tell the color. Two people got out and walked over to a black SUV. From my perspective, it looked like a drug deal. I couldn't really hear what they were saying, but an envelope was exchanged between the van drivers and the people in the SUV." Daisy sipped her beer. "I'd bet money it was the same crappy van."

"How would you know?" Winston asked.

"It sounded like it was on its last legs."

"If you saw the van again, would you recognize it?" Winston asked.

"One hundred percent. There's *no way* this is coincidence." Daisy was not to be swayed.

"Did you see the driver?" Jaida asked.

"No. But when Ira and I ran to the metro, one of them got out and ran after us."

"Male or female?" Jaida asked.

"Male."

"What did he look like?" Nick asked.

"I don't know, but he looked tall and strong." Daisy sighed. "I'm tired of talking about all of this. Do you guys mind if we stop?"

"Of course not. We understand," Jaida answered.

Winston clapped his hands together. "So, is anyone

hungry?"

"Starving," Jaida said.

"Famished," Nick said, rubbing his stomach.

"Kind of." Daisy shrugged.

"What do you guys think? Get takeout or go out?" Nick threw out. He patted Daisy on the leg. "Daiz, you need to eat."

"I don't feel like going out. Let's just get takeout, okay?" Daisy asked.

"Whatever you want. We'll go get it," Jaida replied.

With dinner decided upon, Winston and Jaida left.

"What the *hell*? Erin's dead?" Winston said as they left the apartment.

"I know and I feel sick about it, believe me," Jaida whispered.

"And you gave the other four diamonds to the agency, correct?"

"I will."

"You know this means potential disaster for Daisy. Sykes is a ruthless son of a bitch. He obviously thinks she took them."

"I know. And we'll catch him. I know it."

CHAPTER 35

Victor met Rubi Lee and Zeke in the sprawling, empty cafeteria of the American History Museum. They sat at a back table. Steam rose from hot cups of coffee. Victor told them they had the right woman this time.

"Her name is Daisy Taylor. She is currently living with a woman who happens to work in the same building as I do."

"Holy shit. That means you killed the wrong person," Zeke whispered.

They jumped when Victor slammed the table, causing his coffee to slosh from its cup. "Yes, Zeke, apparently that is the case. At this juncture, though, we all should be most concerned with retrieving the diamonds." Victor announced it was time for the conference call with Alex.

On the second ring, Alex answered and spewed, "Victor informed me of the latest developments, and I am not pleased. This is getting sloppy and that means this entire operation is in jeopardy. None of us can afford sloppiness, especially me. Am I clear?"

"Perfectly," answered Zeke and Rubi Lee.

"But where in the hell is this Daisy person keeping the diamonds?" Rubi Lee asked.

"That's the question. I don't know the answer," Alex said.

"We know they're not in her apartment. Perhaps she

gave them to someone else," Victor said.

Rubi Lee asked what she wanted done next.

Alex replied, "You all need to come up with a plan to get the diamonds. Victor, I expect to hear about the plan tonight at home." The phone went dead.

"She was pissed," Zeke said.

"Yes, she is. However, I have a workable plan that I'll share with her tonight."

"Are you gonna tell us?" Rubi Lee asked.

"Before I leave, I will tell you what you need to know," Victor replied.

Rubi Lee rubbed her hands together like a witch. "What if we go after the roommate and Daisy at the same time?"

"You may well have that chance. Which leads me to ask if you own any formal wear."

"Formal wear?" Rubi Lee scoffed at him. "What in the hell's that got to do with getting the diamonds back?"

"Well, do you?" Victor asked again.

"Not really," Zeke answered.

"Senator Boyd's annual Christmas party is on Saturday night. She invites all staff who work in the building. Since it is a faux pas to not attend, I feel certain the two women will be there. You two will attend as my guests."

Zeke scowled at his uncle. "Faux what?"

"A faux pas is a mistake," Victor said. "I saw Daisy outside of the Cooper Building with one of Senator Boyd's aides—a young man. They looked very...comfortable with each other. He will presumably choose her for his date. Therefore, the party will be fertile hunting ground for you two to complete the job."

"Wait. Won't there be tons of people there?" Zeke asked.

"Yes. However, I know where everyone will be seated, and you will watch over her table. Paula will text you regarding her every move."

"How will we get them with all those people?" Zeke started to doubt the success of the plan.

Victor turned to Zeke. "You are sounding doubtful, Zeke."

"Christ, Zeke. If Uncle Vic has a plan, it will work."

Victor glanced at Rubi Lee and said, "Thank you, Rubi Lee." He pulled out his wallet. "Here's some cash for you to buy appropriate party clothes."

"Party clothes? Like what?" Rubi Lee asked.

"Rubi Lee, you will buy a dress. Black is the best choice—and please, not too tight, or short. Try to find one to cover the graffiti on your arms." He turned to Zeke. "A gray or navy suit will do with a subtle tie. I'll be in touch." Victor rose from the table, took his coat, and left.

Rubi Lee stared at the wad of cash in her hand. "I guess we're going shopping!"

"I don't think we have a choice," Zeke replied and rolled his eyes. "I hate shopping."

CHAPTER 36

The cold weather added to Daisy's somber mood. She missed Erin. *This place feels like a tomb*, she thought as she loaded the cooler. The police made several visits to interview the staff about Erin, but nothing materialized from them. *At least Christmas is coming.*

Christmas meant time off from school, bright decorations, and her favorite Christmas television special: the original *Rudolph the Red-Nosed Reindeer*.

I wonder if NT likes this special? She finished up work and hustled to the police station where she was meeting Henderson and Jackie. Nick offered to go with her, and she was grateful for it. She took him up on it and texted him she was leaving soon.

See you in ten minutes, he wrote back.

Ringing phones, tapping keyboards, and people talking greeted Nick and Daisy. "I haven't been in a cop station since the summer we helped solve Uncle Clay's murder," Nick said to Daisy as she knocked on Jackie's door.

Jackie opened the door to her small office. Henderson stood and greeted them.

"Hi Daisy. Hi Nick. Thank you for coming in. Please, take a seat." Jackie motioned to two wooden chairs in her office. Daisy took off her coat and sat on the chair next to Nick.

Jackie began, "I'll cover what we've done on our end

before I begin the questioning. First, we have obtained video footage from the night Erin was found. Cameras are mounted on some of the lamps surrounding the area. However, the cameras are old and may not have picked anything. With that—"

Daisy felt her hopes rise and interrupted, "They may have recorded *something*, right?"

Jackie ignored the plaintive tone in Daisy's voice. "It's possible, but old equipment and cold weather often don't mix."

"Hopefully one of those cameras caught *something*," Daisy pressed.

Jackie asked, "Shall we begin the questioning?"

Daisy took a deep breath and nodded.

"How long have you known Erin?"

"A couple of months. I started working for her in the spring. She had been the manager for a few years," Daisy said.

"Was it out of the norm for Erin not to show up for work?"

"Yes, very much so. Erin loved her work, and she never missed a day while I've known her."

"Have you ever noticed any strange people who *only* wanted Erin to wait on them?" Jackie asked.

Daisy thought for a bit. "Erin is—I mean was—gorgeous and people liked her. But stalkers or creepers? None that I noticed."

"Where did Erin live?"

"About twenty minutes west," Daisy responded.

"How did she get to work?" Jackie asked.

"She drove."

"Did she live alone?"

"Yes."

"Boyfriend?" Jackie pressed.

"She just started to date someone. He lives out of state, though."

"Do you know his name?"

"I was afraid you were going to ask." Daisy turned her lips inward and thought. "I want to say Tim? Jim? Not sure, sorry."

"It's okay. What did she do in her off time?" Jackie asked.

"She volunteered at the local no-kill shelter. Erin loved animals. She was trained to walk the dogs there and she'd spend hours with the cats."

Daisy stretched while Jackie scribbled notes.

Henderson sensed a break was in order and asked, "Before we continue, would anyone like a drink? Water? Soda?"

Nick and Daisy asked for water; Jackie requested black coffee.

"How about we all take a quick break? I'll help with the drinks," Jackie said.

"Thanks, Jackie. We'll be back in a few," Daisy said. She and Nick took a short walk around the station's parking lot. Daisy asked, "Do you think I ought to tell Jackie I think it's strange that *two* people connected to the same bar are murdered?"

"Yes, tell her. Like you, I have a tough time believing that it's coincidental."

Daisy kicked a pebble and exhaled loudly. "Bizarre things have happened ever since I moved here. Maybe DC isn't for me, NT."

Nick stopped her and turned her to face him. He lifted her chin and his heart melted. The confusion in her eyes made him ache. "Whoa, back up Daiz. Think about what you're saying. You haven't even been here a *year* yet." *Don't smother her*, he thought to himself.

She waggled a finger in his face. "You know I'm right, though."

"I'm not about to disagree, but don't rush to any decisions, okay?" He waggled his finger back.

"Okay. Let's get this over with."

Back in the office, Jackie resumed the questioning and as she took notes, Daisy shared her observation with Jackie. "Ever since I moved here, strange things have happened."

"Such as?" Jackie asked.

"First, Ira and I were chased by someone in a van. It just so happened to be the same night I wore home a sweatshirt—one with *diamonds* sewn into it. Then I have to—"

"I'm sorry for interrupting, but did you say diamonds?" Jackie asked.

Henderson leaned in and asked, "Diamonds?"

"Yes, but I'll get to that. Anyway, then I had to move, and my new apartment gets trashed and lastly Erin is killed. Can't be coincidental, right Jackie?" Daisy's eyes pleaded with Jackie to offer reassuring words.

"Those are very unsettling experiences you had." She ignored Daisy's question about coincidence. "Tell me more about this sweatshirt."

Daisy relayed the entire story of that evening.

Jackie's hand flew down the page. "Are you sure they were diamonds?"

Henderson shook his head in disbelief.

"No. If they were fake, though, why sew them in a sweatshirt?"

Jackie pressed on. "And you said you returned the item to the bar?"

"Yes. Jaida and I did."

"Who's Jaida?"

"My friend and roommate. She was over for dinner the same night."

"I see," Jackie replied.

Daisy leaned in. "What are the odds of two people being murdered within months of each other, both of whom had ties to the same bar?"

Jackie clicked the pen in her hand and eyeballed Daisy. "Interesting question, Daisy. "I'm sure the odds are slim. But not out of the realm of possibilities. Why?"

"I was wondering if you think their murders are connected."

"I don't know. Coincidences *do* happen, Daisy." A saccharine smile spread across Jackie's full face.

Daisy placed her elbows on Jackie's desk. "Frequently in murder cases?"

Jackie's eyes lifted from the notepad and shot Daisy a withering glance. "Look, I've been a cop for over twenty years and yes, there are coincidences in murder cases." She took her glasses off and rubbed her eyes. "Is there anything else you'd like to add?"

"I hope and pray you find the horrible people who killed Erin. She was a solid, honest person who didn't deserve to die."

Jackie closed her notebook and stood. "No, she didn't.

It's been a long day. Thank you again for coming in. I'll let you know if we find out anything."

"I hope you do. Erin deserves it," Daisy said.

Outside, Nick pulled up the collar of his coat against the biting wind and dug his hands in his coat pocket.

"Jackie's demeanor toward the end of the interview was strange. Didn't it seem like she shut it down quickly?" Daisy said.

"Maybe. Remember, you *did* give her a ton of information for her to think about—especially with mentioning the diamonds."

Behind them, they heard footsteps. "Hey guys, wait up!" Henderson shuffled toward them. "Good work in there. I know answering questions is tough, especially about Erin."

"Thanks, Henderson. I hope I helped," Daisy said.

"Oh, for sure." He squeezed Daisy's arm. "Why didn't you tell me about the diamonds?"

He caught Daisy off guard. "Um. I'm not really sure. Maybe since I returned it, I felt like it was over with. But who knows?"

He looked at her and told her he wished she had told him. "But I understand your thinking," he said.

"Can we change the subject?" Daisy pleaded.

"Sure," Henderson said and turned to Nick. "I'm assuming you received your invite to the senator's party? It's a *not-miss* event."

"The big Christmas thing? I got an email about some party."

"*Thing?* It's *the* event of the season, trust me. Jackie and I are going."

Nick scrolled until he found the invite. "And here it is."

He read the invite aloud and turned to Daisy. "Daisy, will you please accompany me to the senator's Christmas party on Saturday night?" He bowed as he said it.

She stared at him. "Look at you, all dashing and formal. You *do* realize that's this week, right? A few days from now?"

"Oh. I do now." He reread the date. "Short notice, I know. Please?"

She toyed with him. "I'm not sure, I'll have to check."

Nick's arched eyebrows drew into a furrow. "Check what?"

"I may have other things going on. I'll let you know."

Henderson cut in. "Senator Boyd will know you if you don't RSVP. Don't put yourself in that position—especially since you work for her."

"Yes sir. I'll respond right now." Nick tapped his reply into the phone. He turned to Daisy. "Just so you know, I responded yes, plus one guest."

"Hopefully I can make it," she responded coyly. "I suppose I need to find a dress."

"I'll see you two on Saturday if not before."

They said goodbye to Henderson. "Up for a drink?" Daisy asked.

"Sure. It's five o'clock somewhere. Black LaSalle?"

"No. How about another place? I kind of need a break from there."

"I'm sure you do. We'll go to Queenie's, okay? It's within walking distance."

"Fine by me." They strolled down the brightly lit sidewalk.

CHAPTER 37

Senator Boyd threw the annual Christmas party at the renowned American Hotel, once known as The Old Post Office. After its postal heyday, a wealthy woman—a real estate developer—bought it. People feared for the stately, dignified building and what she planned to do to their landmark. Their concerns were quieted when she announced she was going to use the existing structure to create one of the most luxurious hotels in the DC area.

Victor secured two rooms on the eighth floor for Zeke and Rubi Lee. He instructed them to check in by four o'clock because the party started at six. "You will shower and change in your rooms. Paula will text you any information you need. I think you will enjoy this little taste of luxury. Merry Christmas," he told them.

"Holy crap, this place is unbelievable," Zeke commented, staring up at the soaring atrium.

"You're not kidding. They have *running fountains* in here. Must be nice to be this rich," Rubi Lee said.

"We can see everything from up here, just like Uncle Vic said," Rubi Lee said when they stepped out of the elevator.

"Yep. We can watch their every move," Zeke answered.

"I'm ready for a fun night, right little bro?" Rubi Lee asked. "Oh, Paula just texted. She says we need to be downstairs by seven and to hang there."

"You know it." Zeke sounded like a little kid excited about a new toy. "Time to get ready!"

Outside, the air held an icy bite—a perfect complement to the seasonal merriment drifting through the air. Carols wafted from the speakers and welcomed the guests as they descended steps that were adorned with colorfully lit dwarf Christmas trees. Attendees spun through the giant glass revolving door into the opulent and stunning lobby. Four multi-tiered crystal chandeliers the size of small cumulus clouds hung in the soaring atrium. A tastefully decorated Christmas tree stood twenty feet high. Partygoers waited patiently at the two busy bars at both ends of the lobby. A sitting area the size of an Olympic pool commanded attention where countless royal blue and cream plaid couches sat upon enormous colorful rugs. Soft jazz floated from a baby grand piano. Elegantly dressed guests enjoyed passed hors d'oeuvres and sipped a variety of drinks.

Nick and Winston arrived at the party a few minutes after it started.

"Wow, this place is amazing," Nick said as he gaped at the magnificence of the building. "Do you see Daisy or Jaida anywhere?"

They both scanned the crowd. "Not yet. I texted her when we left and she said they were running a little late. She'll text when they get here. Let's get a drink," Winston replied.

They strolled around, munched on delicious hors d'oeuvres, and absorbed the scene.

"Man, the bigwigs go all out!" Nick remarked.

"They have the cash for it. Or shall I say, the taxpayers do!"

"I agree. Cheers!"

A few minutes later, Winston's phone buzzed. "They're here."

At the front door, more guests were arriving, Jaida and Daisy among them. Jaida was a stunner in a gold sheath floor-length dress. Her mocha skin glowed like the dress. Her dark curls were a fusion of braids and loose tendrils twisted into a relaxed updo. Sparkling sapphire earrings were a subtle and classic touch to her ensemble.

Daisy wore a strapless, black satin dress with thin silver threading patterned throughout the bodice. Her hair flowed in soft waves past her shoulders. A thin, silver jeweled headband was a perfect balance to her dress. Exquisite radiance emanated from her.

I knew she was beautiful, but wow. Nick ran his eyes up and down Daisy several times.

"You guys look great," Nick said, "like *really* great."

Daisy basked in his overt ogling. "Thank you. You do too," Daisy responded and hugged him. A spark made them jump. "Static electricity I guess?" Daisy tried. They both knew better.

"Well, don't you guys clean up nicely!" Jaida said and kissed Winston. "Not too bad for rented tuxedos!"

"Would you ladies like a drink?" Winston asked.

"Absolutely!" Daisy said.

Nick held his arm out for Daisy and zigzagged through the crowd.

At the bar, Daisy scanned the crowd. "Seems like all of DC is here."

Nick sipped his drink. "I know. I heard talk in the office that Senator Boyd's Christmas party is epic. It looks like everyone *is* here."

"Apparently," she answered. "Think a lot of VIPs are here?"

"Since ninety percent of the people here *think* they're VIPs, the answer is yes. Besides, they aren't going to turn down free food and drink!"

"Neither are we!"

The band opened with Glenn Miller's "In the Mood." Soon, people filled the dance floor including Daisy, Nick, Jaida, and Winston. They stepped back and watched Henderson joyfully twirl Jackie around the dance floor.

"You kids having fun?" Henderson asked when they all returned to the table they shared.

"Absolutely! How about you?" Nick said.

"Certainly. I spun Jackie around the dance floor, and she was most impressed with my moves," Henderson said.

"Oh, that was you? I thought I was dancing with Fred Astaire!" Jackie teased.

"Darn close!"

After Senator Boyd wished all the guests a wonderful holiday season, Henderson stood from the table and announced he was off in search of surf and turf. "Come on Jackie, time to eat! You all need to get some food too. Don't miss out!"

"We wouldn't dream of it, Henderson," Nick said. He took Daisy's hand and stood. "I'm starving. Are you ready to eat?"

"Oh yes. I didn't eat much today on purpose."

Nick asked Jaida and Winston if they wanted to join.

"Sure. The food looks spectacular," Jaida commented, eyeing the three sumptuous buffets loaded with food from all corners of the earth.

"I'm ready," Winston said and rubbed his stomach. "I can't remember if I even ate today!"

"Typical," Jaida teased him as they followed Nick and Daisy.

Fifty feet away, Victor, Rubi Lee, and Zeke watched Daisy and her friends return to their table with dinner.

Bitterness and loathing simmered in Rubi Lee. *I hate her and her dipshit friends. None of them'll ever know what it's like to live hand to mouth, not go to college, not be better.* She threw down the last sip of her drink. "Don't worry Uncle Vic, we'll take care of her and her friends."

"Good. You have no choice." Victor disappeared into the sea of partygoers.

* * *

Toward the end of the night, Daisy reached over and squeezed Nick's hand. "This was really fun. I need to use the ladies' room. I'll be back."

"Sure thing," Nick said.

"Girls, I'm headed to the bathroom. Anyone else need to go?" Daisy looked at Jaida and Jackie.

"Not me, thanks," Jackie said.

"I'll go," Jaida said.

When they left the table, Jackie and Henderson made small talk with Winston and Nick while enjoying the food.

"Zeke, Paula just texted. Daisy and her friend are headed our way."

Rubi Lee and Zeke hustled down the stairs to the bathrooms at the end of the hallway. She told Zeke to wait in the men's room adjacent to the women's restroom. Tucked in the shadows, Rubi Lee watched Daisy and Jaida meander down the long marble hallway toward her. Suddenly Jaida stopped; Rubi Lee saw her say something to Daisy then walk back toward the party. Rubi Lee dashed across the hall, entered the bathroom, and waited in a stall.

Daisy entered the opulent bathroom and placed her drink on the sink before entering the stall. She pumped out the gardenia-scented hand soap and washed her hands. Behind her, a stall door swung open. Daisy glanced up from the sink and saw a petite dark-haired woman in the mirror. Daisy offered a smile as the woman extended a thin, tattooed arm to turn on the water. Her sleeveless evening dress did nothing to hide the rainbow of images twirling up her arms.

"Your tattoos are pretty," Daisy remarked as she dried her hands. Something about her awakened Daisy's memory.

"Oh, thanks. Kind of been collecting them," Rubi Lee responded, but gave Daisy no eye contact.

"I can tell." Daisy looked at her harder. "I feel like I've seen you around. Maybe at the Black LaSalle?"

"I don't think so."

Daisy finished up quickly. "Just a guess. Anyway, have a good night." She turned and started to walk toward the door.

"Yeah, I will."

Daisy did not get far. A hand grabbed her by the hair and violently snapped Daisy's head back. "You're not going anywhere!" The tattooed woman wrapped her forearm around Daisy's neck in a surprisingly powerful grip.

"Get *off* me!" Daisy yelled and slammed her elbow into

the woman's ribcage. A sharp exhale was music to Daisy's ears. She twisted around and slammed the woman into the marble sink. "Motherfucker!" The woman's eyes rolled back in pain.

Daisy fumbled for her phone and called Jaida. She was only steps from the door when her attacker shoved Daisy with such force her phone flew from her hand and clacked across the floor.

"Bitch! I'm gonna *kill* you!" The woman grabbed Daisy's head and headbutted her. Daisy's head snapped back into a large mirror. Glass shards exploded from the mirror. Blood ran from the back of Daisy's head. Stars flashed in front of her.

Daisy snatched a decorative vase from a table. She screamed and swung it at the woman—a split second too late. She only nicked the side of her neck. Infuriated, the woman cracked Daisy's jaw with a perfectly placed uppercut.

Daisy crumpled to the floor, out cold. Rubi Lee spat on her. "Bitch."

CHAPTER 38

"Where are Daisy and Jaida?" Henderson asked as he sat back down at their table with a plate of filet and shrimp cocktail.

"They went to the bathroom," Nick said.

"Ah, got it." He picked up a pink shrimp and popped it in his mouth. "Mmm, is that good."

Jaida returned and grabbed her handbag off the table. "Be right back."

Halfway to the bathroom, Jaida's phone buzzed—Daisy. She answered, but all she heard was screaming, yelling, and banging. "Daisy! *Daisy!* What's going on?" Jaida yelled but got no response. "Daisy! What's going on?" With the phone pressed to her ear, Jaida raced to the far end of the hall in time to see a bloodied Daisy being dragged out of the bathroom by a woman. A tall man darted from the steps to help her.

"Pick her up! We have to get her in the elevator to get the hell outta here!" Jaida heard the woman yell. He ran over and clumsily lifted Daisy from the floor.

"Daisy!" Jaida screamed and ran toward them. "Hey, stop! *Stop!*"

Rubi Lee whipped around with her knife ready. She pressed it to Daisy's throat and threatened, "You come any closer, I'll cut this bitch up!"

Jaida looked at the glowing orb of the elevator light. One floor until the doors opened and Daisy disappeared.

By the crazed look in her eyes and steady hand, Jaida knew this woman meant business. *It's the same people from the airport!* Jaida thought as she backed away, palms up. "Fine, fine. I'll stay right here. I won't come any closer. Please don't hurt her."

"Shut the fuck up. I'll do whatever I want with her."

Ding! Rubi Lee followed Zeke into the elevator. Jaida locked eyes with her. The woman took her knife and made a slicing motion across her neck.

* * *

Nick had gotten restless. "Hey Win, I know women take a long time in the bathroom, but this seems *really* long."

"I'm sure they're gabbing, but let's go anyway." Down the hall they went in search of Daisy and Jaida.

Around the bend they saw a man and a woman backing into the elevator. Jaida was standing with her hands held up. Nick's heart stopped in his chest. Daisy was flung over the man's shoulder; her head bobbed like a puppet's. The elevator stopped on the ground floor. Rubi Lee and Zeke hustled out.

"Daisy! Stop! Hey you, stop!" Nick yelled and they ran toward the elevator. "What the hell is going on, Jaida? Who are those people?"

Jaida shook like a bowl of jelly when she answered Nick.

"What the *hell*? She's been *kidnapped*? We have to get Daisy!" Nick yelled. "We're losing time!"

Winston told Nick, "I'll go back to the table and tell

Jackie and Henderson. But keep your phone accessible!" Winston yelled.

Nick and Jaida ran outside to see Rubi Lee and Zeke hustling toward a beaten-up white van parked on a one-way street behind the hotel. He called Winston, "*Get out front now!* They're dragging her into a white van!"

Oh shit! A white van! Nick took off running after the van.

"I'm getting a taxi! Keep me in the loop!" Jaida yelled at Nick.

Breathless, Winston explained, "We have to get out of here! Nick and I just saw Daisy being carried into an elevator by two people!"

"What do you mean, *carried*?" Henderson asked.

"Are you sure that's what you saw?" Jackie asked.

"Yes! She was slung over some guy's shoulder! She was all bloody!"

Immediately, Henderson's police training kicked in and he asked for Winston's number. "I'll track you." He and Jackie headed to the front door.

I'll get our coats. I'll see you out front!" Jackie said to Henderson.

* * *

The guests were oblivious to the mayhem occurring outside.

"You look stunning as always, Senator," Judge McKinney observed as Alex greeted him. A crimson floor-length dress wrapped around her athletic body and accentuated her toned shoulders. Her teardrop diamond earrings garnered much attention and were the perfect addition. "Thank you,

Judge."

"As always, this is a wonderful party," Judge McKinney said to the senator, dabbing sweat from his brow. "I hope this band keeps playing. I ate so much I need to keep dancing!"

"Judge, if anyone likes a good party, it's you. You're the champion of enjoying yourself—sometimes a little too much."

"You're so right, madam. The apps are delicious, where did you get them?"

"The grocery store, where else?" she shot back.

Alex caught her husband's eye. She excused herself from the judge and mingled through the crowd until she met up with him.

"Enjoying the party?" she asked him.

"I always enjoy a good party as long as there is plenty of food and booze," Victor responded.

"Don't drink like a fish. You can't afford to make any mistakes—especially tonight."

"Don't worry, Alexandra." He shook his cell phone. "I've got everything under control. My operatives are in the building, and they'll send a signal when they have her."

Alex pasted on her fake senator smile and nodded to guests walking by. Between clenched teeth she said, "Those two idiots better not screw up again otherwise we will have to put an end to our relationship. An *irrevocable* end."

Victor patted Alex's shoulder and gave her a kiss. "Just keep your cell phone on. I'll text you the code word *Stella* when it's done."

Fifteen minutes later, as Alex was mingling, her phone vibrated. She politely excused herself from her and checked her phone. *Stella. Oh Victor, you never disappoint.*

At the bar, she smiled broadly as she ordered a double martini.

"Judging by the smile on your face, you're in a good mood," Jake noted.

"What's not to be happy about? A great party, lots of friends, and I just received some wonderful news. Nice suit," she commented, looking at Jake's blinking Christmas suit.

"I wore it just for you. Great news, huh? Cheers!"

"Eat, drink, and be merry, Jake!" Alex sauntered away to her table where other bigwigs relished their after-dinner drinks. She was greeted with predictable compliments.

"Hell of a party, Senator!"

"You outdo yourself every year!"

"Can't wait till next year!"

"I'm glad you all are having fun. After all, tis the season! Cheers!" However, her fun was dashed when she looked down at the new message on her phone. *Son of a bitch.*

CHAPTER 39

Nick raced to the ground floor first and charged through the door. A fresh coat of snow had fallen, and more floated down from the sky. He saw new footprints heading off to his right. Winston arrived seconds later and told him Henderson was helping to find her.

"Jesus Win, someone took her!" Nick was ready to vomit.

"I know!" He pointed to the footprints.

They followed the prints and when they turned the corner, an old beaten-up white van was hastily trying to pull out of a tight parking spot. It wedged itself free, spun out on the snow-covered road, and plowed down the one-way street. Nick and Winston were in its crosshairs.

"Jump!" Winston grabbed Nick's collar and pulled him out of the way. "We need a car!" They ran for the front of the hotel, the same way the van went.

"Come on! The street is a one-way and there is only one way out!"

The van was like a bull in a china shop, smashing into parked vehicles and ripping side mirrors off in its wake.

The valet attendants ran over and were riveted by the commotion. Winston took advantage of their inattention and grabbed a set of keys from the valet station. He hit the unlock button and to his left, a horn honked, and lights flicked on.

"Nick! Get the hell in the car!" He pointed. "Strap on the seatbelt!" He cut the wheel hard to the left and the car bounced off two parked cars.

"Stop! Stop!" the attendants yelled, as they chased them.

"Sorry fellas!" Winston yelled and punched the gas.

Seconds later the white van sped past with its rear bumper hanging loose, dragging on the ground.

Winston floored it and the car pitched blindly into traffic, forcing several cars to swerve out of the way.

Nick's hands hurt from gripping the dashboard. He hung on for dear life and yelled, "Win, watch out!"

"Hang on!" Win screamed as he ran a red light and just missed nailing a metro bus.

"Can you see the van, Nick?"

"Three cars ahead! Watch out!"

Winston jerked the wheel left then right, narrowly missing a stopped taxi.

Winston handed Nick his phone and ordered him to call Henderson. The phone flew from his hand when Winston slammed on the brakes to avoid hitting a bus. They were rear-ended and thrust forward.

Nick hit his head on the windshield and felt a trickle of blood. He wiped it away with his hand.

"You all right?" Winston asked.

"Fine! Keep going! We have to get Daisy!" Winston and Nick sped away in hot pursuit. From the floor, Winston's phone vibrated.

"Are you all okay? What the hell is going on?" Jackie asked.

Nick filled her in on their chase. "I'll be in touch!"

* * *

Daisy came to as the van sped off. Her head throbbed; her hands were cut and bloodied. Dread and fear threatened to smother her. *What is going on? God help me!* Survival mode kicked in and she fought to free herself from the iron grip of her captor, but he was too strong. The van suddenly careened out of control. Daisy screamed as she and Zeke were tossed around in the back like ragdolls as the van weaved in and out of traffic.

"Watch what you're doing!" Zeke screamed at Rubi Lee.

"Shut up!" she shrilled and clung to the wheel, trying to control the van on the slippery road.

Bang! Rubi Lee smashed into the back of a smart car. Zeke bellowed at her to go around it. The van bucked as she threw it into reverse, backed up, then plowed past. The little car had no chance and was shoved aside like an unwanted toy.

The sudden lurch caused Zeke's grip on Daisy to weaken. Her strength and wits temporarily restored, Daisy took full advantage of this. She spun around on the seat and delivered a powerful, well-placed knee to Zeke's groin. Daisy grabbed the door handle and yanked it open. The blast of frigid air stunned her.

She screamed as a hand jerked her backward. With all her weight, she lunged forward and propelled herself out of the van. She felt the back of her dress rip, but she didn't care. She was in a fight for her life. She sprinted over frozen ground when she realized she was just outside Margaux Ford Park. *Thank God! The park! Get to the office!* Her entire body screamed in pain, but adrenaline pumped through her to the point where she did not feel the cold on her feet. She heard footsteps and labored breathing behind her. She quickened her pace.

"Oh no you don't!" Zeke yelled as he dove to tackle her. A stream of expletives left his mouth as he slipped and fell.

Rubi Lee flung the van into park and leaped out. She hoped to catch Daisy, but Daisy was quicker and made it through the entrance to the park. Fortunately, Daisy knew the pathways and ran toward the center of the park.

Rubi Lee caught up to Zeke and yelled at him, "You idiot! Ya lost her!"

"Just shut the fuck up!" He panted and looked down. "I'll follow the footprints. You get the van!"

Rubi Lee ran back to the van, jumped in, and sped over the sidewalk through the gates to the park. One taillight was broken, one of the headlights like a human eye hanging from its face, but it ran. Rubi Lee kept her eyes on the path in front of her until she spotted Zeke, who had caught Daisy. *Yes! Good work, little bro!*

"You thought you'd escape from us?" Zeke panted into Daisy's ear as he watched the one-eyed van bump over the turf toward them.

She didn't respond. Daisy knew he wanted to see her fear, smell it. Yielding to them was out of the question. She stayed calm and tried to predict what these two cretins were going to do. Daisy had to figure out how to buy time.

"Aw, your party dress is ripped and your hair is a mess. Poor baby." Rubi Lee tsked. "Guess you won't be looking too pretty for your boyfriend. But it won't matter, because he ain't ever gonna see you again, right Zeke?"

Daisy leveled her breathing and stared at the pale,

skinny shrew-like woman in front of her. "I know where I've seen you," she whispered.

"Oh yeah, where?" Rubi Lee said.

"At the bar where I work," Daisy panted. "What do you want with me?"

"You know damn well what we want. We thought the other redhead had the diamonds, but she didn't," Zeke said.

Daisy's mind kicked into high gear. *The other redhead? Erin! They killed her!* It came tumbling out of her mouth: "*You* killed her! Why? What did she do to you?" Rage filled her.

"*We* technically didn't kill her. But we did watch, and it was entertaining."

Daisy struggled to keep from throwing up. "What do you want from me?"

"Don't play dumb with us. You know damn well what we want!" Zeke yelled.

"What're you deaf? I already told you I DON'T know!" Daisy's rage stomped out her fear.

Rubi Lee rolled her eyes. "You're forcing me to do this." She pulled out her gun and pointed it at her head. "Let me spell it out for you. You took the diamonds from the sweatshirt. We want them back. Get it?"

Daisy's mind flipped like the pages in a cartoon sketchbook.

All the pieces fell into place: the chase with Ira, the sweatshirt, the break-in, Erin's murder. She thought, *Please God, help me buy time.* She knew if these two soulless people killed Erin, they would kill her too.

"You're not going to get away with this, trust me." Daisy glared back. She fought off the weakness she felt.

"Oh yeah? You willing to bet your life on that?" Rubi Lee hissed.

"Yes. I. Am. You piece of shit."

Rubi Lee looked at Zeke. "You hear her? This bitch has an attitude." Rubi Lee slapped Daisy across the face. Daisy spit out blood but kept a poker face. "I'll go and make sure no one's near the van. Stay here. I'll text you." Rubi Lee trudged off.

Daisy struggled to ignore the cold. Her face stung from the slap, but she stayed calm. Zeke shifted his stance from one foot to the other. *Good, he's cold too*, Daisy thought. She hoped the cold would lessen his vice-like grip on her. *Please God, let everyone be looking for me*, she prayed. *Be positive. They're coming for you.*

When Zeke's phone buzzed, he threatened, "Don't even think about runnin'. I'll hunt you down like a wounded animal, understand?" He released one arm and pulled his phone from his pocket. He hung up and grunted, "Let's go."

Daisy's hope of being rescued eroded with each step across the frozen ground. The white van sat forty yards away like a monster waiting for its prey.

CHAPTER 40

"There it is! Going into the park!" Nick yelled and pointed. Poor visibility and snowy roads caused the car to fishtail dangerously. The van turned into the park. His heart galloped in his chest. "Hurry up!"

Winston eased up on the gas to survey the scene.

Nick whipped his face to Winston. "Why are you slowing down? We have to get her!"

"Nick, we need to stay calm. We don't know if those people are armed. We need a plan. That's the one way we can help Daisy." Winston killed the lights and followed the van's tracks. *Jesus, it's the van from the airport*, Winston thought. *This is very bad.*

Roughly a hundred yards away, Zeke held Daisy by the hair and Rubi Lee shuffled to the van. Visions of slasher movies ran through Nick's head.

"Daisy! I can't sit here!" Nick undid his seatbelt and had one foot out the door when Winston grabbed him.

"Nick, *stop!* They don't know we're here and if they find out, they may kill her. And like I said, they could be armed. We need to stay calm and think this through."

"You're *killin'* me, Win!"

"I'm sorry. More importantly, we can't panic."

Nick looked at him like he had five heads. "*Don't panic?* How can I *not* panic with her out there?"

"I'm sorry. But you need to trust me with this, okay?"

"What? You've been involved with a hostage situation before? How the hell do you know what to do?" Nick yelled.

Winston looked hard at his friend. "Nick, just *trust* me."

Something in Winston's tone caused Nick to listen. "Fine. So what do we do now? Where's Jaida?"

"She's on her way and she called the police."

"Do you have my phone?"

Nick handed it to him, tapped quickly, and gave it back. "Now we wait."

"*Wait?* Wait, for what?" Nick's panic raced like a trapped bird.

"We wait for help. Henderson and Jackie now know we're here. They're going to secure backup."

"You sure?"

"Yes. If we confront those people, they may kill us, and I'm not planning on being dead for a while, man." He smiled. "Help is on its way." Winston patted Nick on the back.

Nick was crawling out of his skin. Sweat poured down his back and his heart raced.

"I gotta get out of this rolling sauna." Outside, he paced in small circles in the snow; terrifying scenarios ran through his head. He glanced back at Winston who was checking his phone. *Now's your chance. I just got her back in my life.* He turned around and looked one last time at his friend.

* * *

Out front, Henderson bellowed at a quivering attendant, "What do you mean there is no valet service?!"

"Sorry sir, apparently someone stole a car and smashed

into several others. The police have shut us down while they are sorting it out," the attendant stammered.

Henderson looked out into the parking lot and saw a police officer. He grabbed Jackie's hand and they trotted over.

Henderson asked the officer, whom he knew, "Jeff, what happened here?"

"Hello sir, ma'am. Allegedly, two men stole a car and crashed into several other vehicles and sped away. Crazy."

Jackie asked, "Were they young men, one tall and the other wearing glasses? Evening clothes?"

The officer checked his notes. "Yes, that is the description the attendant gave me."

Jackie continued, "We know them. We need to get to where they are. So, we're taking your squad car." She held out her hand.

He put the keys in her hand. "Yes ma'am! Good luck!"

Jackie handed Henderson the keys. "I'll wait here."

"Okay, be right back."

Henderson pulled up. "Ready?"

"Yup!" she replied.

He flipped on the sirens, lights and punched the gas hard. "Feels like old times!" Henderson tossed Jackie his phone and asked her to locate Nick and Winston on the tracking app.

"It looks like they're at Margaux Ford Park. Get going!" Jackie replied.

"Buckle up, Jackie, I ain't messing around!"

At the park, Henderson fishtailed outside the office and jammed the car into park. In the office, Henderson and Jackie hatched a plan: Henderson would search for the others, she would wait for backup.

"Roger. I'll be in touch!" He threw on his parka overtop his evening coat.

* * *

Jaida barely escaped the mayhem in time. Outside in the cold, she hailed a cab and texted Winston she was outside the hotel.

Winston shot back he and Nick were in hot pursuit of a white van heading toward Margaux Ford Park. *I knew it was the same van. Please God, help us save Daisy!* she thought as she responded to Winston.

Inside the cab, Jaida hollered at the driver to step on it. "GO! We can't waste time!" Jaida hollered.

The driver hit the gas and spun out.

"Jesus Christ! Just get me to the north gate of Margaux Ford Park without killing us!"

His eyes lit up like a kid at Christmas who got a puppy from Santa. "Damn, bring it on! I always wanted to drive like I was in a cop chase!"

Jaida pulled out her phone and said, "It's Campbell. Get me a night scope and a long range, ASAP! Meet me at the north gate of Margaux Ford Park in ten minutes. Don't be late! One more thing, boots and a parka . . . because I'm in a cocktail dress and it's snowing!"

The car swerved to a stop at the north entrance. "Man, I haven't had that much fun driving in forever!"

Jaida threw several twenties at him. "Thanks, and Merry Christmas!"

"Merry Christmas to you!"

Frigid air bit at her as she picked her way over the snowy ground. According to her phone, Winston and Nick were at the opposite side of the park. She knew that advancing from the opposite side gave her better position. She called Winston to see if they found Daisy. He told her she was within eyeshot but her situation looked dire.

"What the hell does that mean?" She saw headlights and waved. "I'll call you right back." She ran to the truck and someone handed her the equipment.

"Night scope, long range?" she questioned as she took off her shoes and grabbed the boots from her colleague.

"Yes, just as you requested. Here's the parka. By the way, nice dress."

"Thanks, I guess. Rather than ogling me, you need to leave and wait for orders."

"Yes ma'am!"

She called Winston back. "What's the situation?"

"Same as before. Daisy is being held captive and from my vantage point, the three of them appear to be talking. No doubt it's the same van and perps from the airport."

"I knew it! I just *knew* it." For a split second, Jaida was wracked with guilt. "We have to do something, Win. She could die, and I don't want her blood on my hands," Jaida replied.

"Hell no. I called the cops and asked Henderson to secure backup. For now though, I'm trying to keep Nick from doing something stupid."

"Please do. I'm sure he is flipping out, right?"

"Big time. It'll be even worse when he realizes what is *really* going on with you and me."

"Understandable," she squinted at a light a block away.

"I think I see the light in the park office. I'll make my way over and lock into position."

"Okay, you sure you're going to be okay?" Winston asked.

"Oh yeah, I'm more than okay," Jaida replied, snapping the night scope in place.

"Okay, good. When we— Nick! Get the hell back here!" Winston yelled. "*Shit! Shit! Shit!* He just took off toward the perps! Stick to your plan!" Winston yelled into the phone. "Get back here, man! They could kill you!" Winston yelled and ran after him.

"I don't care! I love her and I have to save her!" Nick yelled and plunged forward into the park, his quarry in his crosshairs.

CHAPTER 41

We have a situation . . . get out here ASAP.

Alex shook her head and steadied her breathing. *Stay calm, you have no choice.* She replied, *Where are u?*

Victor responded, *Back of the hotel . . . third black SUV parked to the left of the Dumpster.*

On my way.

Alex Boyd rose from the table and headed toward to the back of the hotel. Jake was returning from the bar and asked her if she was okay.

"I'm fine. I just need a fix," she laughed and pulled out a pack of cigarettes from her bag.

"Okay, 'cause you look rattled," he replied.

"I'll be back," she lied. Looking around, she exited from the side door and found the SUV. Victor opened the door for Alex. "What in the *hell* is going on?" she shot at Victor. The SUV lurched forward and raced off into the night.

"Apparently, they saw Zeke and Rubi Lee leave with Daisy."

"How did this *happen*?" she hissed. "Jesus Christ, Victor."

"Darling, please stay calm. It does not matter *how* this happened. What matters is that we take care of it."

"You damn well better be prepared to take care of it—to the point of elimination. Got it?"

"Yes, I'm prepared," Victor answered, pulling his coat aside to reveal a gleaming Glock 19.

* * *

Daisy's energy started to deplete. Her feet were frozen, and her thoughts were cloudy. *Am I hallucinating or do I hear sirens?*

"Oh man, cops are comin'! We need to get her out of here!" Zeke yelled.

"Look! I see a light through the trees over there!" Rubi Lee pointed toward a faint light.

Daisy almost wept with relief at the lovely shriek of sirens.

"What's the quickest way?" Zeke said.

Daisy spoke up. "I know how to—"

"Shut up! No one asked you!" Rubi Lee spat at her. She waved a small stiletto blade in the air. "I'll warn ya again, if you talk, I'm gonna cutchew!"

"We need to get outta here, now!" Zeke yelled.

Daisy saw her opening and dug deep for energy. "Do you mean the park office? There's a garage there too."

Zeke and Rubi Lee looked at each other, then turned to Daisy. *Good, keep buying time*, she thought.

"Yeah, whatever the hell it is." Zeke narrowed his eyes at Daisy.

"Cut through the middle." Daisy pointed up ahead of where they stood. As he looked, Zeke was blindsided and knocked to the ground by a crazed Nick. Pain exploded in Zeke's leg as he crumbled to the ground, screaming. He tried to roll over, but the pain momentarily controlled him. Nick straddled him and rained an assault of punches to Zeke's head.

"You bastard, leave her alone or I'll *fucking* kill you!" Nick bellowed and kept pummeling Zeke until he heard Rubi Lee.

"Stop or I'll slice her throat!"

Nick looked up and saw the glint of a blade resting against Daisy's pulsating throat. Nick howled as Zeke used an old wrestling move and reversed positions. All two hundred pounds landed on his right shoulder. Enraged, Zeke pounded his large tattooed fists into Nick's head. Blood flew from Nick's ear and flecked the white snow.

"Leave him alone!" Daisy cried. "He didn't do anything to you!"

From behind, Rubi Lee hissed, "No one gets away with hurtin' my little brother, got it?" The cold tip of the knife found its way into Daisy's skin.

"Please," Daisy gasped. "I'll go with you if you let Nick go. Please. You need me alive to help you. Just let him go."

With Nick squirming under him, Zeke looked at his sister and gasped, "She's right. She's worth more to us alive than dead."

Rubi Lee held Daisy with one arm and slid the blade down Daisy's spine with the other. "You try anything, I'll plunge this into your kidneys."

Daisy knew it was fight or flight time. She opened her mouth and sank her teeth into Rubi Lee's arm. Stunned, Rubi Lee released Daisy. She wheeled around and landed a perfect hook into Rubi Lee's face. *Crack!* Blood and teeth flew from her thin-lipped mouth. Rubi Lee stumbled back into the snow. Daisy's hand ached, but it wasn't over. She lunged at Rubi Lee who rolled away and reached into the top of her dress. Nick saw the glint of metal before Daisy.

"Daisy, she has a gun!" Nick screamed.

It was life or death for her and Nick. Daisy looked at her beloved and bloodied friend. With a primal scream, she charged at Rubi Lee who was frantically trying to cock the weapon. Rubi Lee was too quick—she cocked the gun and pointed it at Daisy.

* * *

The golf cart sputtered to life after a few stomps on the pedal. Henderson zipped up the plastic siding to block the cold of the night. He punched the red button on the dash and the garage door rose. He flicked on the headlights and propelled the cart into the snow, looking for Nick's location. The thumping of his heart and the bad feeling deep inside his chest scared the hell out of him.

As Henderson rounded a corner, he saw the beaten-up van parked on the circular walkway around a memorial garden. The doors gaped, one headlight hanging by wires. He saw a figure carefully approaching the van from behind. Henderson squinted harder—it was Winston, who gave him a thumbs-up and pointed at an area near the Welcome Center's office. Henderson saw with horror the predicament Nick and Daisy were tangled in. He beckoned Winston over to his cart.

"Just what *in the hell* is goin' on here?" Henderson whispered to Winston, who slid onto the seat next to him.

"Daisy got snatched at the party. We followed the van out here where Nick charged out after her before I could do anything!" Winston explained.

"Well, *we're* gonna do *somethin'* to save those two!" Henderson commanded. "Follow me from behind, but stay crouched down so the perps don't see you, got it?"

Winston nodded. "Loud and clear. When you get there, I'll stay here, and you distract them."

The tires spun under Henderson's stomp on the gas pedal. Behind the cart, Winston tried to stay low and keep his balance on the slick ground. Diesel fumes made him gag.

From the icy blackness, they all heard it: the sound of the golf cart. "Put the weapon down!" All four heads swiveled toward the headlights.

Winston stayed crouched behind the cart. "What's goin' on here?" Henderson asked from the driver's seat.

"This!" Rubi Lee whipped her gun around and pulled the trigger. The hot orange flash, the scream of pain.

"Henderson!" Daisy's world suddenly froze. She watched her dear friend grab his chest and crumble to the ground.

"You *bitch*!" A primitive animal-like surge came over Daisy. She turned and body-slammed Rubi Lee. The gun flew like a grenade into the darkness toward the van. Rubi Lee skittered across the ground like a crab, trying to escape. Daisy chased her and stomped on her back and was ready to land another when Nick grabbed her and held her tight.

"Let me *go*! She shot Henderson!" Daisy screamed and flailed.

Winston crouched over a shocked Henderson and yelled, "Stop! Forget about them! The cops'll get them! I'll take care of Henderson! You two go to the park office where you can shelter. I'll tell the authorities to look for a white van!" Winston grabbed handfuls of snow and held it against the bloody hole in Henderson's shoulder.

"Help me, man." Henderson gripped Winston with his good hand. "Good Lord, help me. The pain—oh Win, the pain!" Henderson began to shake.

"Stay calm. I got you, Henderson. Everything is going to be okay. Just stay calm." Winston helped Henderson off the ground and into the cart. "I called 911. They're on their way."

"Don't leave me!" Henderson begged.

"I'm here, Henderson. I'm not going anywhere."

* * *

Zeke hobbled to the van and yelled, "Forget about the gun! Get in the van and go after them!" He watched Nick and Daisy disappear in the swirling snow.

"Get in!" Rubi Lee screamed at him.

"I'm tryin', my knee's broke!" Zeke slid the side door open and collapsed inside. Rubi Lee stepped on the gas, following the footprints Nick and Daisy left in the snow.

Daisy and Nick limped past the Susan B. Anthony statue. He held her tightly. The snow slowed their pace. The office was not far away, but to their broken bodies, the distance felt like a marathon.

"Daisy, we can get help in the office," Nick tried to reassure her. He held her tightly around the waist with her arm slung across his shoulders. Her breath became labored. "Come on, Daiz, stay with me! Only a few more feet."

Breathlessly, she replied, "I hear sirens." She looked toward the center of the park where the night sky was bisected by blue and red lights. "I need to stop for a sec." She paused, then to Nick's horror, collapsed on the ground.

"Daisy! Oh my God! NO!"

She wrapped her cut-up hands around her throbbing, bloody head and whispered, "I don't think I can make it. You go on. I can wait here."

"Daisy, I'm not leaving you, ever." He knelt and gingerly hoisted Daisy from her fetal position. His shoulder shrieked with pain when he pulled her close to his chest. Blood from her head stained his shirt. He knew she was perilously close to losing consciousness due to blood loss. Footing was treacherous as he carried her over the bumpy, white earth. *Please let her be okay. Please, God.* Adrenaline pounded through his body and pushed his throbbing legs closer to the park's office. *Don't slip, Nick. Stay calm and go slowly.*

Nick prayed Henderson's office was unlocked. *Thank God!* He pushed the door open and fumbled blindly for a light switch. He flicked on the light and gently placed Daisy on the well-worn woolen chair by the desk. He searched the closet and found a blanket he wrapped around Daisy's shivering, exposed shoulders. In the small bathroom, he grabbed a few towels and wrapped her feet.

"This is a nightmare, NT," Daisy whispered. "Henderson's dead."

"He's going to be okay—I promise." Nausea washed over Nick as Daisy's head drooped down. "Don't sleep! Stay with me, Daiz! We're gonna be okay." *Please God, help us. Don't let her die!* Salty tears slid down his face as he stroked her forehead.

Daisy laid her head back and closed her eyes, "NT, I'm so tired."

He knew the signs of a concussion. "No, no, don't sleep! Stay awake Daiz, stay with me. I'll get us out of this." He fought to keep the panic out of his voice.

"Promise?" she asked, sleep heavy in her voice.

"Yes. I'm calling now." He picked up the receiver from the phone and dialed 911. But it was dead. The cord had been severed.

"What the . . . ?" he said aloud.

"Looking for this?"

He turned to his left and saw a figure standing in the door, dangling the other half of the cord.

"Jackie! Oh, thank God! We need help!"

"No, Nick. That is not going to happen. We have you right where we want you," Jackie replied.

He looked at her, confusion swirling in his brain. "We? What do you . . . ?" A loud slam made Nick jump. Battered, Rubi Lee looked like she went ten rounds in a boxing ring. Zeke hobbled in after her.

"You fuckers are ours now!" She pulled her gun out. "You thought you were safe? Hardly!" She cackled. "You ain't goin' anywhere except to an early grave. Same with your bitch girlfriend. Pick her up, Zeke." Rubi Lee squeezed the trigger and shot a bullet into the wall several feet from where Daisy sat.

Daisy whimpered at the blast as Nick jumped to shield her. "Are you insane?! You could have killed her!"

"Back off, Romeo, or I'll make *you* squeeze a bullet into her brain!" Rubi Lee shoved him into the desk chair.

Zeke hobbled over and pulled Daisy out of the chair. He dragged her limp body across the floor like a stuffed animal.

Nick's blood pumped through his hammering heart; his

body was electrified. He leaped out of the desk chair to stop Zeke, but Rubi Lee cocked the gun.

"Hold it right there."

He turned to Jackie for help. "Jackie?" he cried out. "What's going on? I thought you—"

Speechless and terrified, Nick stared at Jackie, then Rubi Lee and back to Jackie.

"*Jackie?* Who the *fuck* is *Jackie*?" Rubi Lee yelled, eyes darting back and forth. "Your name's Paula!"

Jackie's mind raced. She knew Rubi Lee would not hesitate to pull the trigger and shoot all of them. She thought quickly. "Jackie's a nickname," she lied. She gestured at Daisy. "Take her to the garage where Vic wants her. I'll take care of this one." She glanced back at Nick.

Rubi Lee said, "I don't really give a *shit* what your name is. Get rid of him!" She waved her gun at Nick. She glared at Daisy. "Come on, Zeke. Get her to the garage."

When Zeke, Rubi Lee, and Daisy were gone, Jackie forced herself to look into Nick's blazing eyes. Fear and determination radiated back at her.

"But you're a *cop*, Jackie! What're you *doing*?" Nick trembled with anger.

Jackie met his eyes. "Not anymore. That life is over." She tightened the silencer on her weapon and took aim.

CHAPTER 42

In the garage, Zeke dropped Daisy on her back. She struggled to sit up from the cold floor. Her head felt like a bowling ball. She fought to lift it. When she did, she was eye level with six sets of tires. Tractors, lawn mowers, and snow blowers stood at attention along the opposite wall.

"Oh, my head," she groaned.

Zeke grabbed her pale face. "Mornin' sunshine. None of this needed to happen if only you told us earlier what you did with the diamonds you stole."

"Diamonds? I told you, I don't have any diamonds," Daisy whispered.

"Stop lying!" Rubi Lee screamed as she jerked Daisy's head up.

"Stop hurting her!" Nick cried from the office where Jackie kept him hostage. "She doesn't have any goddamn diamonds!"

"I . . . I don't know what happened to them." Daisy's eyes fluttered.

"Wrong answer. Do you want to try again?" Rubi Lee pulled her hair. "We can do this all night if you want."

Daisy whimpered, "Stop! Please!" The horrifying reality sunk in. The fissure in her chest exploded open. She sobbed.

Rubi Lee cocked her head and listened. "I hear the cops. We need . . ." She fell silent after she heard what sounded

265

like two muffled shots coming from the office. She yelled over her shoulder, "Did you get rid of him?"

Jackie appeared from the office door, grim-faced. "It's done. He's dead," she answered.

Daisy fought to process what she thought she heard Jackie say. In her heart, she knew what happened. The sobs intensified the pain in her body. Daisy sagged to the ground. She gasped for breath at the thought of her dear NT dead. *No! NO! NO!* Her emotions asphyxiated her, paralyzed her. She lay motionless.

"Is she alive?" Rubi Lee asked.

"Check her pulse." A cold finger pressed against her neck.

"She's alive," Zeke replied as Daisy blinked. Among the gasoline cans, shovels, and rakes, she saw two pairs of shoes and one pair of boots. She closed her eyes again. *Please God, just take me. I can't hang on anymore.*

"Paula, did Uncle Vic say he was on his way?" Rubi Lee asked.

"Yes, he should be close."

"Meanwhile, we should find something to wrap the dead guy in before—"

Rubi Lee was interrupted by the groans of the garage door opening. It seemed like an eternity until it reached its rusty resting spot. Rubi Lee, Zeke, and Jackie braced themselves and pointed their weapons at the door. The snow had intensified and sirens approached the park.

A stocky figure appeared out of the still darkness. The snow fell hard, obscuring his face.

Zeke lifted the pistol and commanded, "Stop right there or I'll blow you away!"

The figure moved closer. It was Victor.

Zeke lowered the gun. "You scared the crap out of us, Uncle Vic! Where's Alex?" Zeke breathed.

"She'll be along. After you sent me the signal, I thought everything was under control, but obviously it's not." His eyes glued on Daisy; he approached her slowly, head cocked to the side. "I see you have our redheaded friend." He leaned down and stroked Daisy's hair and took her chin in his hand. "Did she tell you where the diamonds are?"

At first, Daisy did not move, did not say a word. She was someplace far away. Someplace in the recesses of her mind where it was safe and warm. Victor clapped his hands in front of her face. Her eyes fluttered and in a barely audible voice, Daisy said, "I swear I didn't take any diamonds."

"What about your pretty roommate, Jaida? Do you think she took them? Come now; tell me her whereabouts," he took Daisy's jaw in his hand and squeezed.

Why would Jaida take them? She tried to maintain consciousness.

"Well?" Her chin sank to her neck. "The longer you avoid telling me, the worse it will get for you and your friends . . . well, those who are still alive." Victor stood and wiped his hands on a handkerchief to avoid dirtying his tuxedo.

"What are you going to do with her?" Rubi Lee asked.

"Keep her here." Victor tortured her with his words. "We know all about you. We know you tend bar at the Black LaSalle, Don Gaylord's favorite bar. Or as you called him, Moneybags. We know your three—or shall I now say two—friends work at the Cooper Building and we know your roommate Jaida is a brilliant computer engineer. If she's that good at fixing computers, then I'm sure she is an equally talented thief."

What? Jaida a thief? NT dead? Confusion and fear whirred into a horrible mix and poured over Daisy. She stared at him, trying to place his face. Her concentration and strength were trickling out of her like water from a hose. She inhaled. "The diamonds were . . . in a sweatshirt Jaida and I returned. I have no idea if she took any of them. She went . . . to the party with us tonight, but . . . I . . . I don't know where she is."

"Victor, she could be telling the truth, you know," Jackie dared to say. She blinked and cut her eyes to Rubi Lee and Zeke, then back to Victor. *Don't let them sense your fear.* "I'm only going to leave if you make it worth my time." She knew Victor had a gun and would shoot her as easily as he would a rat. Gun in hand, she held it steady at Victor.

Victor stared. "Put the gun away. Knowing you as well I do, I came prepared." Victor reached into his jacket pocket and tossed her a thick envelope. "Your work here is done. The documents and cash you need to disappear are in this envelope."

Envelope in hand, Jackie cut through the garage to the office. She opened the closet door and whispered, "Stay quiet, they think you're dead."

From under the coat he was hiding, Nick jumped out of his skin when the door opened. "Please don't shoot me!"

"I'm not going to shoot you."

"How can I trust you?" Nick stammered.

"I didn't shoot you before, did I?" Jackie replied.

Nick stared at her. "Oh my God. You're *part* of this. Why?"

"Why? *Money.*" She waved the envelope and looked at Nick. "If you want to stay alive, do not leave this closet." She shut the door and hustled out to the parking lot to the cruiser she and Henderson used earlier that night. She started the car, pulled down the visor, and looked in the mirror. She yanked off her wig and scratched her head. Tiny clumps of hair appeared in patches on her otherwise bald scalp. An online gambling addiction was her comfort when her husband left her years ago. The heinous addiction drained her savings and made her hair fall out. *Sykes came along at the right time, but I'll be damned if I'm going down for murder.* She hit the gas and watched the park and her years working intel for Victor disappear in the rearview mirror.

* * *

In the garage, Zeke, Rubi Lee, and Victor watched the taillights of the cruiser Jackie and Henderson arrived in fade into the night.

Zeke asked, "What are we gonna do with her?"

"Get rid of her. It's Jaida we need to find!" Victor answered.

Rubi Lee's eyes lit up. "Oh, I'll get rid of her, trust me." Daisy felt the cold blade go from her left ear, over her throat and down her breastbone. Rubi Lee cackled, "I can see your heart pounding. Good, I like my vics bein' scared!"

"Stop right there!" a female voice commanded from the cold.

Rubi Lee, Zeke, Daisy, and Victor turned toward the open garage.

It was Alex. She stood, feet apart, dark hair dotted with snow, gun held at them. "This has gone far enough! You two are done!" Her eyes blazed at Zeke and Rubi Lee.

"Now, Alex," Victor began. "Sweetheart, don't—"

She pulled the trigger. The ear-shattering bang froze time. Zeke never knew what hit him. He dropped to the ground like a brick, blood pouring from what was left of his head. Rubi Lee dropped her knife and raised her hands. She looked down in horror at Zeke and slowly backed away. "Uncle Vic, you gotta tell her not to kill me!" she whined and backed farther into the garage.

Victor flicked his eyes at Rubi Lee, then stared down at his nephew. "For God's sake, Alex! Did you have to kill him? Why not just shoot him in the leg for Christ's sake?"

Alex stared at him. "They're worthless and we sure as hell didn't need another screw-up. Time to cut our losses and find others. I'll take care of her," the senator said, turning the gun on Rubi Lee.

A sharp *pzzzt* broke through the frigid air, followed by a scream. Victor grabbed his chest and fell to the ground.

Before anyone realized what happened, another *pzzzt* pierced the night.

"AHHH!" Alex screamed. The gun flew from her hand. Something warm ran down her wrist. The bullet grazed her arm; blood dripped to the floor. She clutched it to her chest and ran to Victor. Quickly, Rubi Lee backpedaled into the rear of the garage and hid behind a large tractor.

A dark silhouette came into the dim light. The rifle she carried was aimed at Alex.

"You killed my husband!" Alex shrieked. She knelt by Victor's body and cradled his head in her lap. Blood poured over her arms and legs.

Jaida ignored the guttural sobs of Alex and kept the rifle aimed at her. "Get up. Unless you want to end up like Victor," Jaida said calmly.

Alex ignored her and continued to clutch her dead husband's head. "You killed him!" Her howl rattled windows.

"I said get up," Jaida said through clenched teeth.

Alex tenderly laid Victor's head down and slowly rose to her feet.

"Hands up, turn around, face the wall," Jaida commanded. Alex obeyed.

Daisy thought she was dreaming. "Jaida, Jaida," she moaned. "What's going on? I can't . . ."

Daisy's whimpering made Jaida feel sick. She pulled out her phone and dialed 911. Jaida knelt and put Daisy's head in her lap. "Shh, hush Daisy. You're going to be fine. Don't talk. Save your energy." Jaida bit down hard on her inner cheek to stop from crying.

"What is going on, Jaida? Please tell me," Daisy murmured. "Why do you have a rifle? I don't understand . . ." Her eyes rolled back in her head.

"Come on Daisy, stay awake. We're gonna get you to the hospital."

The EMT unit arrived. Jaida motioned them to hustle Daisy into the ambulance. They came in and gently lifted her onto the gurney and took her outside.

With the rifle still leveled at Alex, Jaida said, "I'll be right there, Daisy, as soon as I can—I promise."

Daisy felt herself being lifted and placed on a kind of bed and loaded into a warm ambulance. A slam of doors, the murmur of a soft, yet unfamiliar voice and the shrill sirens registered in a faraway place in her brain. The pain was beyond anything she felt; fighting it was futile. Darkness overcame her and the last thing she saw in her mind's eye were the faces of her mother, father, and her beloved NT.

CHAPTER 43

Winston watched the ambulance drive off. He knew Henderson was in good hands, but he said a prayer anyway. He sprinted to the garage. He knew to observe the scene before taking action. He circled around to the side and watched.

Several uniforms, guns drawn, approached the outside of the garage and entered. They saw no one at first and sent the all-clear. Farther in, they walked into a bloody mess. Two bodies were strewn on the ground, blood pooled on the floor. Senator Alexandra Boyd was facing a wall, hands above her head.

Jaida watched from the shadows, stepped out, rifle at her side. "Don't shoot," she said to the officers.

One of the officers commanded, "Drop the rifle!" Weapon aimed on her.

Jaida dropped her rifle to the floor and raised her hands.

"Identify yourself! Show your ID!"

Jaida reached into her parka and held out her ID. "Special Agent Jaida Campbell. US Customs," she responded. "Officer, I am going to ask my partner to step inside . . . Agent Wang, please step into the garage!" she yelled.

Winston stepped into the garage, his arms raised, ID in his hand. "Agent Winston Wang! Don't shoot!" He put his gun on the floor.

The officer spoke into the walkie talkie, "We have a situation here and need backup ASAP!"

"Officer, there's no need for backup. We're US Customs agents. We have been working undercover for over two years to take down a diamond smuggling ring."

Alex pointed at Winston and shrieked, "He's a *liar*! Officer, I am Senator Alexandra Boyd! These two kidnapped me and my husband! My husband tried to free us, and they . . . they shot him." Alex sobbed loudly.

More police showed up, including Captain Barrett who demanded an explanation for the carnage before him.

The officer who spoke to Alex took charge. "Captain, these two"—he pointed to Jaida and Winston—"claim they are US Customs agents, undercover." He shifted his attention to Alex. "Senator Boyd's husband was murdered in what she says was a botched kidnapping. The dead man there"—he pointed to Zeke—"allegedly drove the van in which the couple was kidnapped."

"Thank you Officer Little, good work. Please get the medics in here and secure the area. I can take it from there."

Captain Barrett pulled out his phone. "Get me the customs department and ask for Commissioner Knight." He continued, "Ma'am, I am calling for identity confirmation. I think I have two of your agents in a police situation. One says her name is Campbell and the other is Wang. Can you please confirm?" He eyeballed them and nodded. "Thank you, ma'am. I'm sorry for the late call. Good night."

He looked at Jaida and Winston and turned his attention to Alex.

"So, tell me Senator, what *really* happened here?"

Alex's ashen face told the whole story.

* * *

In the stuffy closet where Nick was hiding, time dragged. Sweat poured down his face as he prayed. *Please let Daisy be alive. Please let me see her.* The winter coat he crouched behind blocked all sound and light and smelled like must. His heart skipped over itself when a moth flittered across his face.

"Stay quiet, they think you're dead." He said aloud. He knew he had to stay calm.

Nick waited at least an hour. *I can't stay in here any longer. If I die, I die.* He had to know if his Daisy was alive and get her help. What about Henderson? All of them? *Don't think like that, she's fine. Be positive.*

Slowly, Nick opened the door to ominous silence. The door to the garage was ajar; the frigid air poured in. He winced in pain as he approached the door. He peered in. *Oh my God!* His stomach churned at the massive puddles of blood pooling on the floor. The scene reminded him of an ancient sacrifice. The powerful metallic smell filled the garage and made him gag. He did not allow himself to think the dark thoughts pushing into his head like an army.

"No, no, no!" he screamed. *She's not dead. No. But what hospital did they take her to? Central Hospital is the closest; only five blocks away.* With no regard to the weather, he took off running. His dress shoes did nothing to help him gain traction in the snow. He pounded the pavement to the rhythm of *I know she's alive, she must be ... I know she's alive, she must be.* Before he knew it, he saw the hospital.

CHAPTER 44

Emergency vehicles, police cars, and general traffic swarmed like hornets at the emergency room doors. He bumped and twisted his way through the crowd and entered the emergency area. Bandaged people, crying children, and other sick people waited to be checked in or go to triage. Nick kept looking at the swinging doors that led back to the emergency area, hoping to get a glance inside and possibly see Daisy. The nurses at the desk were overwhelmed. He pounced on the opportunity like a lion on a sick gazelle and hustled to the ER doors but was stopped short.

A stout, dark-haired nurse held up a chubby hand. "Stop right there. Nobody comes back here without authorization."

"I'm sorry, Nurse Monica. I'm not thinking clearly," he explained, reading the ID tag clipped to her scrubs. "I've got to find my friend . . ." His anxiety rose with each swing of the door. He peered over her curly hair. "Daisy! Daisy!" Nick's scream was futile. He soon found himself outside in the glare of the waiting room, ushered out by a large security guard.

He asked Nick, "Man, why are you pushing your way into a restricted area? Look at you! You look like a bad horror movie!"

Nick ignored it. "My friend was injured in a horrible accident and I have to find her!" Nick said, breaking down into tears. "Oh my God, what if she's dead? She has no family here, please help me!"

Nick's distraught emotional plea sank in with the security guard. He put his arm around Nick to give him some comfort. "It's all right, man. What's her name?"

"Daisy Taylor. Redhead, tall, wearing a black dress."

"I'll go inside and see what I can find out. Sit awhile and have some coffee." He led Nick to the waiting area and brought him coffee. "Stay here, I'll be back."

Nick fell into the seat and rubbed his head. *Weren't we all just at Senator Boyd's party? How's it possible it's still the same night?* He took a sip of his weak brew, shook his head, and breathed deeply. *Please God, let her be okay. Let Henderson be okay too.* He laid his head on his crossed arms and tried to make sense of what was going on when he felt a tap on his shoulder.

"Hey, you okay?"

Nick looked up into the creased face of the friendly security guard. Nick was terrified to ask, but he had to. "Well?"

""I found out more for you. There was a gunshot victim brought in around the same time as an unconscious girl. A redhead," the guard said from behind.

He leaped up. "You said a redheaded girl! Daisy! Was she alive?"

"Don't know. Seems the police are keeping these events under wraps."

At the front desk, he asked again if a Daisy Taylor had been checked in. *Tap, tap tap.* The nurse scanned the screen and confirmed what the security guard told him—that a redhead was brought in, seriously injured.

He held tightly to the counter to steady himself. "Thank God."

The nurse met Nick's eyes. "Are you her husband? Family?"

"I'm her friend. Her parents aren't here. Please help me. Please."

"Do you have ID?"

Nick jammed his hands in his pockets and only found money. "No. Please. I need to know if she's at least *alive*."

"Fine. Stay here." In their whispery, medical way he spoke with Nurse Monica, who glanced at Nick.

He walked back. "I'm happy to tell you she's alive. We can't let you see her because you have no ID."

Nick felt his whole body relax at the news. "Thank God. I understand. I'll come back with my ID."

"Do you know her parents?" he asked.

"Yes. I'll call them. Thank you again for your help."

"You're welcome."

Nick needed some time to organize his thoughts. He found the hospital chapel and sank into a pew. *Thank you, God, for saving Daisy. Please help her recover completely, please.*

CHAPTER 45

It had been a long two days, but Daisy recovered, waking from her injuries. CT scans revealed no traumatic brain injury, and Daisy was released from the hospital within a week. She and Gussie moved in with Nick and Winston during her recovery.

The next day, the doorbell rang. She was happy to see Henderson's cheery face when she opened it. "Hi Henderson! What a nice surprise!" Daisy was careful when she hugged him.

"Easy on the shoulder. I'm still sore and have to wear this sling," he said.

"Is that Henderson I hear?" Nick said, coming downstairs.

"Yes, it is. Winston texted me and asked me to meet him here around five," Henderson answered.

Daisy looked at Henderson, tears filling her eyes. "What happened to you?" she asked.

"Remember when I came upon you and Nick being held captive by the two perps?"

"I sure do," Nick said.

"Yes, sort of," Daisy answered. "No, not really." She shook her head.

"I didn't know what was happening either, but the next thing I knew I felt like my arm was tossed into a woodchipper. I was shot by one of them. Luckily their aim was off. I think Winston called the ambulance. Thank God he did, or I may not be here."

Daisy was horrified. "Henderson, this is all my fault! They could have killed you! I'm so sorry!"

"Now young lady, don't you dare. *None* of this is your fault and I'm sure we will learn exactly what happened."

"Yeah but—"

"Now hush. None of this is your doing, understand?" He held her face in his hand.

"Okay, okay. I'm just so thankful that you're alive and feeling better."

"Same goes for you. I did visit you in the hospital, but you were asleep most of the time."

Nick said, "Henderson, I have to ask. Did you ever suspect Jackie was part of this? A big part?"

Henderson exhaled and regarded Nick and Daisy. "I'd be a liar if I said no. When I think about it—which I did while lying in my hospital bed—there were some subtle signs I chose to ignore."

Daisy prodded, "Like what?"

"Well, she had two phones, but I chalked that up to her being a cop. She sometimes was a no-show when we planned a date because a 'meeting' ran late. Stuff like that. I enjoyed her company and cared deeply for her, so I let those things slide. I guess I was a fool."

"No, you weren't, Henderson. She fooled the entire precinct and all of us," Daisy said.

"Damn right she did. We had a relationship and I deserve to be told face to face. Was she that hard up for money?" Anger and frustration bubbled to the surface. "She played me well. I was just a foolish pawn in her game—a game where three of us almost died," Henderson lamented.

"Don't be so hard on yourself, Henderson. You trusted her—we all did. Even though she saved my life by telling me to hide in the closet, she's still a criminal."

The doorknob turned and Winston walked in. "Glad to see everyone is here. Sit down; I'll make us some coffee. I have some news to share."

A few minutes later, over a cup of coffee, Winston began.

""I won't pull punches. I am an undercover US Customs agent."

Nick choked. "*What?* What are you *talking about?*"

Winston took a deep breath. "Nick, it's the truth. I've been undercover for several years now. I know what I'm about to tell you will sound insane. But please know, it's the truth and you must trust me."

Nick digested this. "We're roommates and best friends! How could I not know this?"

"Don't be upset, we *are* best friends and that will never change." He patted Nick's hand. "During my senior year, I applied to be a US Customs agent. The money was right, I wasn't married, and I knew I fit the profile of an agent."

"You're a *security analyst*, not an agent."

"Come on man, put two and two together. *Undercover.* I *do* analyze security measures with a focus on domestic issues. I was put on this investigation two years ago."

Nick rubbed his eyes. "Investigation? Please tell me about it since Daisy and Henderson were almost killed—in a freakin' *shootout* no less!" He gestured at them, who sat in silent shock.

"Sorry Nick, I know your head is spinning. The short

story is that it is an ongoing investigation into a dangerous and lucrative diamond smuggling ring. I'm not at liberty to discuss details, which I'm sure you understand."

Daisy stared at Winston, her mind reeling. "Oh my God! The sweatshirt and the diamonds! Holy crap! I stumbled onto this and they think I stole them! It all makes sense now."

Nick leveled Winston with a simmering glare. "So, you *knew* all along? And now she's recovering from a *brain injury*?" He wanted to punch Winston.

Winston stared back. "I'm so sorry. We did everything we could to avoid catastrophe. In this line of work, not all things go as planned. Daisy is tough and will be okay, especially with you caring for her. Henderson is okay, too." He paused, looking at Henderson, Daisy, and Nick. "You all must understand *no one* ever meant for any of you to be involved in the events of the other night. Ever." Winston's sincerity was tangible. "I feel sick about what could have happened and for that, I apologize." He continued, "Jaida and I were part of a two-year undercover investigation into a global and profitable diamond smuggling case. It's over. The ring was run by Senator Boyd's husband, Victor Sykes. And she was a major play in it too."

Nick's jaw hit the floor. "*No way!* Senator *Boyd*? Holy crap!"

Daisy's head swiveled to Nick and slapped his knee. "And to think, NT, you worked for her! Wow," Daisy said. "And Henderson, you were in the same building as she was!"

"I know. I can't believe it either." Nick shook his head. "She seemed so normal, but she was corrupt like so many others."

"Alex Boyd ran part of the operation by providing Victor with access into restricted areas, names of VIPs, plus the use of government cars and property. Sykes was reselling illegal goods such as ivory, diamonds, and even exotic animals to his wealthy clients as well as to people in the upper, top echelons of government. I started two years ago, and Jaida came into the investigation over a year ago. I needed someone who had a vast wealth of computer expertise. She was a perfect fit and she was in the top tier of her firearms class."

Henderson sat back on the couch and puffed his cheeks. "That's a lot to absorb."

Winston turned to Henderson. "Yes. We knew diamonds were being smuggled into the country by two, if not more, of Victor and Alex's mules. One of the mules was Don Gaylord. He brought them in from Russia and—"

Daisy sat up. "Don Gaylord? Moneybags! The police came and asked us all about him! Jackie too!" she yelled. "Sorry Winston, I interrupted. Please continue."

"Thank you, Daisy. As I was saying, he passed them along through various means—such as the sweatshirt, a belt, or even a baseball cap. Gaylord was murdered most likely by Zeke and Rubi Lee Dixon, niece and nephew of Victor Sykes and Alex Boyd."

Nick's eyes grew as large as dinner plates. "*What?*" Nick said. "The two crazy people who drove that white van! They're *related* to Senator Boyd?"

"Yes. And only by marriage," Winston said.

"And the one I saw from my window that night," Daisy said.

Henderson added, "Then they are most likely

responsible for killing Erin *and* destroying Daisy's apartment."

Winston continued, "Correct. Daisy, you happened to come along at the right time in the right place—the Black LaSalle. In March, we had the Black LaSalle under surveillance because we knew it was a drop point for contraband and, by sheer accident, you took home the wrong—or right—sweatshirt." He took a breath. "When you and Jaida became roommates, it made our job easier. The night you found the diamonds in the sweatshirt was our jackpot. Soon after, Jaida discovered incriminating evidence on Victor's laptop. At that point, we were closing the web. Unfortunately, Erin was kidnapped and killed and"—he glanced at Daisy—"as you said, it was supposed to be you."

An iciness ran down Daisy's spine. She inhaled sharply. "I knew it. Too many weird things happened in a short time to be coincidental."

"How did Erin get mixed up?" Nick asked.

"Well, Victor sent Rubi Lee and Zeke to get the redhead at the bar, and they grabbed Erin instead of you."

All three were speechless. Nick reached over and hugged Daisy around the shoulders.

"Sykes knew some diamonds were missing and incorrectly assumed Erin had them—but she didn't," Winston said.

"Who did?" Daisy asked.

Winston sighed. "Jaida did. The night you found them in the sweatshirt." He could tell Daisy's mind was racing when she cocked her head and looked at him. "She was following orders."

Daisy gawked at Winston. "*What?* She lied to me. And

Zeke and Rubi Lee thought that *I* stole them," she whispered.

"I'm so sorry, Daisy. In a manner of speaking, yes. She took them to the agency to cross-reference them with the entire shipment. You'll never know how horrible she felt about this."

Daisy stood up and began to pace. "So those scumbags killed Erin? If it weren't for me wearing home that damn sweatshirt, she'd be here! Oh my God."

"Daiz, easy. You don't know that for sure. This is not your fault," Nick said.

"He's right, Daisy," Winston said. "Fast forward to the senator's Christmas party. They were smart because they checked in to a room, dressed appropriately, and mingled. And when you were snatched, we had an all-out race against time to save you."

"I put up a fight, trust me. But then I woke up in a van?" Daisy put in.

"Correct. Nick and I chased the van with Jaida close behind. In the park, the situation became extraordinarily dangerous. Henderson was shot, Nick almost died, and Daisy was losing blood. Thankfully, Jaida executed her job perfectly and took out Victor. The cops arrested Alex Boyd and hauled her off."

A thought suddenly occurred to Daisy. "Hold on a second. What about Rubi Lee and Jackie? Did they get killed?"

"The police apprehended Jackie outside of town. As for Rubi Lee, we believe she slipped away during the shootout. We have an APB on her with her description at every police station in the city and into Virginia and Maryland."

Daisy leveled her gaze on Winston. "I looked into that face of evil. You *need* to find her. And soon."

"We will, don't worry."

Henderson asked, "What are those diamonds worth?"

Winston shoved his glasses back on the thin bridge of his nose. "At least two million. They were brilliant, raw, and from Russia."

"*Damn*," Henderson exclaimed.

Nick let out a low whistle.

Daisy stared off into space and quietly mumbled, "But . . . we *all* could be dead."

"Daisy, I can't deny that. But you're not. We're all here and we will move past this," Winston said.

She nodded thoughtfully. "You're right. Thanks for telling us, Win."

"Yeah, thanks man. What are you going to do now?" Nick asked Winston.

"As of now, I'm stepping away from any undercover work. The agency has granted me some much-needed R and R."

"What about Jaida? I thought you two were an item?" Henderson asked.

"We invented a credible front as a couple. It seemed very natural for us to be an item, given our *occupations*." Winston used air quotes.

"And you were quite convincing!" Daisy said. "What's Jaida's plan?"

"Eventually, she'll return to working for the agency in the capacity of cyber-security."

"I don't know whether to be angry or relieved. Jaida *knew* I was in danger, and so was she. I understand why she needed to keep this quiet, but I considered her a close friend, practically a sister."

"Believe me, Daisy, she was torn apart by putting a dear friend in danger and fulfilling her job requirements. She wanted to be here, but she couldn't be."

"I feel empty. I thought we'd have a long friendship." Daisy shrunk back into the couch.

Winston replied, "I have something that may make you feel better. Before I share that with you, though, I will never be able to apologize adequately for putting you all through this. Jaida and I and the department never thought in a million years we'd bring the smuggling ring down the way we did. These criminals are smart and crafty and dangerous. They have shattered and destroyed many lives."

"We're all glad this is over, and the bad guys are caught. More importantly, we're all okay," Nick said.

They sat in contemplative silence until Henderson spoke. "This may go down in the history of the biggest case of my career that I *wasn't* assigned!" Henderson chuckled and glanced at his watch. "Kids, this old man needs to go home, rest, and reset. I'll see you later at the Black LaSalle anniversary party." He stood and hugged his friends.

Winston was quick to follow. "I'm with Henderson. Daisy, this is for you." From his pocket he handed her a USB key. "I'll be in touch. Take care of each other. I love you guys." They hugged at the front door and watched Winston hop into an idling SUV.

CHAPTER 46

"What do you think is on here?" Daisy asked, turning the USB key over in her hand.

"I think we need to find out." Nick reached his laptop and inserted the key.

Daisy smiled when a prerecorded video showing Jaida's beautiful face appeared on the screen.

Jaida waved. "Hi Daisy," she spoke softly. "First, I want you to know how deeply *sorry* I am for all of this. I never ever meant for you to suffer like you did. I hope you can forgive me. I also want you to know how much I miss hanging out with you. I miss your thousand-watt smile, silly laugh and our girl time."

Jaida wiped a tear away.

"I'm sure you are upset with me after what you learned. I don't blame you. I wish I could explain everything to you in person because you deserve it. But I had to go," Jaida explained. "By now, Win has filled you in that I'm an agent and we were involved in a very dangerous case with horrible people."

Jaida looked to her right for a brief second.

"When we found those diamonds, our relationship was irrevocably changed. I so desperately wanted to protect you, but I could not give up my identity. I hope you understand that now."

She stopped and leaned into the camera.

"Daisy, you are—and *always* will be—the sister I never had. I love you like you're my own blood and I never intended for you to get caught up in the violence and terror. Never. I unintentionally put your life in danger, and I am sick to my stomach you were hurt."

The small tremor in her voice pulled at Daisy's heartstrings.

"After that night, I was put on administrative leave while the investigation took place. Winston gave me updates on your condition every day."

Jaida wiped her eyes.

"Daisy, I hope you can forgive me, and we can reconnect as time goes by. I have arranged for you to stay in the apartment for the next year, rent-free. I know deep in my heart that you will be a successful news reporter and I wish you all the luck in the world as you pursue your dream. Don't let Nick get away—he's a good one. Love you sister. I'll see you again someday."

She then held up a little sign that read: *I left you a gift in the apartment.* ☺

Nick glanced at Daisy, who wiped away her tears. "You okay?"

She nodded. "I will be. Watching that makes me think I'll never see her again."

He pulled her over to him and stroked her hair. "You'll see her someday, I know it."

Daisy rubbed her eyes. "I wonder what she means by gift?"

"We'll only know when we get to your place. I'll get changed for the party and call for an Uber."

At Jaida's apartment, Daisy asked Nick to feed Gussie. "I'm going to take a quick shower and change."

"Sure."

* * *

Daisy wandered into her room, opened her closet, and selected a deep garnet dress and black heels. *I wonder what Jaida left. Bath salts? Eucalyptus perfume?* She glimpsed and saw nothing new in her room nor her bathroom. *I'll find it eventually.*

After a hot shower, Daisy applied makeup, put her hair in a twist, and dabbed on pink lip gloss. She looked in the mirror and thought she needed something else. She took a silver necklace, fastened it, and assessed her look. *Earrings.* Daisy knew she had a pair of silver hoops in her jewelry box. She opened her dresser drawer, popped open the top of her jewelry box, and saw two small envelopes staring up at her. One had her name on it and the other Nick's.

She scowled at them. *What the . . . ?* She opened the one with her name. "Oh my God," she whispered to herself. "NT, come here!" she yelled.

"What's going on?"

"Look." Daisy held out her hand.

Two diamond stud earrings glittered at him from her palm. "Oh, wow. They're beautiful. Where did you get them?"

She handed Nick the envelope with his name on it. He slowly opened it and shook out two glimmering diamonds into his palm. "Are these real?" He brought his palm closer to inspect them.

"This is the gift from Jaida," she murmured. Carefully, she put the earrings on. Daisy turned to the mirror and admired the shimmering stones. "They're breathtaking, aren't they?"

"Yes, like you. They're fit for a queen."

"What are you going to do with those two?" she asked.

"Oh, I think I have an idea," he coyly replied.

He stood behind Daisy and watched her admire her earrings. She tilted her head and cast her eyes upon his reflection.

"Is that a fact?" She turned around.

He wrapped his arms around her waist, pulled her close. "Yes, it is." He kissed her deeply. She did not resist.

Acknowledgments

Thank you to Kristen Hamilton, my editor. Your guidance, knowledge, and care are deeply appreciated. Thank you!

Special thanks to these three dear friends for their time, suggestions, and patience: Lauren McKinney, Cheryl Flail, and Ed Flail.

Thank you, Nick Woodfield, for enlightening me as to where in DC my younger characters would "live."

Wayne Reid, thank you for educating me about diamonds and methods used to transport them—legally and illegally.

Thanks to Annie Ripley and Karen Sullivan for the medical information.

A heartfelt thanks to my friends and family for asking, "How's book two going?"

Lastly, thank you to my readers for your enthusiasm and support. I hope you enjoy *Hot Ice, Cold Blood.*

Made in the USA
Middletown, DE
03 September 2020

16689227R00166